ANXIOUS

To my second mom I love you and I am so thankful to call you a friend. — Michael Dunn

Michael Dunn

ISBN 978-1-64458-965-6 (paperback)
ISBN 978-1-64458-966-3 (digital)

Copyright © 2019 by Michael Dunn

All rights reserved. No part of this publication may be reproduced, distributed, or transmitted in any form or by any means, including photocopying, recording, or other electronic or mechanical methods without the prior written permission of the publisher. For permission requests, solicit the publisher via the address below.

Christian Faith Publishing, Inc.
832 Park Avenue
Meadville, PA 16335
www.christianfaithpublishing.com

Printed in the United States of America

Chapter 1

Alex

Whap!

A branch smacked me in the face, as I shimmied up the trunk of the tallest tree possible. My face was pressed up against the rough bark, and I'm pretty sure I ate a bug, but this was going to be worth it. Plus, a little protein never hurt anyone.

"I think he's part squirrel," my buddy Ian shouted to my other friend Jack.

"Nah, I think he's part 'I'm as dumb as a rock.'" Jack grinned up at me, as I grabbed another branch.

"As soon as I get this up and running, you two are going to have a fine view of my pretty butt." I managed to somehow get to the next highest branch without falling to my death. A rope was tucked into my belt, slapping my legs.

The sun broke through the branches, making scattered splotches of golden light dance over the forest. Ian was down below me, dancing from foot to foot, his blond hair a curly mess on his head, his blue eyes focused on me. Jack stood, his long brown hair pulled back into a man bun, an unnaturally calm expression painted on his tanned face, his hands shoved deep into his pockets. Whenever he was nervous he'd do that, or get excessive gas, which really drove the ladies wild. He was about as smart as a brick, but he'd do anything stupid if I asked him to.

I got to the top of the tree and let out a happy sigh. I could see my neighborhood from up here, plus the school far off in the distance. Ian and Jack both lived a block away from me, which made it convenient when I got any harebrained ideas like this one.

"Alexander Lance Dayton!"

Dang, I'm in trouble. My eyes glanced down to see my willowy, dark-haired sister, who I loved to death. Raven had her arms crossed, sitting on her horse, Mayfly, with a look on her face to scare a grown man.

"Get down here! Mom's going to kill you!" Raven slid off Mayfly and let the horse graze. She rested her hand on the animal's long, brown neck.

Ian and Jack chuckled under their breath like eight-year-old girls at a sleepover. Instead of listening to my little sister, I smirked at her.

"Throw it up, Ian." I ushered toward a pair of bike handlebars he'd been holding for a few minutes.

The metal bars whirled through the air like a flying saucer. I reached out and grabbed them, my feet slipping slightly.

"Alex!" Raven's voice rose in pitch as she watched me nearly tumble. Mayfly's head rose sharply, her ears perking. After I could breathe again, my heart sounding like a bad rap song, I looped the handlebars through the rope and tied it up on the strongest-looking branch possible.

"Raven, I'm fine." I laughed at the panicked look on her face. She told me all the time, the only reason why I was alive was her—it was probably true. I was supposed to be the responsible one, according to her, since I was older by a year. At fifteen, I figured you only live once, so why do boring stuff.

"I can't look." I heard her squeak. She hid her face in Mayfly's neck.

I grabbed the handlebars as Ian and Jack started whooping, encouraging me to kill myself—great friends. I jumped off the branch, praying I'd tied the other end tight enough. I let out a man scream as I soared across the zipline I'd rigged up on the fly. My sister screamed like a zombie was after her, making Mayfly twitch her ears toward her in interest. After a few seconds, Raven started laughing. It was a good thing that horse didn't spook easily.

"You're insane!" she said.

The wind whipped my dark hair around my face, the trees blurring by as I weaved between trees. I got to the end of the line and jumped into a net, I'd also rigged up, and fell out into a heap on the ground.

I spat leaves out of my mouth, standing to my feet.

"I hate you right now." Raven stood before me, her arms crossed, but she was grinning. Mayfly lazily ate the little bit of grass she could find nearby, ignoring all of us. "Now, let me try that."

I was shocked. Normally I had to bribe Raven to do anything daring.

"A'ight." I shrugged and grabbed her in a big hug, getting leaves all over her sweater. My sister was a bit of a freak, wearing hoodies in the summer and all. I knew underneath all those layers Raven was fit and probably could take out my friends in a fight. She'd been in gymnastics since she was three years old, and I had been in Wing Chun. As a kid, I'd watched the *Ip Man* movies and had begged my parents for fighting lessons until they caved. Raven and I had practiced fighting together for years, and I'd even shown her some moves with the butterfly knives. She wasn't half bad.

"The little lady is going to try!" I called to Ian and Jack. I frowned suddenly and looked up at the handlebars. "Hmm…how are we going to get those back to the other side?"

"Why don't you tie a string to them?" Raven asked.

"This is why I keep you around." I pulled another rope out of my belt and threw it over the edge of the handlebars. I dragged it back to the first tree.

Raven pulled herself up the large maple, one branch at a time, looking determined, and making it look far too easy. Once she reached the top, she grabbed the handlebars, threw me a nervous glance, and soared across the forest with a high-pitched shriek. I watched her with pride. She landed in a heap in the net and rolled out into a pile of leaves, her hair a mess.

"Told you not all my ideas are going to kill me." I grabbed her hand and helped her to her feet.

"One out of a hundred is not exactly good odds." Raven swiped at the leaves, pulling me in a big hug. As she hugged me, something rustled in the brush nearby. It caught my attention, and I craned my neck to see what it was. The edge of a tail flickered in front of my vision for half a second and then disappeared.

Squirrel? A tingle ran down my spine, and something inside of me felt more curious than I ought to feel about a forest rat. I shrugged it off. As I spotted Ian about to take off on my zipline, whatever that feeling was, lifted.

"What is it?" Raven turned her head toward the brush I had been staring at a second ago.

"I dunno." I shrugged.

"Come on, I can tell when something bothers you." She continued to look at the brush. "Is a big, scary bear going to eat us?"

"Probably. But I can run faster, so it doesn't matter. It'll eat you first!" I gave her a light shove and ran back toward Ian and Jack.

"You're such a jerk!" Raven laughed, catching up to me.

* * * * *

I walked to the barn behind our house, helping Raven put her horse away. Mayfly swished her tail back and forth as I brushed her down, while Raven took her saddle off. We often did this together. Even though I wasn't exactly into horses like Raven, I thought Mayfly was pretty awesome. Of course I wouldn't admit that to Ian or Jack, since they thought liking horses was a girly thing. I'd rode a few times, but I tended to stick to my dirt bike to get around.

"Thanks, Alex," Raven said. She gave her horse some food and water, and we turned to go back to the house.

"You have gymnastics tonight?" I walked casually beside my sister, the light wind rustling my hair.

"They canceled practiced tonight."

"Well, I can show you a few new moves I learned the other day. Want to check them out?" I nudged her.

"Sure." She grinned at me as we stepped onto our wrap around porch.

"See, we didn't die today. Right?" I turned around and grinned at her, running my fingers through my dark brown hair, walking backward up the steps.

Raven shook her head at me, passing me to go into our three-story Victorian-style house. To anyone who drove by, we looked like we lived in a big, green dollhouse. In the front, we had split steps with a round turret in the center. Everything was etched in fancy white trim and spirals. Mom was into that stuff, and secretly I think she had been born in the wrong era. Dad called her a professional "dust collector" because everything she owned was old and dusty. He'd stopped joking though when she sold some piece of junk for ten grand. She loved to rub that in his face.

I went through the front door, and instantly the smell of something gooey and chocolatey hit me.

Dang, Mom is going to make me fat. I slapped my stomach as I headed toward the kitchen to see what she was making. Dad was hunched over his computer, rubbing his forehead, trying to get his brain to fall out I suppose. My dad's a professional writer, though I tend to think he stares at his computer and swears for a job instead.

Dad had written historical documents, articles, and a few books over the years. He and my mom ended up meeting through a mutual friend. Mostly because his friend tricked him into the date—telling him there was old, dusty documents to read. While my dad wasn't necessarily a hermit, he holed up in the house quite often like Raven.

My mom, on the other hand, loved a good party. In fact, we'd had to designate a section of the house for parties because she threw them about once a week.

"Alexander, come here," my mom said from the kitchen. I hurried toward her, the smell getting stronger.

"Taste this."

Before I'd even fully stepped into the kitchen, my mom shoved a spoon in my mouth. Something warm, buttery, and chocolatey exploded on my tongue. *This woman is going to make me a chunk for sure.*

"What is that?" I stared at her with wide eyes, probably looking like a lunatic wanting more happy drugs.

"It's Mom's surprise!" My mother did a little twirl, still holding the wooden spoon with my drool on it. My mom was built like Raven, small and feisty. Her hair was a lighter shade than mine or Raven's and was usually up in a fancy bun braid thing. Like I said, she was born in the wrong era and enjoyed dressing and looking like it.

"You should make surprises every day." I smacked my lips to encourage her. "Except, you're going to make me fat." I grabbed my stomach and gave it a shake, though there really was nothing to shake.

"Momma?" Raven came into the kitchen and reached for a cup. "You and Daddy are coming Wednesday, right?"

Raven had signed up for a poetry reading at a local coffee shop and hadn't stopped talking to me about it since.

"Of course. I'll peel your dad's fingers from that keyboard." My mom nudged her head toward the direction of my dad.

Raven gave her a shy smile and darted off to her room.

My mom watched her leave for a moment and then turned to me. "All right, Alexander, I believe you gave me my stamp of approval for my mom's surprise. Why don't you wash up, and we'll eat it before dinner?"

"You don't have to ask me twice." This is why I loved my mom—she loved to break the rules.

* * * * *

"I'm getting closer, Penny," my dad said as we sat around the dinner table. Mom had made some chicken fettuccini—another attempt to fatten Raven and I up. I had just shoved a giant bite of garlic bread into my mouth.

"What exactly are we talking about, Ben?" My mom smoothed out her napkin, a look of great patience on her face. Mom was used to Dad randomly bringing up a topic that she was clueless about.

"If I could find the exact geological location, on our old property, I'd have all the evidence I needed to put the puzzle pieces together." My dad tapped his long fingers against the wooden table, his slightly graying black hair mussed from him rubbing his forehead.

My dad loved rambling. It happened a lot. I exchanged a look with Raven, who attempted not to giggle. Dad didn't actually want us to respond; he was simply spouting out loud about his latest project.

"The facts aren't adding up yet, and I think that some of my sources are fabricating things." He scrunched his forehead and ruffled his hair again, making it stand up like he'd just gotten out of bed.

"Um hmm," Mom said, taking another bite of her fettuccini. She winked at Raven and I, and we all pretended to listen to Dad go on for another five minutes. He'd been working on this project for about six months—some sort of legend or curse in our family. Part of his curiosity had to do with his own father—who was proclaimed clinically insane. When my father was a child, his dad had often rambled about other worlds, angels, demons, and evil creatures, until my poor grandma had him committed. Supposedly there had been sightings in our family history of what Dad called 'Shadow Man', and anytime someone saw this so called 'Shadow Man', they'd go missing or insane.

Dad really needed a better name, because Shadow Man reminded me of a three-year-old's boogieman hiding in the closet. Every time Dad found out more information on the subject, it seemed people clammed up or ended up in a padded white room. I was interested in his project, but not enough to pay too close attention. He only had small pieces of a giant puzzle.

"Dad, you think you can help me with my dirt bike tomorrow morning?" I said after a moment of silence.

"Huh, oh, yeah, of course I can." He seemed to come back into the real world. "You going to go riding with Ian and Jack?"

"Yeah." I didn't tell Dad that we were planning on checking out the paranormal hotspot he'd been researching for months now. Supposedly the Dayton bloodline had always lived on that property—up until Mom had wanted to buy the house we lived in now. Whether because the place creeped her out or she just wanted her own space, I don't know. We still rented out the ancient house on the property to a nice couple. My friends and I were going to camp on the hotspot for the night and see if any of the legends were true.

Mom rubbed Dad's back, giving him an affectionate kiss.

"Gross," I said under my breath, but of course really I was happy Mom and Dad weren't like most my friends' parents—divorced or screaming like cats in a bath.

"Oh, you want a kiss too?" Mom baby talked me, leaning over and trying to attack me with kisses.

"Ah!" I held up my hands as she came after first me and then Raven. By the end we were trying to ward Mom off with garlic bread.

"Don't forget, I need you two's help running the store Saturday and Sunday. Your dad and I are going on a romantic getaway—"

"Again, gross, no one cares." I plugged my ears like a five-year-old.

"I think it's cute, Mom," Raven said with a smile, kissing Mom's cheek and hugging Dad. "And of course, we'll help you."

"Suck up," I muttered and elbowed her lightly. She smacked me in the stomach.

"Umph. Remind me not to teach you anymore Wing Chun."

"This is all *Karate Kid* movies." She gave me a devious smile.

"So you'll watch the store and make sure everything is locked up, right?" Mom raised an eyebrow at the both of us.

My mom ran a successful antique store. I absolutely loved staring at creepy dolls that were going to kill me in my sleep; it was fun. Raven would sit there and draw when the store wasn't busy. Both of us had our fill of stimulating brain activities.

"Thanks, you two. Plus, I snuck in a little meeting with an antique seller on the way. It could be an incredible piece to sell for our store—pray he sells for a good price." Mom tried to get us again with kisses, and Dad joined in, making the garlic bread attack even less successful.

"Go! Get out of here. We don't want your kind anymore!" I threw a hunk of bread at them as they ran off to their room to finish packing.

"I'm so glad we had kids!" Mom called over her shoulder.

"To be your slaves!" I said, throwing a final piece of bread at Dad and hitting him right in the back of the head. He returned the throw and managed to nearly knock over a lamp.

"You need to work on that aim, slugger," I said.

Raven's hand was over her mouth, and her blue eyes shimmered with laughter.

"I want to be like that one day."

"What? Gross?" I scooped up my plate and put it into the dishwasher.

"It's not gross, Alex. You like it." She came over and put her own plate into the dishwasher. "You're just too much of a boy to be romantic."

"I'll take that as a compliment." I cleaned off the rest of the table and headed to my room for the night to look at my funny apps.

I stepped into my room, swooped up my phone, and plopped down onto my bed. I'd barely clicked on the first app, when I got a tingling sensation in the back of my head. It was the same feeling from the forest. *Who's watching me?* I set my phone down, peered in the corners of my room, looked in the closet, and finally stuck my head out the window. *I'm being a paranoid little girl.* I scanned our yard below, trying to spot anything weird. The corner of our hedges rustled, and again I spotted that tail.

"So a squirrel is stalking me? Awesome." I laughed at myself and plopped back down on my bed.

Chapter 2

Raven

As I walked into the coffee shop, I inhaled the rich aroma and chill atmosphere. Out of the corner of my eye I saw the mini stage and microphone, and my mind drifted to my upcoming poetry reading. I'd been trying to perfect my poems for months now, and I prayed they were finally good enough. Alex had been encouraging me for the last several months to take a risk with my poems, so I'd signed up for the Wednesday reading. Between gymnastics and horseback riding, I tried to make time for my art as well.

My friend Ella was meeting me here to hang out for the day, and I could tell by her texts she was excited to talk to me. I spotted her loosely curly red hair and smiling face and waved. Ella had been my best friend since the first grade, and we rarely went a day without texting. She was in gymnastics with me, but lately everything she talked about was her boyfriend Jaden.

"Hi!" Ella stood up and gave me a big hug, her brown eyes sparkling. "You won't believe what's been happening lately!" She waved her manicured fingers around. Ella loved to shop, get mani-pedis, and spend her dad's money almost more than he could make it. We were an odd pair. Me with my very basic outfit: hoodie and jeans, and Ella with her fashionable, designer clothes and salon style haircut. Alex had asked me once why I liked Ella, and I guess it was mostly because she was bubbly, fun, outgoing, and I wanted some of that to rub off on me, and we both shared the same love for gymnastics. Plus, she reminded me of Alex in certain ways.

"Jaden made out with me last night," Ella said the words in an attempted whisper, but failed miserably. She clapped her hands in excitement and leaned in toward the table. "Do you think he's the one?" Her eyes lit up dramatically, and I saw a deep desire buried inside of her gaze.

"He could be, El. You do seem to really like him."

"I'm scared sometimes too though. I used to really like Dan and look how that turned out." She leaned back against her chair, suddenly looking bummed out.

"Hey, just because that doofus didn't see what a good thing he had, doesn't mean that Jaden won't realize it." I gave her a smile.

"You are so smart, I love you." She reached over the table and kissed my cheek, startling me. "Let's get coffee!" She jumped to her feet, her red curls bouncing as she did. She strolled to the counter, her heels clicking. I envied the risks Ella took all the time in the area of romance. I had yet to have a boyfriend, and anytime I liked a guy, it seemed I'd get shy about approaching him.

"I'd like a vanilla frappe, please," Ella said, smiling at the guy behind the counter. I stole a peek at him. Instantly my heart spasmed in my chest. What was wrong with me? He was cute and had an amazing smile. I hadn't seen him in here before, so I figured he must be new to the café. He wore a black shirt with a name tag, and his dark brown hair was styled in a side swoop. He had beautiful, crystal blue eyes. I glanced at his name tag and felt a thrill go through me. *Colten*. I wasn't sure why, but even his name made me react in a weird way. *Stop being such a dumb girl*, I told myself, but I couldn't help glancing at him as often as I could while Ella paid for her order.

When it was my turn, I stepped up to the counter, a ball of nerves in my stomach.

"What can I get you?"

"A number," I said the words before I could stop them. I nearly choked on my tongue. Why had I just said that! He gave a chuckle.

"I mean, can I have a mocha frappe, please?" I felt mortified. I did want his number, but wow, could I have been a bit more subtle about it? He punched in my order with a smile. I handed him a ten-dollar bill and stared at my hands. Ella nudged me from behind, and I looked back up. Colten held out my change, a warm expression on his face.

"What's your name?"

"Raven Dayton." I had no idea why I said my full name.

"I'm Colten, and we'll get that ready for you in no time." He gave both of us a nod and went over to the coffee machines.

"What was that?" Ella whispered, grabbing my elbow and dragging me over to the side.

"What was what?"

"That, that!" she said, nudging her head toward Colten. "Did you just ask that guy for his number?" Her eyes were huge and round, a devious smile on her face.

"I dunno, I guess, yeah, maybe…" I tripped over my words, feeling stupid.

"Raven Dayton, I didn't know you had it in you!" She gripped both of my arms, raising her eyebrows. "That was bold, girl." She pulled me in a huge hug and let out a squeal.

"He didn't give it to me, Ella, so my bravery was lost on him." I pulled her a little way from the counter, so Colten wouldn't overhear us.

"That is not the point. The point is—you actually asked for a guy's number. I feel like a proud mama right now." Ella waved a hand in front of her face. I let out a giggle. A minute or so later, Colten set our drinks up on the counter. When I grabbed mine, I saw a number scrawled along the side. I let out a gasp and turned and looked at him. He winked at me and went back to the counter to wait on another person.

"Ask and you shall receive," Ella said, walking with a strut back to the table. "I am so freaking proud of you right now. You have no idea." She sat down, setting her drink on the table. I rubbed my fingers over the number and blushed.

"Put that in your phone now. Or so help me." Ella waved at my cup. I shook my head, smiling as I did. I inserted the number in my phone to satisfy her but figured I wouldn't call it.

"So are you still having those freaky dreams?" Ella sipped at her drink, her eyes wide. I'd told her about a few detailed dreams I'd been having for a solid month now.

"Well, yes, and no." I played with the edge of my cup, stealing a glance at Colten.

"How can it be yes and no?" She giggled at me.

"They're not as freaky now, but I still have them. I see shapes more than anything." I wasn't entirely sure how to explain to her what had been happening for a while. I'd tried to tell my mom about them, but she was usually out the door too quickly.

"I thought you told me some of them came true." Ella was fully engaged now, staring at me, her coffee gripped in her hands.

"Yeah, they did, but it was just stupid stuff. Like, I saw Mom making brownies, and the next day she did. It's not that weird though." I was trying to shrug it off, but I wasn't telling Ella everything. I wasn't just seeing everyday life stuff. Shadowy figures seemed to be infiltrating my dreams more and more. This morning I could have sworn I saw one. It made me nearly scream. My mind drifted to what Dad had been researching. *Maybe I'm going to end up in the coo-coo bin with our other relatives.*

"You're not telling me something. Spill it." She crossed her arms.

"It's weird, Ella."

"I love weird." She took another drink of her coffee and leaned in closer.

"Okay," I said with a laugh. I brushed my hair from my face. "I'll be seeing normal people in my dreams, and then suddenly they will be clouded by shadowy-demon-like people. And I swear I saw one this morning as I woke up."

"Oooh!" Ella clamped a hand over her mouth. "No way! That's so freaky."

"I was trying to tell my parents, but I swear I have to make an appointment with them sometimes."

"Your dad loves that stuff. You should definitely tell him," Ella said.

I leaned back in my chair, sipping my coffee slowly so that I could think for a moment. Dad did love weird stuff, but for some reason this shadowy stuff felt way more real than the things Dad talked about. *It's because it's happening to me. I never asked to see demons.*

"Maybe you're clairvoyant!" Ella slapped her hands down on the table, startling me. I laughed nervously.

"Uh, Ella, what is that?" I'd heard of the word but wasn't familiar with it.

"They see visions that come true. Raven, it would be awesome!" She caught the look on my face and went somber for a moment. "I'm sorry. It bugs you, doesn't it?"

"Yeah, it does. It creeps me out." I turned my attention away from her, staring at the pictures on the wall in the café. She let me have a moment of space to sort my thoughts out.

"Clairvoyant or not, I still love you." She put her hand over mine. I turned my attention back to her.

"Thanks, Ella."

* * * * *

Wednesday rolled around, and I stood on stage, my notepad in my hand, my knees practically knocking together. A small podium stood in front of me, and I rested my notepad on top of it. I'd practiced the first poem, a million times, but I still didn't feel comfortable quoting from memory. The café's lights were dim, but I could still make out the faces of my family and the couple friends I'd conned into coming. I cleared my throat and looked down at my paper.

His hair as white as a dove's wing
His eyes as bright, golden as a ring
His voice shakes mountains, calling me home
His breath is warm, like an ocean's gentle foam
Here beneath his gaze, I am free to fly
Underneath his embrace, I can reach the sky
The golden flecks dance, reflected in his hair
Beneath the breeze, his skin so fair
I wonder who he is, why does he call me?
I dream of him coming, reflecting nightly

ANXIOUS

Could he be love, wrapped up in one soul?
Could he be light, peace of mind without a toll?
I hope one day I meet him, this golden-hearted one
So that I may reflect him and feel his warm sun.

I finished the poem and snuck a peek up at the crowd. They stared at me with wonder, and a splatter of applause erupted, mostly from my family. My eyes wandered to the left, and I saw a figure standing there. Brown hair, blue eyes, and a giant smile. *Colten.* My stomach clenched, and suddenly I felt like a nervous wreck. Thank God I had only signed up for one poem. I hurried from the stage and into the arms of my family.

"That was beautiful, Raven," my mom said and kissed my head.

"So, do you have a secret boyfriend I don't know about?" Ella said with a wink. "Who is this white-haired boy?"

I gave a laugh. "I have no idea. I had a dream about him, and as a result I wrote that poem. The weird thing is"—I stared at her a second—"Don't laugh, okay?"

"Just tell me!" Ella squeezed my arm.

"I swear he's real." I rubbed my forehead, flushed with embarrassment. "But it's not like I'm in love with a made-up guy. He's not—" I felt like I was digging a bigger hole for myself.

"What? He's not what?" Ella persisted.

"He's not like a romantic thing," I finished with a lame shrug. "It's something else. A feeling I guess."

Dad came up to me and hugged me, kissing my cheek. "You were brilliant, Raven. I loved it." His eyes lit up suddenly. "You know, in our family history there is a legend similar to the boy you wrote your poem about. Is that where you got your inspiration from?" He put his hands on my shoulders.

"Um, not really. I had a dream about him."

"Hmm..." Dad looked lost in thought, and I could already see him mentally typing something on his computer about the legend of the white-haired boy. I wanted to tell him about my other dreams.

"Dad—"

"How about we get ourselves some ice cream and head home?" Mom said. I stole a glance over my shoulder to see Colten staring at me. I wanted to go talk to him, but my nerves jumped all over the place at the thought. Alex noticed where my eyes stared and elbowed me gently in the side.

"You like?" He tilted his head with a grin.

"Shut up." I smirked and shook my head.

"Go talk to him, Raven," he said and nudged me again.

"What if he hated my poem?" I played with the ends of my dark hair.

"And what if he loved it, and you'll fall madly in love?" He tossed his head back dramatically.

"You are such a dork." I shoved him and started walking toward the door. "Let's go get ice cream."

* * * * *

I closed my eyes that night, Colten's face drifting in and out of my thoughts. I'd looked at his number a thousand times already, imagining myself texting him something. I wish I could be as brave as Ella or Alex about stuff like that. Alex had been with one or two girls, but nothing serious. He was too busy having fun and being crazy to settle down into anything just yet.

I'd dreamed about having a boyfriend since my friends and I used to cut out pictures in magazines and tape them up in our room. I smiled at the memory of me pasting famous singers and actors all over the walls and imagining them kissing me. Now, the only face I could see was Colten's. *Then text him!* I told myself with a laugh. I reached for my phone and stared at it for a few seconds. I quickly put it back on my nightstand. *Maybe tomorrow.*

I closed my eyes again. As I started to drift to sleep, I heard the shuffling of feet. My eyes jerked open, and I saw a shadow leaning over top of me. I slapped my hand over my mouth to stuff down a scream. I scrambled for something to hit the shadow with, but the only thing I found was a glass of water. I splashed the figure in the face and scrambled backward on my bed.

Warm light filled my room, and for one second the figure was illuminated. The face of a fair-haired boy swirled in the midst of golden rays of light. "The realms need your help, Raven. Only your bloodline can crossover…"

"Who are you?" I barely could get the words to come from my lips. His image flickered in and out like an old black and white film. *Am I actually seeing this?*

"King Michael of the angelic realms." And with those words he vanished.

I flipped on my lamp, staring at the place he'd just been. *I just saw an angel.* I turned my head slowly, examining my entire room. *I thought they were bigger.* I let out a nervous laugh, pressing my hands over my rapidly beating heart, trying to make sense of what had just happened. I wrapped my arms around myself. *I've lost it.* Whatever this was, I had a feeling it was only the beginning of it.

Chapter 3

Alex

I plopped the tent down on the leaf-infested ground, stretching as I did. Ian and Jack weren't here yet, but I figured I'd set up our site for our investigation tonight. I'd told my parents I was going on a mini camping trip with my two best friends, but I hadn't told them where. I unrolled the tent and set it up within a few minutes.

After I did, I pulled out a camp chair and plopped into it. I stared up into the tree branches, wondering what it was about this place that made my family bloodline see weird, freaky things. Dad had been studying the testimonies of our ancestors around the area, but most of them had ended up in the coo-coo bin. Ian, Jack, and I were just stupid enough to not really think this through like that. I leaned forward, massaging my chin for a moment.

"Dang, you're going to permanently break something by thinking that hard." Ian's voice broke through my thoughts. I jumped to my feet, pretend punching my friend.

"Ah, you or Jack will clean up the mess." I gave him a shove. A second later Jack jumped on top of the both of us, nearly bringing us both down into the leaves.

"Ah! Ghosts!" he screamed like a maniac. He looked around the campsite and nodded. "We are going to create havoc tonight!"

"If we can get a picture of these demon-shadowy things, we'll be rich." Ian pounded his chest.

"Yeah, right." I shook my head at him. "You can't even stay quiet for five seconds. How are you not going to spook off a ghost?" I grabbed my sleeping bag and shook it out, throwing it into our tent.

ANXIOUS

"But from what you've told us, Alex, this just happens to your coo-coo family." Ian wiggled his eyebrows. "I always knew you were one fry short."

"Me? You're claiming me one fry short? Who ate the chips under his bed last night?" I moved forward like I was going to attack him, and he jumped back.

"We gonna snuggle tonight, Alex?" Ian wiggled his eyebrows.

"Come here, bro." I leaned in with a kissy face. He shoved me away with a laugh.

"I love cuddling." Jack opened up his arms, his brown hair falling into his eyes.

"Cuddle with the bugs." I plopped back down in my chair and closed my eyes. "Do you really think anything weird is going to happen tonight?"

"Guess we'll find out." Ian opened another chair and plopped into it. "I brought the holy water, crucifix, and garlic just in case."

"Perfect, if we were hunting vampires, genius," I said.

"We don't know what we're facing. My Aunt Millie anointed our house with smelly oil to ward off demons, ghosts, vampires, and fairies. Maybe you should spritz us down with some WD-40 to keep the ghouls away." Ian wiggled his fingers at me.

"Let me get right on that, but with my luck I'd probably summon a demon instead," I said.

"Maybe we could feed him marshmallows and keep him as a pet." Ian leaned forward in his chair. "It'd come in handy with that bully Vince in school."

"That'd go over well with the folks," I said with a laugh. "Hey, Ma, I need to feed my demon some souls…got any spare ones?" I laughed again at how stupid this conversation was turning.

"Anyone going to build a fire?" Jack looked between the both of us.

"You are not touching anything." Ian pointed a finger at him. "You'll burn down the whole forest with your pyromaniac ways."

"I swear, I'll be careful." Jack rubbed his hands together, looking jittery.

"No, Jack. We know your tricks." Ian gave him a glare. "Besides, we don't need a fire. We're trying to attract the ghosts, not scare them away."

"How do you know they're ghosts?" I said with a laugh. "They could be werewolves."

"Shadowy-demon men are not wolves," Ian said matter-of-factly.

We continued to argue about whatever these shadow men were for a while.

Jack suddenly slapped Ian on the arm. "Shut up."

The sun had started to set, and even though I wasn't easily spooked, I could feel something lurking nearby.

"Do you see that?" Jack pointed far off in the distance, his body stiff with fright.

"No. You're just making crap up, Jack." Ian glanced past Jack, but I could tell he was a little bit freaked out too. He reached for his crucifix, which stuck out of his pocket.

"I swear to God I saw something move over there."

I tried my best to see through the dusky light, but it was hard to make anything out but the shadows of the trees.

"We should go check it out," Jack said, standing to his feet.

"Fine." Ian also stood, throwing me a look. I shrugged and headed toward the direction of the area Jack had seen something. For some reason, I knew there was something there. It wasn't that I saw anything; I felt it. It reminded me of when Raven and I were kids and she'd attempt to sneak up on me. I could always sense her before she got close enough to scare me. Ian and Jack were about as stealthy as a herd of elephants. We walked for a while until Jack stopped.

"It's gone. You goons scared it away with your loud-crunching feet." He crossed his arms over his chest. "Let's go make smores." That was how quickly Jack's attention span turned. I continued to examine the woods, sweeping my head back and forth, trying to get a glimpse of anything. Jack and Ian turned back around, but I stood there for a few more seconds. I could still feel something nearby. It hid itself, but it was still there, as if waiting for the right moment to reveal who it was to us. *Or eat us.*

My mouth went dry, and I licked my lips. I turned to go when I heard a soft whisper ripple through the tree branches. I strained my ears to hear the words, but it was hard to make out. Ian and Jack had nearly made it back to the campsite without me. Again, a murmur of words rippled through the trees.

That what you seek is already near. That which you desire is already here. You are the creator of your own reality. We are the protectors of the realms, we need you.

My body stiffened at the words, and I nearly squeaked in fright. I wasn't one to be ruffled easily, but the sound of those haunting voices made me on edge.

A shimmer of something caught my eye, and I could have sworn I saw several glowing figures glance at me from behind a few trees. When I took a step closer they disappeared into a shimmer of gold dust. *Angels?*

"That was freakin' weird." I hurried back to the campsite. I either had experienced what others in my family ancestry had witnessed, or I'd had some pretty bad hotdogs earlier today. Whatever the case was, I was quickly becoming a believer.

* * * * *

Something cold touched my arm, jerking me out of my deep sleep. Ian and Jack were curled up like little babies. What had touched me? I looked around the tent, willing my heart to stop its crazy, frantic beating. *It's nothing. Nothing touched you.* Something rustled outside, and again I froze. I wondered if what I'd felt and heard yesterday had come to finish the job. I climbed out of bed, unzipped the tent, and grabbed a nearby branch as a club.

I did a quick sweep of our campsite, but I didn't see anything disturbed. It could have been a squirrel or something out for revenge. I smirked at my own thoughts and lowered my club. I was overreacting that was for sure. I heard another sound and saw a ripple in the air, almost like you'd see from a heat mirage.

What you believe is what you see.

I heard the words as clear as can be, but I didn't want to believe that I'd actually heard something.

"What do you want?" I said in a mere whisper.

If you believe, you will create what you so desire. We are always watching... We need your help... The realms need you.

What I desired was to see who or what was talking to me. I no sooner thought the words, when the forest lit up for half a second. White figures, cloaked in golden light, swayed in an invisible breeze. I saw beautiful faces, fair skin, and white hair on each of them. *They look like elves.* Or at least that's the first thing I thought before my mind kicked into reality. *Maybe Jack was right, and these are ghosts.* My skin prickled with fear, and I gripped my club tighter.

Suddenly, a beam of light burst from their backs, going straight up into the air, and trickling down around the tall, ethereal beings, as if shielding them. Unlike pictures I'd seen of angels, these wings swirled and seemed to be alive. The light from their backs blurred together as if one giant barrier of light.

Holy crap, those are angels. Wow. I could have stared at them all night. *Now I know how those shepherds felt.*

We are the Endrita, angels of the other realms, a voice whispered, tickling my ear.

"Hey...uh...okay." I took a step back, brushing a hand over my ear. "Whatever you are, we didn't mean any harm coming out here. I got no beef with angels."

We help protect everyone from the demon horde the Daegal. We need your help. Only your family can cross over into the realms.

A dark feeling swept over me at the word *Daegal* and I shuddered. My knuckles started to turn white. I was officially creeped out now. *Demon horde...what did I get myself into?* I took several steps back toward the tent to wake up my two friends. The moment I touched the zipper, the white entities disappeared into golden dust. *I just saw freaking angels, and they want my help.*

"This keeps getting freakier and freakier by the moment." I slipped back into the tent, climbed beneath my sleeping bag, and pretended I hadn't just seen what I'd seen.

Chapter 4

Raven

"That's the fifth time that doll has plotted to kill me today," my brother, Alex, said in a deadpan tone. I gave him half a glance and continued drawing. My brother was nuts. I knew he was bored, but there wasn't a whole lot we could do in Mom's store. I'd already rearranged everything twice, and Alex had borderline drove me crazy a few times.

"Alex, maybe you should clean the bathroom." My lips turned into half a smile as I erased part of my drawing of a weird-looking woman. It looked terrible. Lately it seemed all I could draw were these strange-looking people inspired from my dreams. I started to sketch something that looked like wings and paused. *Seems like that fits.*

"Can I?" Alex put his hands together and batted his eyelashes at me, pursing his lips like a girl.

"I'll even let you spray the air freshener when you're done." I heard him get up, and I stuck out my finger. "Don't eat it, no matter how fruity it smells."

"I'm out." Alex raised his hands up and backed away, making me laugh. This was why I loved my brother—he always knew how to make me laugh. In school, Alex was well-liked, even if some of the kids thought he was a bit "out there" with his antics. His two friends were pretty idiotic, but they made him happy, so I couldn't razz him too much about them. I knew Alex was smart, even if his grades sucked.

"What is that?" Alex's face was suddenly right next to mine, his breath on my cheek. "She looks like a freak."

"Alex," I said under my breath. "Can you not be you for five seconds?"

"Can't."

"Why?" I tapped my pencil.

"It's in my contract. Annoy sister for life. Check."

I put my pencil down and turned to face him. There wasn't anyone on this planet I loved more than my brother. Of course, I loved my mom and dad, but Alex, despite his craziness, understood me. He constantly supported me in my art, writing, and anything I was brave enough to try. I wrapped my arms around him, surprising him.

"I love you." I hugged him tight, smiled, and went back to drawing.

"You're going to make me blubber doing crap like that." He pretended to wipe tears from his eyes, but I knew he'd needed a hug. Alex and I had this weird connection from the day we were born. I could sense and feel what he needed, even if he didn't say it. Mom and Dad loved us both like crazy, but Alex couldn't show his deeper, affectionate side to them—it was too "babyish." But, for some reason, he'd always open up to me.

"I'm not cleaning the toilet, so don't try that again." He wandered away, picking up the random, weird stuff Mom was selling.

Ding.

I turned to see a guy walk into the store. The instant I saw him, I put my pencil down. Alex gave me a side-glance, and I knew what he was thinking before he said a word.

"Hmmm…" was all Alex said.

"Shut up." I blushed and grabbed my pencil again. I tried not to stare, but it was pretty hard not to notice the cute guy walking around an antique store. It was Colten from the café. Why was he in here? Finally, after what felt like an hour, he came over to the counter.

"Hi."

I slapped the picture in front of me, startling the brown-haired, blue-eyed boy, who had muscles far too big for a teenager.

"I'm good," I said, and then nearly kicked myself. He hadn't said "how are you," he'd simply said hi.

"How can we help you?" Alex cut in, saving my butt. I turned about five shades of pink, wishing I could slide under the counter.

"I'm looking for a birthday gift for a girlfriend." As he said the word *girlfriend*, he gazed at me, and I swore he looked amused—like he held a secret I didn't know about.

My stomach twisted. Of course, he had a girlfriend. He was far too good-looking to not have a love life—unlike me.

"What does she like?" Alex came out from behind the counter, throwing me a "sorry" expression as he led the guy away.

"She loves old stuff." Again, as he said the word, he threw me a glance. My heart spasmed in my chest. *Why does he keep looking at me if he has a girlfriend? Why did he give me his number?* I watched the back of him, shutting my drawing book and letting out a sigh. For the last few months, I watched the friends that I did have get into relationships. They'd go off to camp, or meet a guy in some random place, and suddenly before I knew it, they were gushing all about their latest Prince Charming. It's not that I didn't want a guy; I was just terrified they'd think I sucked.

When Alex came back, he didn't say a word to me. He just sat there, quiet. Which I figured he knew I needed. There had been a couple guys I'd liked last year, but none of them seemed interested in me. While Alex swore I wasn't ugly, I found it hard to believe that any guy would find me attractive.

"Thanks, man. I gotta run to work." Colten left, empty-handed, throwing me one final look. The moment his eyes landed on me, I felt the flutter of a million wings all over again. I was still confused about why he'd give me his number when he had a girlfriend. Until it struck me. He hadn't had a girlfriend when he gave me his number, I was just too late. I slumped in my chair. I'd waited too long to contact him.

"It's seven. Let's close this joint and grab some coffee. I'm going to send Mr. Butcher a quick text to let him know where we are. Mom wanted us to check in with him." Alex wrapped his arm around my shoulder and squeezed.

"Kay." I packed up my drawing stuff, straightened a few things in the store, and followed Alex toward the door as he sent a message to our neighbor. We shut off the lights and locked it up tight. As we headed toward the coffee shop, Alex was far too quiet.

"What are you thinking?"

"Stop worrying so much, Raven." My brother's shirt rippled in the wind.

"I'm not."

"Yes, you are. I don't have a girlfriend either."

"I don't want a girlfriend," I said with a smirk.

He gave me a light shove. We reached the café, and we stepped inside. I inhaled the coffee smell with a content sigh. Alex ordered a triple espresso, while I ordered a caramel macchiato. I spotted Colten in the back but prayed he didn't see me. After we got our drinks, we both sat down, sipping them. I'd only had a couple swallows when the door to the coffee shop flung open. A man stood, panic-faced, his shirt buttons torn off, and a smear of blood on his cheek.

"That's Mr. Butler," I said to Alex.

"Alex, Raven," he said in a choked voice.

I felt the air leave my lungs.

"You two need to come with me." What little hair he had was a complete mess, and the wrinkles on his face looked even deeper.

Alex grabbed my hand, squeezing so hard it hurt, but I didn't pull my hand away.

"Let's go," I said. As I stood, I bumped the table, knocking my coffee over. Alex's hand slipped from mine as I swore under my breath, running over to get a napkin. Colten was suddenly beside me, grabbing napkins. "It's okay. I got it."

"Just leave it," Mr. Butler said in a panic. I exchanged a look with Alex, tingles of fear spreading over my entire body.

"Thank you," I told Colten. He nodded to me. Alex grabbed my hand again. I jerked my head, as out of my peripheral vision I saw a swirling black image of a shadowy man grinning at the both of us. *What was that?* My body started to tremble. *Demon.* The vision of the golden-colored coffee dripping down the table transformed in my mind to a deep shade of red—blood.

Chapter 5

Alex

Our house wasn't far, and Raven and I ran the entire way. Mr. Butler tried his best to keep up with us. He attempted to tell us what was going on, but all he could say was a bunch of nonsense. I spotted our green dollhouse, and the instant I saw it, I felt a heaviness hit my chest, dragging me into an abyss on the inside.

"Alex?" Raven's voice was barely a whisper as we stopped running. We stared at the house for several heartbeats. I'd never heard Raven's voice sound so scared and childlike. I had to be brave for her. I could hear Mayfly whinnying in the background somewhere.

"Come on." I pulled her after me, up the stairs, but I couldn't bring myself to move quickly. I pushed open the front door, the hinges squeaking. I stepped into the entryway of our house and into the living room. A strangled cry came from Raven's mouth, and I found myself making the same heart-wrenching sound. My stomach lurched into a million knots, bile burning my throat.

I had to turn away for a moment. Two figures lay in a pool of blood. The only thing I could think was, *Mom is going to be so upset about the stain.* I clutched Raven's hand, but I barely felt her fingers squeezing mine. Mr. Butcher came in, just behind us, a complete wreck, pacing, crying, and blubbering on the phone.

The floor was scratched, as if someone had been dragged, trying to escape their fate. Old papers, yellowed with age, were scattered all over the place. Little bits of glass were strewn about the floor—like small diamonds spilled haphazardly. Several family pictures had been knocked off the wall. Where the images of our faces had been was holes—as if someone had shoved just their fingertips through it.

I recognized my dad's nice suit—the one he wore when he was trying to impress someone, and my mother wore her prettiest dress. But the two figures on the floor weren't them—it couldn't be them.

Raven started shaking beside me, and finally I felt the pain ravaging through first her and then me. The link, we shared, created a mass of chaos, on the inside of me. My knees hit the floor, and I scooped up the bodies of my two parents. Mr. Butler screamed something at the both of us, but Raven was beside me too, sobbing, clutching our parents, burying her face in their chests.

"I tried to stop him, I tried! He killed them both before I could get help for them." Mr. Butler paced again, wringing his hands, crying. His body trembled, his eyes wide with terror. "Something was wrong with him—his face—" Mr. Butler shuddered. "He was too strong."

"Shut up," I said under my breath, clutching the bloody bodies of my parents, feeling a giant, sucking hole taking all my air.

"He was raving mad—I tried to stop him!"

I heard the door open and shut behind us, and suddenly Raven and I were ripped away from the bodies of our parents. Something shattered in the middle of my chest, and I let out a scream. It barely registered in my mind that Raven also screamed, fighting her way toward the bodies of our parents. I punched one guy in the face and shoved another out of my way.

"Leave them alone!"

Men in uniforms grabbed me, holding me back, holding Raven back. How could this have happened? Why would someone break in and murder my parents?

"I'm sorry, son. Come with me." A tall, brown-haired officer wrapped his arms around me, holding me tight against his chest. I struggled to get free, wanting to touch them, wanting to know they were okay. They had to be okay.

"Alex!" I heard Raven scream, and I turned to see her also restrained in the arms of a police officer.

"Let me go to my sister. Now."

The man released me, and I rushed over to Raven's side, pulling her tight against my chest. She sobbed, shuddering, her fingers digging into the back of my scalp.

"Why did this happen? Why didn't Mom and Dad just let the man take whatever he wanted?" Raven's dark hair plastered to the side of my face, my tears making it stick.

I didn't say anything. I just held her.

* * * * *

Outside on the porch, Raven sat numbly beside me, a blanket wrapped around her shoulders. I had one arm around her, but I barely felt a thing. The police officers had talked to Mr. Butler, and it seemed to all of them a cut-and-dry case. A man had broken into our house and murdered my parents. Mr. Butler had tried to give a detailed description, but it seemed he talked mostly gibberish saying stuff like "his face shifted" or "he seemed to be a blur." So now we had nothing—the one man who saw the murderer couldn't even describe him. Anger scratched through me at the thought.

"This can't be real," I whispered under my breath. I rested my head up against Raven's.

"Who would do this—" Raven's voice broke into a sob. I pulled her against me, my heart a spastic mess on the inside. Something crushed my chest; I couldn't seem to get enough air, my hands tingling. *Am I having a heart attack?*

"I can't breathe." I buried my face in her hair, trying to get control of myself. Darkness crowded in the edges of my mind, spreading. *I should have been there to stop that man. I should have been there.* I thought about my years of training. *I could have taken him down.*

"Alex..." Raven's voice trembled. I knew I needed to pull myself together for her. I couldn't lose it like this. A hand twisted my heart on the inside of me, and images of my parents dead, sprawled out on the floor, flickered like a horror movie in my head.

"I'm fine." I was anything but fine, but I couldn't let Raven deal with my panic too. I had to be strong for her. Raven held me, and I let her, trying my best not to let her see my fear. What was going to happen to the two of us?

"I can feel what you're feeling, so stop hiding it," Raven said, and she looked me in the eyes. Her tears made my heart churn harder in my chest, racing out of control to the point I thought I was going to vomit.

"Raven, I don't know what they're going to do with us."

"It doesn't matter. I have you." She buried her face in my neck. "As long as I have you…"

My heart finally slowed back down, my breathing still tight, but manageable. I kissed my sister's head, brushing her hair back from her face like my mom used to do when we were kids.

After what felt like hours, the same police officer, who had restrained me, came over to the both of us.

"I'm really sorry." His eyes filled with compassion as he looked at us. "Do you two have any relatives close by?"

"Uncle Jim," I said without thinking. My dad's brother lived in our city, but Dad always called him the "black sheep" of the family, and we never saw him.

"All right. Let's give him a call."

I somehow managed to give him the phone number, since Dad had given it to me once, and the man talked for a while, glancing at us every so often.

"I want Mom," Raven whimpered against my shoulder, her tears dripping onto my shirt. So did I, but I somehow couldn't get my mouth to say it. It felt like we sat there for hours, waiting.

The policeman, whom we found out was named Tom, bent down to the both of us, putting his hands on our knees. "Your uncle is on his way. We'll figure this out. It's going to be all right."

Raven and I nodded, knowing that nothing would be right again.

Chapter 6

Raven

I heard the squeal of tires and watched as a black Mustang pulled up to the front of our house. I winced at the sound. *This is Uncle Jim's car?* I had half expected a beat-up pickup truck, not this. The way Dad had talked about his brother, I thought he'd be some sort of deadbeat. He obviously had money, and money to burn. Our family had always had plenty, and part of me realized if anyone was to rob a house, ours would be the one to rob. We've always had high-class, antique furniture, art, and artifacts all over the place.

My eyes traveled up to the sky above me as it turned shades of orange and pink as dusk manifested. A light breeze rustled my tangled hair. Alex sat beside me, fighting the darkest feelings I'd ever felt from him, and I struggled to catch my breath as well. I couldn't shake the image of Mom and Dad sprawled out, looking like they'd been through a war and back again. How could someone have done that to my family? Why, why had they done it?

Only your bloodline can cross over... The words of King Michael came scrambling into my mind. *That was just a dream. It had to be.* Dark spots danced behind my eyes, and I felt my lungs struggle to get enough air. I'd felt anxiety, from time to time, but nothing like this. *Will I ever feel normal again?* My brother's panic rose by the second, and I didn't have the energy to help him.

The door to the Mustang opened, and I watched as a tall, slightly overweight man, with dark hair and blue eyes, get out. He looked a lot like Dad, but I could see a hardness in his face. His lips were pressed into a straight line, and his eyes darted to first Alex and then me. A shiver ran over my skin at the sight of him, and I had no idea why. Dad hadn't talked much about his brother, Jim, and I figured there was a good reason why he kept him away from us. We'd only seen him about three times in our lives.

Uncle Jim stopped about five feet from the both of us. He wore a black business suit, and I could practically smell money on him. He didn't talk for a solid ten seconds. The police officer spotted him and walked over.

"I'm Officer Tom Williams, you must be Jim Dayton?"

"Yes." Uncle Jim looked annoyed by the entire ordeal already.

"I'm sorry about your loss, sir. Please come with me." Officer Tom led our uncle away.

"He hates us," I said, the instant they left earshot.

"You don't know that, Raven," Alex said.

"Did you see the way he looked at us? Like we were some sort of dog poop stuck to his shoe?" I wrapped my arms around myself, rocking back and forth. "I wish you were eighteen."

"Me too." Alex grabbed my hand and squeezed.

The two of us sat there in silence for what seemed like forever, until Uncle Jim and Officer Tom came out. Uncle Jim headed to his car, while Officer Tom knelt before us again.

"Did your parents have wills?" His voice was soft with compassion.

"I don't know," I said. Alex was silent beside me.

"We'll get this all squared away, but in the mean time you're going to stay with your uncle. All right?"

The both of us nodded. What else were we going to do? Demand our parents be brought back to life again?

"Worry about getting packed later. You two get some rest." Officer Tom patted each of us, and Alex and I numbly stood to our feet. We walked, hand in hand, toward the Mustang and got into the backseat. The leather seats below me were cool and comfortable, and I could smell vanilla in the air.

"Don't touch the windows," Uncle Jim said, and started up the car. With a rev of his engine, he pulled out of our driveway.

The ride to Uncle Jim's house was silent. I couldn't shake the knot in the pit of my stomach, and on more than one occasion I wanted to vomit. I heard Alex's shortness of breath and wished I could help him deal with it.

After ten minutes, we pulled up into the driveway of a massive, modern-looking home. It had to have been over four thousand square foot, with hundreds of windows, and a three-car garage with a balcony above it. The steps leading up to the house zigzagged, and the lawn was picture perfect. I spotted a swimming pool to the left and let out a little gasp. Uncle Jim was very well off. He pulled into the garage and killed the engine.

"Take your shoes off, and don't touch anything." He got out of the car and headed inside without waiting for us.

"He sucks," Alex muttered as he opened the door. I got out and followed my brother close, still feeling sick to my stomach. Something about this place, about Uncle Jim, made me feel weird and queasy.

I stepped through the entrance of the house, my hands balled up into two tight fists. A little gasp escaped my lips as I saw the high ceilings, gorgeous white and navy furniture, and a white, spiral staircase winding upward. A fireplace with ornate white stones climbed one entire wall, and several white rugs lay precisely about. Alex had stopped just a few feet in front of the door and stared at everything. Uncle Jim had disappeared from view. I approached Alex, and we both continued to stand there, unsure of what to do now.

"What does he do for a living?" Alex said in a breathless voice.

"Rob banks?" I said and received half a smile from my brother.

"Probably." Alex stepped a few feet more into the room.

"Take your shoes off!" a voice screeched and nearly made me pee my pants. A tall, thin woman, with blond hair styled to perfection came around the corner, holding a fluffy, white dog.

I slipped my shoes off, and Alex followed suit. We continued to stand there, frozen. The woman's eyebrows flexed into an annoyed expression.

"I'm Lillian, and you must be Alex and Raven." She held out a dainty hand like she wanted us to kiss it. I shook it, and she looked me over with a sneer. "Hmm…"

"Your bedroom is this way," Uncle Jim suddenly said, coming into the room without me hearing him. I wanted to hold Alex's hand again, but with Lillian watching it felt weird. The hallways and rooms we passed were just as impressive as the living room. We approached a door, and Uncle Jim turned and walked off, not saying another word to us.

"He's real friendly." Alex shoved the door open, and we came into an open room with two beds, a dresser, and a view of the pool beyond. Alex plopped onto the bed, throwing his hand over his eyes.

"He's Dad's brother?" I said the words before thinking, and Alex peeked one eye at me.

"Probably why Dad didn't mention him much. He's a real sweetheart."

I lay down on the bed beside my brother, staring up at the ceiling. "Is that his wife?"

"She's a ball of sunshine too." Alex kept his hand over his face.

"I guess we did just crash into their lives." I traced the ceiling tiles with my eyes, sorrow weighting my chest making it hard to function.

"Umm…hmm…" Alex reached for me, and I let him hold me for a long time before we both fell into a restless sleep.

Chapter 7

Alex

The next morning, I woke up, my mind racing with a million spiraling thoughts. I should have seen this coming. I could have stopped the thief. I'd been training for years in Wing Chun, and I'd bested most guys twice by size. The one time I actually needed what I'd been taught, and I hadn't been there. My chest burned with pain, and I couldn't seem to catch my breath and calm myself back down.

What were Raven and I going to do? The sunrays danced on the floor, looking like long fingers reaching for the both of us. Raven was still asleep, her face angelic and childlike. I wanted to take away her pain, and I had no idea how to deal with any of this. I felt my skin tingle with sweat, and I turned on my side, burying my face in the sheets. We'd slept in the same bed. There was no way I was going to leave my sister alone for a minute.

A loud shout pulled my mind back to the present moment, and Raven stirred beside me. I pulled her into my arms, holding her, wishing I could go back in time and stop everything that happened. What had transpired on Mom and Dad's getaway? Why had they been back early? I shut the thoughts off, the feelings that rose too painful to deal with. Tension balled up in my chest, and the back of my neck ached. Another shout resounded, and Raven moved again, her eyes slowly fluttering open.

"Wh-what is that?" She snuggled against me, and my heart stung.

"I don't know. I'll go check." I untangled myself from her, pulled on a shirt, and headed out toward the living room. Before I'd even reached the living room, I could hear Uncle Jim shouting.

"I'm figuring it out. It's not like I ordered my brother and his wife to get murdered." Uncle Jim's body was tense, his fingers curled into fists as he faced Lillian.

Something struck my stomach, and I nearly vomited at his words. *Murdered.*

"Jim, this is ridiculous. We both hate children." Lillian's eyes were narrowed into slits. "You're far too busy, and I'm not wiping their snotty, little noses."

"I know that." Uncle Jim shifted where he stood, and I could see that he wanted to slug something. He turned around and noticed me, his blue eyes sparking. "How long have you been listening to us?"

I felt frozen. "Long enough." Furious words roared through my head, but I bit my cheek to stop myself from saying them.

"That thief really threw a wrench in my life, kid." His words were short and clipped. I stared at him, unable to believe that he was so callous toward his own brother's death.

"We can't have kids here." Lillian's face twisted into a sneer, her fingernails clacking against the glass end table.

"His parents are dead, Lillian."

The word *dead* sounded so cold on his lips that it felt like a physical blow to the chest.

"This is a disaster." Lillian stood to her feet, brushed off the front of her white dress, and left the room. Uncle Jim ran his fingers through his hair, paced for a second, and followed after her.

What is wrong with these people? I stood there, alone. A few seconds passed, and I heard the sound of my sister's footsteps. She came and stood beside me.

"Alex?" She didn't need to say anything else as pinpricks of tension climbed over my entire body. How could we live here? They clearly didn't want us around.

"I feel sick." Raven put a hand on her stomach, her face looking ashen.

"Go lie back down." I led her toward the room, helped her back into bed, and lay down beside her. I felt like a helpless baby, and I hated it. My phone buzzed beside me, and I swiped it off the nightstand. It was a text from Ian—I guess word got around fast. I didn't bother to read it, throwing my phone back on the nightstand. I didn't want to think about it. Ropes of tension tangled in the back of my neck and back, a lump formed in my throat. All I could hear was Uncle Jim's words, *His parents are dead, Lillian.*

* * * * *

Something startled me back awake, and I reached over to find Raven gone. My heart sped up, and heat washed over my entire body. *Everyone's gone.* My fingers dug into the sheets, and I tried to catch my breath. I threw the covers off of me and leaned over the side of the bed. *This is my fault. I could have been there to stop it.* A sharp dagger twisted in my chest. *I could have stopped him.* I don't know what had happened between my parents and this thief, but if they'd seen Raven or I, I knew my dad would have given up anything to have us all safe. He loved us. He loved my mom. Why would a man just kill them for some hunk of junk he could sell? Fury boiled in my limbs, making heat climb up my neck. My limbs grew taut as I thought about how I'd have taken him down in a minute flat.

I heard a noise and looked up to see Raven standing in the doorway, pale-faced, and looking like a little kid.

"I was hungry," she said in a tiny voice. "But then all I could think about was how Mom used to make us pancakes."

"Raven..." My throat constricted, and I turned from her, forcing my tears back.

"This is really happening, isn't it?" She walked toward me with slow steps.

"Yes." I got to my feet, stretched, and wrapped my hands around the back of my neck. "Do we have any other family members anywhere?" I racked my mind trying to think. There wasn't much to our family tree.

"I don't think so." Raven sat on the bed, staring out the window at the pool.

"I don't want to live here—I wish Grandma was still alive. Or that Grandpa wasn't crazy." My mouth was dry, and a headache formed in the front of my skull.

"I don't think they want us here either. You'd think that Uncle Jim would have more compassion, considering his brother—" Raven's head fell into her hands, and her shoulders started shaking. My own grief overwhelmed me, and I went to her, crying with her. We both crawled back into bed, not wanting to face the reality of our situation.

You failed. You're alone. You could have stopped him, the thoughts tormented me as I tried to fall back asleep beside Raven. *You should have been there. It's your fault.* A hard ball built inside of me, and my jaw clenched, aching.

"What about Mayfly?" Raven said in a whisper. "What's going to happen to her and the house?"

"We'll figure it out. I promise. I won't let them take her from you." I prayed I at least could save my sister's horse. Somehow, I managed to fall asleep, Raven's ragged breathing filling my ears.

* * * * *

A cold finger brushed my face, jerking me out of my exhausted slumber. *Who touched me?* My heart stopped for a moment, and I glanced, with nerves tight, around the room. Shadows filled the corners, and a swirling darkness danced in and out of my peripheral vision. I squeezed my eyes shut, wishing the aching emptiness to dissolve, wanting my world to be right again—wanting my mind to stop playing tricks on me.

There's no one there. You're delusional.

Alex…this is your fault…, a cold voice hissed.

I pressed my fists up against my forehead, trying to shut out the voice that ravaged my mind.

"What are you?" I said into the darkness. When nothing spoke back, I shoved my pillow over my head.

ANXIOUS

A couple hours later, I woke again, starving. Even though my stomach lurched, the very thought of food sounded revolting. I grabbed Raven's hand, helped her out of bed, and motioned for her to follow me. We went down the hall, into the living room, and somehow managed to find the kitchen in this maze of a house. Uncle Jim sat at the table, drinking a cup of coffee.

"You're finally up." He gave us one glance each and continued to basically ignore us.

"I need to feed my horse," Raven said in a quiet voice. Uncle Jim just threw her half a glance and shrugged.

"What is your problem? Don't you care that your brother just died!" I couldn't help it; this man was a heartless idiot.

"Of course I care." Uncle Jim stood to his feet, his face a dark storm of anger. "You think I don't care that my only brother just got himself murdered? I'm furious—that's what I am. How could that thief be so—so—heartless? Plus, now I have the responsibility of his two brats. Do you really think I wanted two kids to take care of and put through school?" Uncle Jim's face flushed with fury, his fists shaking. "Lillian doesn't want kids. What do you think I'm supposed to do now? Kick out my older brother's kids? She's threatening to leave me—now that I have the two of you to babysit."

I stared at him, every word a kick in the gut. We were unwanted.

"Do you understand the inconvenient situation I'm put into now? Your dad didn't even treat me like a brother anymore, and now I have his baggage to deal with." Uncle Jim left, leaving me feeling dumbfounded, and the pressure of his words on my mind. I threw a glimpse at my sister. Every ounce of color was drained from her face. She trembled, looking as lost as I felt.

"Don't listen to him." I had no idea what else to say or do at this point.

"I'm going home. I have to take care of Mayfly." Raven stood there trembling, her arms wrapped around herself.

"I'll go with you. I'll call a cab."

Chapter 8

Raven

My hand rested on Mayfly's nose, my face pressed up against it. My horse could feel my sadness, and she nuzzled my cheek gently, letting out soft snuffing sounds.

"I don't know what we're going to do with you, girl," I said, choking on my words. I kissed her nose, tears gathered in my eyes. She looked at me with her big brown eyes as if telling me it was okay. I glanced over my shoulder, spotting her saddle. Part of me wanted to ride away as far as I could go—ride until my life felt right again. A warm hand pressed up against my back. My brother rested his head against my neck, and together we stood there with my horse.

"I promise; I won't let them take her. I promise." Alex's words did little to soothe me. Clearly, Uncle Jim didn't want us. He wouldn't want a horse too, even if I could take care of her myself. I'd lately been practicing gymnastics on the back of my horse, and I'd been getting pretty good at it. Alex had often called me a circus freak, because I could balance and flip on Mayfly now. I wanted to ride her at least one more time.

"I have to ride." I strolled toward her saddle and picked it up. Alex gave me a tortured look.

"Raven—"

"This may be the last time ever. Uncle Jim doesn't want us, let alone a horse." I put the saddle on the back of Mayfly and strapped it down. I put the bit in her mouth and stroked her nose. Alex didn't say another word as I climbed onto Mayfly's back. I sat in the saddle, and for a moment I could forget that my entire world was completely shattered.

"I'll ride with you." Alex walked over to where he kept his dirt bike and climbed onto it. The moment we left the barn, I felt like the world was normal again—the feel of Mayfly, Alex beside me, the blur of the trees, and the caress of the wind. All of it seemed so *normal* but digging beneath the surface I felt everything tipped on its end. We rode for what felt like hours, until Mayfly got tired and Alex was nearly out of gas. I walked Mayfly back into the barn and slid off her back. I removed her saddle, rubbed her down, and fed her. Alex put his bike away and stood beside me.

"We'll figure this out." Alex gave me a hug.

"I know."

* * * * *

"You can't keep the horse." Uncle Jim stood in front of our house, his arms crossed. We'd been packing up our stuff for hours, and all of us were growing tired and crabby.

"Do you have any idea what that horse means to Raven?" Alex's body bristled, his eyes flashing.

"I don't care. I don't have room for a horse, and it's going to be too challenging for you to keep it here alone. I'm not going to run you back and forth every day to feed it."

"I'll take a cab." I lifted my chin, feeling defiant.

"You'll run out of money, and I'm not shelling out dough for some smelly animal." He walked down the steps of our house.

"You know what? You're a d——" Alex started to say before I grabbed his arm.

"It's fine. He's right." I cast a look at the barn, thinking about all the times I'd had with Mayfly. I had already called my gymnastic teachers and dropped out of gymnastics. Losing my horse—well, it just seemed like that was how life was going to be now.

"Raven, I won't let him do that to you." Alex had fire in his eyes, and I knew my uncle was going to land on his butt in a moment.

"It's fine, Alex. We can't expect life to be the same now. I already backed out of gymnastics."

"You did what?" Alex grabbed my arms, turning me to face him. "You love gymnastics."

"Yeah, I used to. I can't expect Uncle Jim to pay for it now and bring me to all the practices and meets." A heaviness went through me.

"I already put an ad up online," Uncle Jim informed the both of us. I saw my brother get a look in his eye again to knock my uncle out, so I stepped forward.

"I get to choose who she goes to." At least I could make sure Mayfly ended up in a nice home.

"Fine." Uncle Jim shrugged. "You have someone coming in a few minutes."

The shock of the news hit me. I already had to say goodbye so soon? An emptiness sucked me down, and I almost started to cry right there. Alex's arms were around me, and he pulled me to his chest. He held me for a long time, until a truck pulled up to the house, toting behind it a horse carrier. These people weren't messing around. I forced my tears into a hard ball in my stomach.

Uncle Jim greeted a nice-looking woman, and I saw someone else climb out. When I got closer, shock rippled through me. *Colten.* He turned and spotted me, looking just as shocked as I did. I hadn't seen him since the day in the café, but I was sure he'd heard about my parents' death. He gave me a sympathetic smile and made his way over to me.

"Hi," he said, holding out his hand. "I'm Colten. Just in case you forgot." He nodded to my brother.

"I'm Alex, this is Raven." Alex shook his hand.

"Nice to meet you, guys. I'm sorry for your loss. I heard what happened." His eyes locked onto mine, but I couldn't hold his gaze without bursting into tears.

"Is your mom wanting to buy our horse?" Alex said for me.

"Yeah. She's a real horse nut. She's great with them. I ride too." He threw me a glance, and my heart squeezed tight. "Is she your horse?"

"Yeah." The word came out in a whisper, and I wiped several tears from my eyes.

"I'm sorry." Colten fell silent for a moment. "I promise we will take really good care of her."

I watched as the woman led Mayfly out of the barn. My heart shattered into pieces, and I let out a sob. Alex grabbed me in a hug and held me as I wept into his arms. I felt awful, crying like that in front of Colten, but I couldn't help it.

"Mom, Mom, wait a minute." Colten jogged over to his mom and said something I couldn't hear. I looked up, seeing Mayfly standing there, looking at me with her kind expression. Colten grabbed her reins and led her toward me. He paused when he reached Alex and I and handed the reins over to me. I threw my arms around my horse, my tears smearing on her mane. Mayfly nuzzled my cheek, snuffling against me.

"Bye, Mayfly," I said, tears trailing down my cheeks. Alex's hand was on my back, and I could feel Colten standing nearby. When I looked up, I saw a painful look on Colten's face.

"I promise, we will love her, and um, Raven—" He drew in a deep breath. "Please call me. I know we don't know each other well, but that day I gave you my number I meant it." He held my attention.

"Okay," I said quietly. I finally let Mayfly go, my chest caving in on me. Alex held me from behind, his chin resting on my head.

"We'll get her back. I don't know how, but we will." He gave Colten a nod. "Hey, man, here's my sister's number." Alex rattled off my number, and I saw Colten put it into his phone. "Call her."

"Thanks." Colten gave us both one final nod, waved, and walked toward his mom and Mayfly. I watched him until he climbed into the truck.

"Why did you give him my number?" I asked.

"Because you need it." Alex kissed the back of my head. "Plus, if the guy's a creep, you know someone who can flatten him in about five seconds."

"I can keep up with the best of them," I said, attempting to smile.

"I know you can. Who do you think taught you?" He kissed my head again and held me tighter.

* * * * *

Thud.

I dropped the last box into the moving van, my heart tanking with the sound. Mayfly was gone. I threw a glance at our house, wishing I could rewind time and treasure more of the moments I'd shared with my family. All of it was gone now. Part of me was thankful that Mayfly was now living with Colten. Even though I didn't know him, I trusted what he said—he would take care of my horse. *Maybe I will call him.* The thought didn't send happy feelings shooting through me like the first time I'd seen him. Instead I felt like a shell, just moving without feeling in life.

The last few days had passed by in a blur, as Uncle Jim made funeral arrangements, the police had questioned us about our parents, and several visitors had come out to see Alex, me, and Uncle Jim, bringing flowers and food. Everyone we knew seemed awkward when they approached either Alex or me. I knew they were uncomfortable with the fact that my parents had been murdered, and they didn't know how to express their sympathy for the two of us. Our entire world was shattered, and nothing felt like it used to. I didn't want to leave our house behind, despite having several nightmares about the images I'd seen the night we'd found our parents.

A hand touched my back, and I jumped.

"Come on, we're ready to go. Uncle Jim is waiting." The conversation he'd had with our uncle kept looping in my mind, making even more queasy feelings in the pit of my stomach. I kept waking up in the middle of the night, my gut in a mass of knots. No matter how many times I went to the bathroom, the feeling of nausea wouldn't leave me alone. The funeral was going to be tomorrow, and I didn't want to face the facts—my parents were dead.

Alex gently led me to Uncle Jim's car, and I got into the backseat. He'd hired a moving van to take care of everything in the house and had put it into a storage unit for now. He'd planned on selling most of everything Mom and Dad had owned to help pay for the funeral. Luckily, Alex and I had been able to take what we wanted from the house before Uncle Jim had gotten to it. I'd found an antique mirror hidden behind some old coats, as if someone had quickly tucked it away. I slipped it into my purse, wondering if this was the item Mom had met a seller for—since I didn't remember ever seeing it before. Uncle Jim had put Mom's antique shop up for sale and planned on putting the money into a trust fund for Alex and me.

Despite not liking my uncle very much, at least he wasn't stealing everything from us. I got into the Mustang and leaned up against the back of the seat. We just had to get through tomorrow, and then maybe our life would somehow fall into some sort of normal routine.

"After tomorrow, I need to talk to the both of you," Uncle Jim said from the front as we headed back to his house.

"Okay," I said. I shoved a pair of earbuds in my ears and cranked up the volume of my phone. All I'd been doing lately was listening to music, and I'd never seen Alex so mindless. He never sat still, and ever since the night of our parents' death, he was like a zombie.

We got back to the house, and all three of us made our way inside. I slipped my shoes off and headed to Alex and I's room. There was plenty of space in this giant house, but Uncle Jim had never offered us our own rooms, and Alex and I didn't want to separate anyways. When I got into our room, I let out a sigh.

"Is it stupid that I just want tomorrow to be over?" I said, partially to myself, partially to Alex.

"All the people, flowers, food; it's like ripping open a wound every five seconds, so yeah, I get it." Alex sat down beside me.

"How are you doing?" I turned to face him, sitting cross-legged on the bed.

"I should have been there, Raven." His jaw clenched, and I saw him ball one fist.

"Alex, there is no way you would have known. Plus, Mom and Dad weren't even supposed to be home till the next day. How would you have known to go back to the house?"

"I'm the one who suggested going to the café. If we'd went straight home, maybe I could have stopped that thief. I've been training for years." Alex's mouth pressed into a straight line. I'd never seen my brother look so serious in my life. I was so used to my happy-go-lucky brother that it was like looking at a stranger.

"Stop. You can't do that to yourself. It was not your fault." I rubbed my forehead, a headache building. I stared out the window, watching the wind ripple the trees near the pool.

"I could have tried. Plus, I have a bag of weapons in my room I could have used." Alex's body stiffened.

"Alex—" I started to say.

"Alex, Raven!" I heard a voice call and flinched. Lillian. I barely knew the woman, but I didn't like her. We both stood to our feet and headed toward the sound of her voice.

"Try this apple, dearies," Alex said in an evil witch voice. I gave half a smile—that was the Alex I remembered. The moment I saw Lillian, my stomach lurched into my throat. In her hand was two pairs of shoes—Alex's and my shoes.

"I thought I told the two of you to take your shoes off at the door."

I exchanged a quick glance with Alex. We'd both completely forgotten, and I had deposited my shoes in the living room—tracking into the house.

"Sorry, Lillian," I quickly said, before the woman blew her top off.

"This is unacceptable." She threw the shoes at the floor, spreading more dirt, and stomped away in a huff. I thought it would have been a lot worse than that.

"Well, that was anticlimactic. I thought she was going to grow a pair of horns at the very least." Alex looked at the dirt the woman had created by throwing our dirty sneakers around.

"Has she never heard of a mop or a broom?" I scooped up my shoes and shook my head at the mess.

"Would you even know where a broom is located in this maze?" Alex scooped up his own pair of shoes.

"Nope." I headed toward my room, not really giving a crap about the mess. "Let her clean it up."

"She really will grow a pair of horns if you leave it."

"Why do I care? She doesn't want us here anyways."

Alex's hand rested on my back, and he turned to face me. "Hey, it's going to be okay."

Tears burned in my eyes. "No, it's not. It really is not." I took off to our room, feeling idiotic that I was crying again.

Chapter 9

Alex

The funeral made it real. Greeting hundreds of people, hearing the "I'm sorry for your loss" over and over, made the empty feeling on the inside feel legit. Raven and I both stood before the grave, holding hands, long after everyone had left. We weren't far from Uncle Jim's house, so we'd let him leave without us. I didn't want to walk away, not yet. Once I walked away, I knew the life I had before was as dead as the bodies we'd put in the ground today. *I could have saved you, Mom and Dad. I'm sorry.* I tried not to let my emotions get to me, but here, with Raven, by ourselves, I lost it. I knelt down in front of their graves and sobbed like a baby. Raven soon joined me, until we were both such a mess, I didn't know how we were going to stop.

My head throbbed as the tears flowed, and my fingers dug into the fresh dirt.

"I can't believe he did it. It doesn't make any sense." I punched the ground beneath me. Raven grabbed my arm and turned to face me.

"Alex, I know you're angry, but you have got to stop blaming yourself. You couldn't have stopped him."

"This is my fault. I should have been there." I couldn't seem to shake these feelings no matter how much she told me the opposite. *Alexander…* I thought of the name my mother had always called me. I saw her smiling face before my eyes and could still smell *Mom's surprise.* I didn't deserve the name Alexander anymore. I'd let her down—I'd let her and Raven both down.

"We should go home."

"Raven, we don't have a home." I could have kicked myself for saying the words, but it was how I felt. Raven burst into tears all over again, and I nearly punched myself. I was an insensitive jerk.

I pulled my sister into a hug, feeling her ache and knowing that her thoughts were just as dark as mine were turning.

"It doesn't matter, I still have you. You're my home." She buried her face in my neck, and I felt her tears wetting my skin.

"Come on."

* * * * *

Before Raven and I even entered Uncle Jim's house, I could hear arguing back and forth. Whatever they were talking about had Lillian in a fit. Part of me didn't want to go inside, but there was nowhere else for Raven and me to go.

"This ought to be fun," I mumbled to Raven as I shoved open the door. The moment we stepped inside, I heard Lillian screaming.

"They're not your responsibility!"

Uncle Jim and Lillian both turned to look at us as we stood in the doorway. I slipped my shoes off and set them on the rug. Raven followed my actions, and we walked toward our bedroom.

"Lillian, what else was I supposed to do?" Uncle Jim sounded highly aggravated.

"Put them in the system, Jim. It's not like they're the first kids whose parents have died!" Lillian stood to her feet, looking flushed, and stormed out of the room.

"Lillian!"

"It's me or them, Jim. Make your choice."

Uncle Jim watched her storm out the front door. He turned his eyes toward us, a dark expression flickering over his face. "Sit down." He rubbed his forehead, letting out a heavy sigh.

I knew what was coming. My heartbeat picked up in speed, and a hand tightened my breathing.

"You two have to go." He stood to his feet, pacing, running his fingers through his hair. "I don't want two kids that aren't mine—I don't even want one of my own." He looked up. "I'm not losing my girlfriend over you."

"Where are we going to go?" Raven's voice rose in pitch, white knuckling the front of her shirt.

"I really don't care." Uncle Jim turned to leave the room, when a fierce anger ripped through me. Before I knew what I was doing. My Wing Chun kicked in, and my hands flew through the air. The scumbag thudded to the ground. I couldn't stop myself; a red haze blinded me, urging me to release all my pent-up fury on this guy. I threw punch after punch, my body dancing with each movement.

"Alex!" Something tugged at my arms, urging me to stop. Uncle Jim tried to get to his feet, and I knocked him back down.

"Don't do this!" Raven's shrill voice cut through my blind rage.

I dropped Uncle Jim on the ground, shaking, furious at him and myself for losing all control. He got to his feet and wrapped his hand around the front of my shirt, lifting me off the ground.

"Listen, punk, this is my home, and I don't care if you're my loser brother's kid, I don't have to give up my life for you. It's not my fault your dad got himself murdered."

I nearly attacked him again, but Raven's hand on my arm stopped me. She tugged me backward, tears streaming down her face.

"Alex, come on." She pulled me toward our room, and I felt her entire body shuddering. Uncle Jim picked up his cell phone. I couldn't shake the image of Mom from my mind. Raven practically shoved me into our room and slammed the door.

"What were you thinking?" She gripped my arms and shook me.

"How can one man be so…so—" I couldn't express the fear, anger, hurt, and feelings of betrayal pumping through me right now.

"Selfish?" Raven supplied for me and threw herself backward on the bed. "Because he's not Dad."

"But Dad was selfish, Raven, he should have let that thief take it all. Now instead we have nothing." The muscles in my neck tensed.

"We don't know what happened." Her words were soft.

"Dad was more concerned about material things than what could have happened if he didn't listen." I sat down on the edge of the bed, holding my face in my hands. I rubbed my temples, trying to get my headache, which had quickly formed, to ease.

Raven fell silent, and I knew I'd hurt her by trying to face reality.

"Look, I don't want to believe it either. But something did happen, and as far as I see it, Dad should have let the guy have everything." I brushed her cheek, wishing I could take the fear that was on her face.

"I know that." Raven's body lightly shook, and I knew she was crying again.

"Whatever happens, Raven, I'll be with you. I promise." I hadn't been there for Mom and Dad, at least I could be there for my sister.

Chapter 10

Raven

I woke up, my face feeling puffy, my throat burning with thirst. Beside me, Alex still slept. I reached over to the nightstand and grabbed my glass of water from the night before. My eyes gradually scanned the room, and I spotted my drawing book and journal. I hadn't wanted to draw, write, or do anything since the night my parents died. Now, Uncle Jim was kicking us out. What was going to happen?

Buzz. A text came through, and I swooped up my phone. A text from Colten and one from Ella were on the screen.

How are you? Colten had texted.

I miss you. Please call me, Ella's text read. I wasn't in the mood to answer my best friend's text, so I numbly punched in a reply to Colten. *I'm okay.* A few seconds passed, and my phone buzzed at me.

If you want to visit Mayfly, you can. My mom's cool with it.

The words sent a slight warmth through me but was quickly squelched.

Rap. Rap.

A knock came to our door, and Alex jerked awake, wiping drool from his mouth.

"Who's—" he mumbled. He slid out of bed and went to the door. When he opened it, a woman stood before him, dressed in a business suit, her brown hair smooth and pulled back into a twist.

"I'm Amanda, you must be Alex." She came in without our invitation and took in the room. She spotted me laying in the bed and frowned. "Are you two sleeping together?"

"Well yes, but—" Alex rubbed the back of his head.

I guess it looked weird that siblings were sharing a bed.

"I'm here to bring you both to your new homes. Pack what you need."

"Wait, new homes? As in plural?" I said, straightening. Instantly my heart started to pound like a frightened rabbit.

"I'm sorry, kids, but there are no available homes for the two of you." Her face was smooth of emotion, as if she'd said these same words a million times.

"You can't do that." Alex's hand gripped the woman's arm. She gave him a stern look, her mouth crinkling into a scowl.

"Remove your hand, young man, and yes, I can do that. Your uncle has removed himself as your guardian, so now you are in the care of the state." She ran a light touch over her hair.

A wave of nausea hit me, and I turned to the side of the bed, hot vomit trying to come up my throat. I put a hand over my mouth, forcing the feeling down.

"Please—I'm begging you. You can't rip Raven and I apart. She needs me." I could hear the terror in my brother's voice, matching my own.

"I'm sorry, son, but there is nothing I can do. Now hurry it up. I don't have all day. Pack your things. We'll send for the rest of your belongings once you're settled into your new homes." Amanda smoothed her hair again, brushing invisible crumbs off the front of her.

An iron ball rested in the pit of my stomach. *They're taking him away from me. Everyone leaves me.* My body tremored, something crawling up my throat.

"Raven"—Alex turned to me—"I won't let them do this to us." He grabbed my hand, his eyes searching mine frantically. I knew he could feel my panic.

"How are you going to stop it? We can't live on the street." I somehow managed to get out of bed and started putting my stuff together, my heart starting to feel numb.

"I'll beg Uncle Jim to keep us. I'll do whatever it takes. They can't rip us apart." Without packing, he left the room, and I could hear him talking to our uncle. I didn't hear the words, but I could hear them arguing. After what felt like forever, he came back, his face a mask of fury.

"I'll fix this. I promise." He started shoving clothes into a bag.

After a couple minutes, Amanda came back into the room looking annoyed. "Come on, you two, hurry it up."

I grabbed my bag, shoving my journal and sketchbook inside at the last minute. Each step I took through the house thudded in my ears. I wanted to reach for Alex's hand, but with Amanda next to us, I knew she'd disapprove, so I kept my hand to myself. Without a goodbye from Uncle Jim, we left the house and got into the woman's minivan. I slid the door shut, smelling old food. Alex sat next to me, silent, looking like anyone else but the happy brother I remembered. He'd always been able to pull me out of any bad mood, but now it was like he had forgotten how to be himself. We drove in silence for a good twenty minutes, before the van rolled to a stop. We had gone through a rundown neighborhood; every lawn looked like a near jungle, and toys were scattered everywhere.

"This is your stop, Raven," Amanda said. She parked the van, got out, and waited for me. I grabbed my bag, and Alex and I climbed out together.

"Alex, stay in the van," Amanda said the moment she spotted him. Something screamed on the inside of me, and my body buzzed with terror.

"Please, can't he say goodbye to me?" I held my bag, my stomach in knots.

"Make it quick." Amanda walked toward the house and knocked on the door. An overweight woman with thin dishwater blond hair answered and let her in. She threw a glance at me, and I winced.

"I'll figure this out. I won't let them take you away from me." Alex stood before me, looking furious, but determined as well.

"I know you will." I dropped my bags and threw my arms around him. His heart, pressed up against mine, was beating a million miles a second, and I could feel the sweat breaking out over his body. We held each other for a long time.

"All right. Time to go, Raven," Amanda called from the doorway, sounding rather annoyed.

I didn't want to let go of Alex—he was my lifeline. He was what kept me from completely falling down the hole in my mind. I buried my face in his chest, and he continued to cling to me as well. A few seconds passed, when I felt hands grab me and yank me back.

"Time to go. Now." Amanda's hand on my arm was like iron, her fingers digging into my skin. Again, an inward scream echoed in my mind.

"Please, please, he's all I have left." Tears pooled in my eyes, and fear crowded the edges of my mind.

"I'm sorry," Amanda said with finality. "Say goodbye."

"Where will he live? Can I see him?" I could hardly bear the look on my brother's face.

Amanda ignored my questions. "Get in the van, Alex."

He continued to stand where he was as Amanda gripped my arm, pulling me toward the rather rundown modular before me. I reached the doorway and turned to look at Alex again. I could see him visibly shaking, and I felt his high anxiety building even more. He wanted to protect me, and he knew he couldn't. *Find me, Alex. Come back for me.* Amanda pulled me inside and led me over to a chair and sat me down.

The metal chair beneath me was cold, the windows were dirty, and cobwebs collected in the corners. The house looked like it had been surfaced cleaned, as if someone had been in a hurry to make an impression, but I still noticed the stains, dirt, and neglect that was apparent all over the place.

"Raven, this is your new foster mother, Jill Hannah."

I took in the overweight woman, with thin, dyed blond hair, small brown eyes, and a wrinkled dress, which looked too small for her.

"Hello," I said. My hands twisted together, and my shoulders were tight with tension. I wanted Alex.

"Brandon, grab her bags!" the woman's harsh voice rang, and I found myself wincing. A boy, who looked about thirteen, scurried into view and went out the door.

"Well, Jill, I'll leave you two to get acquainted. When is Nelson going to be home?" Amanda shifted from foot to foot.

"Six." Jill gave me a once over, her beady eyes reminding me of a rat. "It'll give you plenty of time to get yourself settled. You'll be sharing a room with Cody for now, but we'll get you set up with Jamie soon." Jill threw a nervous look at Amanda.

"Make sure she has her own space; you understand the regulations, correct?" Amanda's voice was clipped as she spoke.

"Of course. I have had plenty of kids." Jill gave Amanda a lifeless-looking smile.

"Good." Amanda nodded and turned to go. Brandon came back into the house, hauling my two bags.

"Goodbye, Raven." Amanda turned and left without another word. I stood watching the door for a few seconds, until I realized that this was it. I was now under the care of this other woman, who I didn't know at all, and my life was completely left in her hands.

"I'll show you your room." Jill stood to her feet, wobbling as she walked. I followed her with a timid step, not wanting to admit that everything in this moment terrified me. My body ached, my head pounded, and my throat was dry. We got to a small bedroom, where two tiny beds were shoved against either side of the wall. The floor was covered in Legos, video games, figurines, and CDs—along with crusty plates, cups, and bags of used chips.

"You and Cody will share for a few nights, until we can manage some space in Jamie's room." The woman gave me an odd look, and my chest tightened inside of me.

"Okay." My voice sounded small even to my own ears. Jill closed the door, the sound of the *thud* hitting the inside of my chest.

Welcome home, Raven.

Chapter 11

Alex

I felt cold. Lifeless. My mind was an empty shell as I watched my little sister be placed into the hands of a stranger. I wanted to fight, but I knew there was nothing I could say or do that would change what was happening. Amanda got back into the van and started the engine. We drove in silence for ten minutes, until we reached a modern-looking home, with a metal fence in the front yard.

A couple little boys were playing with a ball, and a black dog nipped at their heels. The sight normally would have made me smile and want to join in on the fun, but all I felt was a sucking emptiness. My mind kept straying back to the look of terror on my sister's face, and there was nothing I could do to help her.

Amanda parked and got out of the van. I grabbed my bags, slid the door open, and climbed out. The sun warmed my face, but I barely noticed it as I walked toward the house. There was nothing amazing about this place, but it looked nicer than the house Amanda had dropped Raven off in. I got to the front steps and sucked in a deep breath. Amanda opened the door and ushered me inside. The living room was crowded with trophies and outdoorsy decorations such as bears, logs, and pinecones. Even the air smelled like pine and cinnamon.

A moment passed, and a pretty woman came bustling around the corner, her blond hair pulled up into a ponytail, and a tennis racket over her shoulder. She wore a tennis skirt and a black sporty tank top.

"Mark! Amanda is here!" she called and hurried out the door, giving me a faint smile.

"Ah!" A man walked around the corner of the kitchen. He was short and a bit bald, but I could see that for his age he was fit. He wore a nice black business suit and a dark red tie. "I'm Mark." He reached for my hand and gave it a good shake. "Come in, come in. Have a seat."

I sat down on the plaid couch, setting my bags beside me. I took in the pine end tables, the handmade wooden lamps with dark green shades, and a ton of bear figurines all over the place. I'm normally not this observant, but my nerves seemed to heighten my awareness.

"I think we're all settled?" Amanda glanced between the two of us.

"Sure." I shrugged, knowing the woman wanted to hand me off and book it out of here as fast as possible. As far as social workers went, Amanda seemed like she had a bug up her butt.

"We'll get Alex all situated. No need to worry." Mark shook Amanda's hand and saw her out the door. Once she left, he turned to me with a warm yet nervous smile. "Follow me, son."

The word *son* unsettled me. My stomach jumped, and I shoved the feeling away. I picked up my bags, and with heavy steps, followed my new *dad*. He led me down a hall, where several pictures hung on the wall of him and his wife playing tennis and several other sports. The two boys I'd seen outside weren't anywhere on the wall. *Weird.*

Mark led me to a bedroom at the very end of the hall, and instantly I felt like I'd entered a closet. There was a bed, a dresser, but everywhere else it was covered in sports equipment.

"Sorry about the mess. This is our storage room. The boys have the other spare room, and my office is off-limits." He gave me a smile. "Are you a sports fan?"

"Not really." I shrugged.

"Other hobbies?" His eyes looked me up and down, probably noticing that I was fairly fit.

"I do Wing Chun, and I like extreme sports." I couldn't seem to put any ounce of enthusiasm into my voice.

A puzzled look crossed Mark's face. "What is Wing Chun?"

ANXIOUS

I pulled my butterfly knives out of my bag and gave a mini demonstration. At the end, Mark's eyes were wide, looking rather impressed.

"So you're a kung fu master?" He lightly laughed. He reached out and ruffled my hair like I was ten years old. "Just keep those things away from the boys."

I set my bags down, shrugged, and turned to face him once again, but he'd already left. I shut the door, sat down on the edge of the bed, and drew in a deep breath. Lately I couldn't seem to breathe deep enough, my chest a constant knotted mess. I'd heard other people describe panic attacks or high-anxiety symptoms, but I didn't want to believe I was like that.

I'd always fought off negativity by laughing, having fun, or talking with Raven. Now I had nothing. I grabbed my phone and scrolled mindlessly through an app that used to make me laugh all the time. I didn't even have my own space—I was storage just like the rest of this crap.

My door suddenly burst open, and the two little boys I'd seen in the front yard came in. They started arguing, grabbing at the same ball resting on the floor. The black dog nipped and barked at their heels.

"I want a turn! You always get the yellow ball!" one boy with red hair whined.

"Nuh-uh! You did last time!" The other little boy, who was skinnier than the first, pulled at the ball.

"Champ! Stop barking! Boys!" Mark came into my room, grabbed the ball, and gave the boys and the dog a shove out the door. "Neither of you gets it." Without another word, Mark slammed the door.

I rubbed my temples, a headache spreading. I scrolled through my different apps—not wanting to allow any of my thoughts to have their way. *You're a failure… You couldn't save them.* My phone dinged, and I saw that a text from Ian came through. I'd been avoiding my friends for a while now, and I still didn't feel like going out and having "fun" at the moment. What was the point of building ziplines or riding my dirt bike now? I knew if I stopped practicing, my Wing Chun would also suffer.

Hey, man, where you been?

I tapped on the reply button, not sure how to even respond to him. *Around,* I texted.

Jack and I are going to the movies. Want to come?

The thought of being around my friends right now opened up worry that they would see beyond my shell and see how sucky I really felt.

Nah, I'm okay. Thanks. I set my phone on the bed and stared up at the ceiling. *If only I'd been there... None of this would have happened.* The thoughts went in and out of my mind making my chest ache. I felt hungry, shaky, and every one of my nerves buzzed with tension. *This is my fault... I'll never get Raven back now. How will I get out of this mess?*

My fingers gripped the sides of my head. This *was* all my fault. If I'd only stopped that thief. Scenes played through my head, each one making the digging feeling in my chest spread. I closed my eyes, resting my head on the pillow next to me. It was still daylight, but all I felt was the emptiness of night.

Alex...

My eyes darted open, tingles spreading over my skin. What was that? Who'd called my name? I shook my head, rubbing my forehead with my fingers. Something moved out of the corner of my eye, and I jerked my head to the side. Was there a cat in here? I sat up, looking between the sports equipment. I reluctantly climbed out of bed, sorting through the random stuff. No cat. I shrugged and plopped back down on my bed.

In and out of several apps, I laid on my bed for what felt like hours, until a knock came to my door.

Mark stuck his head in. "Hi, slugger, do you want some dinner?"

What was with the stupid nicknames? I shrugged, knowing I was hungry, but not caring.

"Lynda made some killer lasagna. Come on, meet everyone." He kept staring at me until I got off the bed. A numbness spread over my chest as I shoved my phone in my pocket. I went down the hall, past the living room, and turned left to an open kitchen. A wooden table sat with log-like chairs. In the center of the table sat a giant candle that looked like Birchwood. The blond woman, who'd rushed out the door without greeting me, set down a glass pan of lasagna. She gave me a quick, nervous smile and slipped into a chair. The two little boys ran into the room, scrambling to find their seats. Mark sat at the head of the table, so I found the last chair, feeling awkward.

Normally to break awkward silences I'd crack a few jokes, but there was nothing inside of me that wanted to talk, let alone say something funny.

"Boys, I want you to meet Alex, your new brother," Mark said. "Alex, this is Garret and Benjamin." He pointed at the redhead first and then the other boy. I gave a little wave, wanting to go back to my room.

"I'm Lynda. Sorry about rushing off earlier, I had an appointment with a friend." The woman smiled, but it didn't reach her eyes. She seemed distracted, as if her mind was lost somewhere trying to find its way back home.

"Tell us a little about yourself, Alex," Mark prompted, scooping lasagna for the two smaller boys and then some for himself.

What was there really for me to say? Hi, I'm Alex, and my parents got murdered? The one relative I did have kicked me and my sister out? I let out a soft gasp, feeling my lungs constrict.

"It's okay, there's no pressure," Lynda said quickly, most likely seeing my panic. I'd never been one short on words, or shy for that matter, but right now I felt like a scared little boy, and I hated it.

"I'm Alex, and I…well…I dunno." I looked anywhere but at the faces of my new *family*. Sadness threatened to overwhelm me, and I felt my emotions building like a geyser about to burst. I practically jumped up from the table and bolted to my room. I shut the door, my breath short, my body sweating. "I can't do this. I can't do this." I couldn't pretend that I was all right. I couldn't pretend that I hadn't just had my entire world ripped from me. *This is my fault. I should have tried harder. I should have stopped that man.* Dark fingers gripped my skull, and my muscles started to ache.

Alex... a dark whisper entered my mind, weaving in and out of my consciousness. Something darted nearby me, and I practically jumped out of my skin. I really did see something that time. It looked like a black ball of fuzz. I pressed my back up against the door, not knowing what to do. Did I check it out, or ignore that it even happened?

It's your fault, Alex. The words hit me in the chest, feeling like tiny daggers digging into me.

"I know it is," I said out loud, and then felt like an idiot for talking to myself. I needed to get a grip. I was surprised Lynda or Mark didn't come after me. Mom would have. She'd make sure I was okay—or she'd somehow get me to laugh so that I forgot all about my problems. *You're not here anymore.* My body flushed with heat, and my fists shook. *This is my fault, Mom, but why did you and Dad not just give the man what he wanted? How could you two have ripped our family apart like this?* My emotions jumped between guilt, fear, anger, sadness, and I couldn't seem to control any of them. I'd never counted myself as an emotional guy, but now I couldn't even figure out what mattered anymore to me. *I have to make sure Raven is safe—that's all that matters now.*

I moved away from the door and laid back down on the bed. A cold sensation pressed down on me, and I let a few tears escape. I didn't want to cry anymore. I'd cried enough.

Chapter 12

Raven

"Get out here and do these dishes," a voice cut into my thoughts. I'd managed to get some of my stuff put away and had thrown away some of the wrappers that were plastered all over this kid's floor. Who was she talking to? I peeked my head out the door and spotted Jill standing at the end of the hall. I turned to finish cleaning up when she called again, "Hey, I said get out here and do these dishes!"

I continued to unpack, thinking she was probably yelling at one of her other kids. Suddenly, the door burst open, and the woman's bulky frame filled the doorframe.

She let out a curse word. "I said get out here and do these dishes."

"Oh!" I stood to my feet. "I didn't know you were talking to me. I'm sorry, Jill." I dusted off the front of my hoodie. She looked around the room with a critical eye and let out a scoffing noise.

"You're going to make Cody mad for touching his stuff. Next time, come when I call you." She left the room, and I soon followed suit, feeling a pinching sensation in my heart. What kind of woman was this? I'd just gotten here, and she was already demanding me clean her horrifyingly messy house?

I stepped into the kitchen and sucked in a sharp breath. It was a disaster! It looked like the dishes hadn't been done in a month. I had no idea how Amanda or I hadn't smelled this when we'd came in. I stepped over several pans that were haphazardly laying on the floor and managed to get over to the sink. Jill stood there, with her arms crossed, her beady eyes taking me in.

"I expect these to be done in an hour. You have a lot of work to do today."

"There's no way these can be done in an hour," I interjected, but then realized I shouldn't have said anything.

"Listen, I am putting you up in my home, and you'll do what I say." Jill's face leaned in close to mine, and I could feel her buzzing anger.

"Okay." I took a step back and started pulling dishes out of the sink. *This woman is crazy.* I stacked for a good fifteen minutes, until the sink was clear enough to fill it with water. I looked around for a dishwasher, but realized I was all on my own.

"Jamie!" Jill called out from where she'd plopped herself onto her couch. "Get your fat butt in the kitchen!"

A minute passed, and finally a girl sauntered into the kitchen, her face a mask of annoyance.

"You have the new girl doing them." She let out a string of curse words at her mom.

"She says she can't do them in an *hour;* it's your job to babysit her. And don't break anything or you'll be short dinner!"

"You never cook anyways!" Jamie kicked at a pan laying on the floor.

"How about you sass me one more time? Let's see how your father handles that!"

Jamie shut her mouth, throwing an aggravated glance my way. "You must be as slow and stupid as you look. It's not like it takes a master's degree to do dishes." Jamie was tall, overweight, and had purple hair with red streaks in it. Her face was caked with way too much makeup, and I saw little marks on her arm.

She cuts herself. Even though I was going through the loss of my parents, I'd never considered hurting myself like that. She noticed where my eyes rested and let out a swear word.

"What are you looking at?"

I loaded up the sink in silence and started washing as quick as I could. Most of the food was stuck on, so it wasn't exactly easy. Jamie rinsed, half the time not getting all the soap off.

"You suck at this. Look, you left food on this plate." She shoved the plate back in the water, drenching the front of my hoodie.

"Why don't you guys do dishes more than once a month then?" I wasn't normally someone who'd snap like that, but this whole thing was stupid. I was emotionally drained and wanted to rest.

"I do other stuff, and Jill is too fat and lazy to do anything," she said the last line under her breath. "You'll see. She's a total—"

Smack!

Jamie staggered to the side, a red mark staining her cheek. Out of nowhere a man had appeared, burly, huge, and with a purplish face.

"You watch your mouth!" He had oil stains on his plaid shirt, and his pants were torn at the knees.

"You say it all the time, Nelson!" Jamie put a hand to her cheek, her eyes narrowing. "Your wife is a fat sloth."

Nelson's beefy hands grabbed Jamie and raised her off the floor, shaking her several times. "Shut your filthy mouth and do what you're told. And you call me Dad, not Nelson." His lips pulled back into a sneer.

Jamie grabbed at his fingers, gagging. I panicked. I backed away from the sink, trembling. I'd never seen such violence before. He dropped her, and she crumpled to the floor like a ragdoll. She wheezed in and out, rubbing the spot the man had squeezed. She stood to her feet, and without another word, she continued to rinse and put away the dishes.

I washed as fast as possible after that, wanting to go to my room, but even that didn't feel safe or familiar. *I want Mom...* The thought left a dead feeling inside of me, and I couldn't seem to find any form of relief of the pressure building under the surface.

When I felt like crap, I would usually find Alex and he'd cheer me up by making me do something incredibly stupid or by showing me memes or funny videos to make me smile again. *Alex is gone.* The empty feeling climbed up my throat. Jamie and I finished the dishes, and I headed toward my room. Before I got very far, I heard Jill call out again, "Come here, Raven."

A quick, staccato beat pounded in my chest. I walked into the living room, seeing the filth coating every inch of this place.

"Nelson, this is our new girl, Raven. Say hello to your new dad." Jill waved her hand as if she really didn't care about what she was saying. Nelson had a smirk on his face, and I tried not to look at him too long, my mind replaying the way he'd treated Jamie.

"Hi."

"Aren't you going to give your new dad a kiss?" Nelson said with a wink. Spiders crawled over my skin, and my body broke out with sweat.

"Ah, Nelson, she's not used to your jokes yet." Jill let out a cackle.

I scurried from the room, hoping that I could have as little as contact with that man as possible.

"Didn't you hear me, girl? I said you had a lot to do today," Jill called as I went down the hall. "Get your skinny butt back here, and I'll give you your list. Jamie already did her duty, and now it's your turn."

I went back out into the living room, reluctant to see what kind of backbreaking tasks this filthy woman had in store for me.

"First on the list is clean the bathroom. Here." The woman thrusted a dirty piece of paper into my hand. "And make your mother some coffee." She gave me a smirk. I fiddled with the list, a crushing weight falling on top of me. This was my life now. I started to walk away when Nelson said, "Make enough coffee for both of us."

I jumped at the sound of his voice.

"Jumpy little rat, isn't she?" Jill said.

"She's not used to having a real man in the house—her father was a pansy from what I've heard." Nelson let out a harsh-sounding laugh. Red-faced, I headed to the kitchen to make these horrible people coffee. Part of me wanted to spit in the pot, but I resisted, trying to find where everything was located. *He's right though—Dad was a pansy. He couldn't even defend himself or Mom against that thief.* A shudder went over my body, and I tried to push the thoughts away. I felt eyes on me, and my entire body tensed. Part of me wanted to look, and another part of me was afraid to. I hurried and made them coffee, leaving as it started to brew.

I walked toward the hallway to find the bathroom. When I came across it, I nearly puked. Mold, old pads, garbage, and dirty towels were everywhere. Smears of something brown were on the walls, and the stench was so horrid that bile rose up my throat. *These people live like pigs.*

"Ha, you got the bathroom on your list too?" Jamie peeked her head in the door. "Cody made a huge dump in there today, so if you lift the lid, you may get a little surprise. He never flushes." Jamie walked away, and I could tell she was happy I'd been certified as Cinderella and not her. I wondered if Jamie was Jill and Nelson's actual daughter or not.

I looked underneath the sink to see if there were any cleaning supplies and found very little. Tears threatened to spill, but I forced them into a hard ball in my stomach. I was hungry, tired, and all I wanted to do was cry, but I couldn't. I couldn't let them see their cruel treatment got to me like that.

* * * *

After a good three hours, I left the bathroom feeling hungry, dirty, and tired. I went toward my room and went to go pull open the door to find it locked. I turned the handle again, but it was definitely locked. I gave a timid knock, hearing rustling around inside.

"Oh, he does that a lot," a voice said from behind me. "He's mad that they put you in his room." Brandon stood behind me.

"I just need my clothes so I can shower and change. Can you get him to open it?" I asked the skinny boy with bad acne.

"He's not going to open it up. You'll have to get Nelson to do it." Brandon shrugged.

I didn't want to go anywhere near that terrifying man. Maybe Jamie would let me borrow some of her clothes until I could get my own. I hesitated by the door a moment longer and headed toward what I figured was Jamie's room. I got to the door and gave a knock.

I heard someone moving around, and Jamie soon peeked her head through the door.

"What?" Her heavy-shadowed eyes narrowed into thin slits. I could smell the waft of strong perfume on her.

"Cody locked me out of our room, and I just need a change of clothes. Can I borrow something?"

Jamie started laughing. "Deal with it." The door slammed in my face. I stood there, in shock, for a solid thirty seconds, before I realized that this life I'd been thrown into was something out of a horror movie. I wasn't going to be given any handouts, no help, and I had to deal with this on my own. I had nowhere to go. *Why did that man have to ruin everything!* Anger exploded on the inside of me, and I wanted to punch something or someone. I'd never been a violent person, and I'd always expressed myself in my art to release the pent-up feelings. Now I had nothing. Not even a space to call my own.

Raven…

A tingling sensation swept over my skin, and I turned my head sharply at the sound of my name. A cold shadow passed over my mind, and I bit down on my lip to keep from falling into a little ball right there in the hallway.

You'll never be happy again.

My stomach knotted, and I felt vomit rise up my throat. I was going to puke, right here and right now, in this hallway. I ran to the bathroom I'd just cleaned and heaved what little I had in my stomach. I clutched the sides of the toilet, shaking, hopelessness seizing my mind. How was I going to survive here? *Alex, I need you.* I not only could feel my fear and anxiety, but I knew he was hurting too. Our bond hadn't gotten any less, even if he was far away.

Please, please, I need help… I didn't even know who I was talking to, but the words continued to build in my head. *I need help.* The sound of footsteps came into the bathroom.

"What's wrong with you?" a sharp voice said—Jill. A hand gripped the back of my head, and she yanked me backward. "I thought I told you to clean this bathroom."

ANXIOUS

My head burned from her pulling my hair, and my body still trembled like crazy.

"I did—I needed to take a shower, and Cody locked our room. I need my clothes."

"Why you puking all over my bathroom, then? You have more to do!" She pulled my hair hard again, and I let out a soft whimper at the pain. She grabbed my chin with her fat fingers and stared into my eyes. "We don't give handouts. You'll get a shower and dinner when you're finished with your list of chores." She slapped me across the face once, hard, and stood to her feet. "Stop wasting my time." She left the room, hobbling, smelling like BO.

My head hit the wall, and I squeezed my eyes shut, wishing that when I opened them this place would vanish. *This has to be a nightmare. This can't be real. I thought they put foster kids into good homes.* I struggled to get to my feet, still feeling nauseated. I somehow managed to get the toilet clean again. After it was finished, I pulled out the list and wanted to cry all over again. There was hours' worth of work, and I was starving, tired, and felt disgusting.

My mind buzzed with a million feelings and thoughts, swirling around, until I wanted to pull my brain out. I made my way through the list of chores, trying my best not to cry, and failing a few times.

At the end of the day, I came to Cody's door again and knocked, not even caring about dinner at this point. It looked like this family didn't make dinner. I saw Jill snacking, and a couple times Jamie left her room for some cereal. The door was still locked. I growled under my breath, a buildup of tension carving a path into my head.

A dark shadow fell over me, and I jumped as Nelson reached over me, brushing the back of me and pounded on the door so hard I thought it was going to bust.

"Cody! Open this door now!"

A second passed, and the door squeaked open. A giant kid, red-faced, overweight, and with greasy dark hair, answered.

"I was just playing video games," the kid mumbled. "I didn't do anything."

"Your sister needs to go to bed. You stop locking this door or else you're going to be in trouble."

I could smell Nelson's breath, and it made me squirm. I probably smelled just as bad though.

"Fine." Cody wandered away from the door. I felt a hand brush my back, and I winced, my skin bursting with a million tingles of fear. I heard Nelson chuckle under his breath, and I hurried to get inside the room. I grabbed some clothes and quickly headed for the shower.

I stepped into the bathroom and locked the door. Alone, I finally let some of my emotions leak out. I searched for a clean towel and found there wasn't any. My face fell into the palms of my hands, and I started to sob. I slid down the wall, an overwhelming sense of loss hitting me. A spiral of dark emotions sucked me down, until I didn't know if I could get up again. After a few minutes of sobbing, I forced myself to get up and jump in the shower.

There was only a thin bar of soap, and nothing else to wash with, so I did my best to feel clean. The water pelted me from up above, and I tried to remember better times—happy times. Alex's face flashed before me, and I started sobbing all over again, clutching my stomach. I choked, gagging on my own sobs, my hair getting in my face.

A dark presence swept over me, and I felt like something was in the bathroom with me. I slid the shower curtain open slightly, and out of the corner of my eye I thought I saw a dark thing move. *You're going crazy, Raven. There is nothing there.*

* * * * *

The next day, I sent a text to Colten and asked him if I could come visit my horse. He eagerly agreed, and I escaped as fast as I could out the door. The moment I stepped outside I breathed a deep sigh of relief. Jill and Nelson were out doing something in town, and their kids were holed up in their rooms. I'd told Brandon I was going outside to ride my bike, which thankfully Amanda had dropped off for me and had left it at that.

As I rode my bike toward Colten's house, the blue sky above me was streaked with smears of clouds. I tried to shake the stress of my situation, ignoring the inner hurricane trying to flood my mind. I forced myself to think about Mayfly and left it at that. I knew I was getting closer to Colten's house when I saw the more crowded streets stretch into farmland.

After another ten minutes, I peddled down a long dirt driveway, with a rather large, white farmhouse resting at the end. A beautiful, new, red barn was off to the left, and a fence encircled the property. I spotted several farm animals and smiled, pulling my bike up to the house. My nerves were high, but my need to see Mayfly counteracted my shyness. The moment I got off my bike, the front door swung open and Colten came down the steps two at a time. He grinned at me, his blue eyes shimmering with excitement.

"Hi, Raven."

"Hi." I couldn't help but smile back at him. I put my kickstand up and walked toward him, shoving my hands into the front of my hoodie.

"I'm glad you came." He looked at his feet for a second and then peered into my eyes. A warm feeling embraced me, and my stomach flipped.

"Do you wanna see Mayfly?" He tipped his head to the side, raising his eyebrow at me.

I simply nodded my head, and he led the way toward the barn. "Thanks for letting me come."

"No problem." His hand brushed my arm, and I nearly jumped as an electric feeling shot through me. I'd never had a boy make me react like this. Even ones I'd liked in school had never made me feel this way. We got to the barn, and I inhaled the smell of horses, hay, and manure. Some people think it smells bad, but I loved it. I felt myself relaxing. Colten led me over to the far stall. The moment we'd stepped into the barn, all the horses had stuck their heads out of their stalls. It looked like Colten's family had at least ten horses.

"What do you guys do on your farm?" I asked as we got closer.

"We teach people to ride, and my mom does therapy for kids as well." Colten stopped in front of Mayfly's stall and turned to me. "Here she is."

The moment I saw my horse, tears flooded my eyes. I couldn't help it. I held her head in my arms, hugging her tight. Mayfly didn't move, letting me cry into her mane. Colten was so quiet beside me that I forgot he was even there for a moment. After I'd had my tear-jerking reunion, I felt embarrassed.

"Sorry," I whispered, brushing tears from my eyes.

"It's okay." A warm hand touched my back, and my entire body flooded with a tingling sensation. What was it about this guy's touch that made me spin?

"Do you want to ride her?" His hand remained on my back, and everything within me didn't want it to ever leave.

"I'd love that." I gave Mayfly another hug, and Colten's hand was suddenly gone. I immediately felt an empty sensation. He headed over to where the tackle was stored, and a moment later came back with a saddle and a bridle. He opened Mayfly's stall and got her ready for me. I watched him work, my heart flipping and dancing. It wasn't even so much what Colten said to me, since I'd met him, but there was something under the surface that whispered to me, *He really cares about you.* It was hard for me to believe, but I couldn't ignore the sensations pumping through me when I was around him.

I'd heard about love at first sight and all of that, but I always thought it was a made-up thing. Now I was starting to wonder if all the fairytales were true. Colten led Mayfly out of her stall and stood her before me with a kind smile. "Here you go. She's all yours."

A flickering happy feeling traveled through me. Colten helped me up onto my horse, and I settled into the saddle with a content sigh. I'd had no idea how much I'd missed this. It was like coming home again. I reached forward and rested my hand on my horse's neck, allowing the warmth of her to travel up my arm. She turned her head and nodded at me as if saying *let's go!* I laughed, the sensation feeling foreign to me.

"I'll come out there with you. Give me a second." Colten jogged away back into the tackle room, and I saw him get a black horse ready to ride. The feeling of sitting in a saddle again did something for me, and for a little bit, I could forget about the tragedy that had struck my life. On the back of my horse I felt like myself again.

"Ready?" Colten's horse came walking up next to mine.

"Yeah." I squeezed my legs and Mayfly started walking. I let Colten lead, since I didn't know where we were going.

"There's a great trail just a little way from here. I think you'll like it." He got his horse moving, and I followed behind him, watching how his back flexed as he rode. *Dang, I got it bad.* His dark hair rippled in the wind, and just watching him ride made me feel warm inside. I giggled at myself, understanding how Ella felt now. It was no wonder she couldn't stop talking about her boyfriend and how he made her feel. I think I finally understood it.

As we rode, the *thud, thud* of the horses' feet felt like soothing music to me. I caught up to Colten and we rode side by side, in silence, for a few minutes.

"There's not that many girls I know who like horses."

"Yeah?" I stroked Mayfly's coat.

"They are all terrified of them. My friend Mallory hates them." He shook his head.

"How could you hate a horse?" Our horses walked into the middle of a forest, the trail well-paved and the leaves rustling in the wind.

"I think she fell off one as a kid." Colten turned his horse to the left of the trail.

"Ah, man, that sucks. She'd probably freak out if she saw me ride." The tension in my body eased away. Talking to Colten felt easy.

"Why?" He turned to look at me, and I was struck again by the sight of his blue eyes.

"I'll show you in a minute." I felt daring at the moment, so I figured why not? "Is there a flat surface coming up soon?" I peered ahead and could see a field approaching.

"Yeah. We're almost there." He looked at me with a curious expression. I got Mayfly going a little faster, and Colten was quick on my heels. Once we got to the flat field, I leaned toward Mayfly's ears. "Okay, girl, we're going to do a few tricks." I began to move my body in fluid motion, standing, swiping my legs into a twist, and turning several times. After I was finished, I heard someone applauding and laughed.

"That. Is. Impressive." Colten's eyes were huge. "I'd fall right on my butt if I did that. How did you learn that?"

"Gymnastics, and a lot of practice with Mayfly. She trusts me, and I trust her." I reached forward and stroked my horse's neck.

"You should compete with her." Colten slowed his horse down.

"I can't do that. She's not mine anymore." I blushed, looking away.

"Who cares. My mom would totally let you. Anyone who can do that with a horse should get a medal." He gave me a half smile. I blushed again and looked at my hands.

"Thanks."

We got the horses going again, and pretty soon we came to a lake. Colten led me along the shore and slowed his horse to a walk.

"I know we don't know each other well, and I know this sounds really corny, but I feel like I know you." He stopped his horse, his blue eyes filled with care. "I like you, Raven."

He likes me? My stomach churned, but I could feel he meant every word he spoke. "I like you too." Awkward silence followed our words, but I didn't care.

"I'll race you." Colten grinned at me.

"You're on." We got our horses going, and I let out a shriek of joy, the sand kicking up behind me.

* * * *

The moment I stepped back into the house, I could feel the tension. Jill sat in the living room. When she spotted me, her eyes narrowed into thin, little slits.

"I heard you were out with the Millard's son."

"Colten?" I asked, wondering how she'd known I had gone riding with him.

"My friend Pauline saw you gallivanting all over the place. Who do you think you are associating with someone like him? There's no way a wealthy boy like that will ever be into the likes of you." Jill shoved a handful of chips into her mouth and crunched. Disgusted, I moved to go into my room and ignore her.

"I'm talking to you, girl. The Millards are relatives of ours, and no good ones at that. You might as well not waste your time. They are bad blood, and their son is an utter loser." She shot a dark look at me. I didn't know what to say, but I knew she was lying to me. I felt angry that she was insulting Colten, but I didn't think it would do any good to try and defend him to her.

I hadn't been with this family very long, but already I knew that they were set in their ways. "Plus, we don't allow our kids to date until they are eighteen." Jill shoved more chips in her mouth. "If you can't follow our rules, then Nelson will gladly put you in your place." She threw me a wicked grin. I simply nodded and headed to my room.

Chapter 13

Alex

Rap. Rap.

I pulled my earbuds out at the sound of someone knocking. I got off my bed and opened the door. Mark stood there, along with Garret and Benjamin, with a basketball in his hand.

"Come on, you're getting outside. You've been holed up in your room for too long." Mark grabbed my elbow and pulled me forward.

"Yeah!" Garret called, dancing from foot to foot. He grabbed the basketball and started dribbling it in the house. A happy spark ignited inside of me for a brief second before it was smothered out.

"Play with the boys awhile, I'll be in my office working." He ruffled my hair, and I felt like I was six again.

I was slightly annoyed that he was forcing me to babysit his kids, but whatever. I grabbed the ball out of Garret's hand and ran out the backdoor. Garret let out a screech, fast on my heels to catch me. The warm air greeted me, and the sunshine blinded my eyes. I bounced the ball on the cement, peering up at the hoop. I wasn't exactly sporty, but I could hold my own I guess. I'd always been more of a fan of extreme sports, not throwing a rubber ball into a metal hoop. There wasn't much adventure to that. I shot the ball, and it bounced off the rim, nearly smacking Benjamin in the head. Whoops. He screamed and backed away. These kids seemed to constantly scream. Garret laughed and ran after the ball. He got it and attempted to dribble it as best as his small hands could.

"How old are you two?" I asked.

"I'm nine," Garret said, still trying his best to dribble.

"I'm seven." Benjamin looked at his feet. "Dad told us your dad and mom were murdered. Why?" Benjamin looked up, his brown eyes looking worried. "He said a thief murdered them. Why didn't your dad fight him with karate like you?"

The questions took me off-guard, and I wasn't entirely sure what to say for a solid ten seconds.

"Dummy, that's not nice." Garret shoved Benjamin. Benjamin's face screwed up into a scream.

"Don't call me dummy! You're a dummy!" He punched Garret in the arm. Garret dropped the ball and gave him a hard push. They were soon both on the ground, pulling each other's hair and spitting. Whoa. These boys had issues.

"Hey, break it up!" I pulled them apart. Benjamin screamed at a glass-breaking volume, and Garret ground his teeth, his fists balled up. "What's the deal? Let's play basketball."

"I'm telling Dad!" Benjamin raced off, still crying at a high volume.

"He's such a baby. All he does is tell Dad everything, and he's not even his real dad." Garret crossed his arms. I guess that explained why there were no pictures of these two boys on the wall. A moment passed, and Mark came out, looking thoroughly annoyed, and grabbed Garret by the arm.

"You say you're sorry right now. We don't treat our teammates this way." He gave Garret a shake. Garret's face balled up into a furious look.

"He started it! He was being mean to Alex!" He stomped his foot.

"Is that true, Benjamin?" Mark scowled down at the little boy.

"No! I wasn't being mean! I just asked him questions!" Benjamin squirmed and let out a shriek of anger.

"Stop that, now." Mark took Benjamin by the arm and led him a few feet away. I couldn't hear what he was saying. All of this seemed blown out of proportion. He was just a kid; I hadn't been upset.

A moment passed by, and Benjamin came up to me with a dejected look on his face. "Sorry, Alex." His head drooped, and he walked away.

"It's fine really. He can play. He was just curious," I called to Mark, but the man grabbed the little boy and led him inside. *Hmm...* I turned to Garret who had started playing all by himself. So much for basketball. My mind wandered to Raven. What was my little sister doing right now? I wanted to see her so badly. I'd tried texting her a few times, but her responses had seemed so short that it got me even more worried. I could feel her hopelessness, and it fed my own.

I went inside and found my phone. *Let's go to a movie. I'll pay, and I think Mark will drop us off if I ask.* I sent the text to my sister.

My phone dinged. *Okay.*

I quickly looked up a movie. I didn't even care what movie; I knew we both needed to see each other. I went toward Mark's office to ask him if he could pick Raven up and drop us off at the movies. I knocked on his office door, feeling slightly nervous.

"Come in," a voice called.

Mark's office was well-organized, and I saw him typing away at the computer. An image of my dad writing came to me, and pain clutched me for a moment. I didn't say anything for a few seconds. Mark turned around and spotted me.

"Did you need something, Alex?"

"Yeah...I—" I took in a deep breath. "I was wondering if I could go to the movies with my sister. Would you be able to pick her up and drop us off?"

"Oh. Well, yeah, I suppose I could do that. What time?" Mark glanced at a clock on the wall.

"The movie starts at 3:30." I shifted from foot to foot.

"All right. That should be fine. I'll get ready to head out. Do you know the address your sister is located?" He stood to his feet, dusting off the front of his suit. I found it odd how he wore a suit, even though he clearly worked from home.

"Yeah." I'd written down the address when Raven had gotten dropped off.

"Do you need some money?" Mark grabbed his keys from a hook on the wall.

"Oh, I...that's okay." I was already inconveniencing him; I didn't want to take his money too.

"I tell you what. It's fine." He reached into his back pocket and pulled out a wallet. He fished out two twenties and handed them to me. "It's on the house. You can always work it off later." He smiled. A warmth spread over me. Maybe living here wouldn't be that bad.

Within just a few minutes, Mark and I were in his car heading toward where Raven lived.

"Are you adjusting well, Alex?" Mark said as he turned a corner.

"Yeah." Not exactly, but it'd only been just a short time.

"Good." Mark smiled. We stopped at a red light, and I wasn't sure what else to talk about. The ride didn't take all that long, and before I knew it, we pulled into the driveway where my sister lived. She came out the door the instant we pulled up, her small purse looped around her shoulder. When I saw her, I almost started to cry. Her dark hair was pulled up into a messy ponytail, and her face looked ashen. She got up to the car and pulled open the door. Once inside, I heard her let out a soft sigh. I wanted to hug her desperately. I climbed out of the front seat and got in beside her. The moment I touched her, her lip started to tremble.

"Hi, I'm Mark." Mark turned around to face us.

"I'm Raven," she said in a quiet voice. I could feel my sister's sadness like a thick, suffocating fog. Mark turned back around and backed out of the driveway. I pulled Raven as tight against me as I could.

"Hi, Alex." Her voice sounded small in my ear.

"Hi, sis. Are you okay?" I could feel her trembling against me.

"No, not really." Her hands fidgeted with her sweater.

"We'll talk soon, okay?" I squeezed her shoulder.

The ride to the theater was quick, and pretty soon Raven and I climbed out.

"What's your number, Alex?" Mark said. I rattled off my number to him as we stood in front of the theater.

"I'll pick you up when you're ready. Just send me a text." He gave us both a warm smile.

"Thanks." I nodded to him, and the both of us watched him drive away. The moment he was out of sight, Raven started crying. I pulled her into a huge hug, holding her for several minutes as she cried. Finally, after she'd calmed down a bit, I grabbed her hand and led her over to a private bench.

"Talk to me." I smoothed her hair back from her face.

"Alex, they're awful." She put her face in her hands, sobbing. I didn't want any public attention, so I helped Raven get to her feet and led her toward the woods located behind the theater. Once we were away from prying eyes, I released her. We found a fallen tree to sit on.

"Raven, tell me." I gripped her arms lightly, and she winced. Pain swam in her blue eyes. Whoever had caused it I wanted to pound to the ground.

"They don't want me to see this boy I like, I'm in the same room as their son, their daughter hates me, and the parents are horrible people. They make me clean everything and hardly give me anything to eat. The dad slaps his kids around, and, Alex, I'm scared he's going to hurt me too. The woman threatened that if I kept seeing Colten her husband would hurt me." Raven continued to tremble, her face growing paler the more she spoke. Anger burst through me, and my neck tensed.

"I won't let them hurt you. And they can't keep you away from Colten, that's not their business."

"What are you going to do? Jill said that Colten's family was bad news, so we can't be together. I have to deal with this by myself." She looked away from me.

"No. No, you don't." I stood up, my hands balled into fists. "I'm going to contact Amanda and tell her to put you in a new home."

A small hopeful look crossed Raven's face. "Maybe…maybe that will work. I really like Colten, Alex. I got to ride Mayfly with him."

"I won't let them do that to you." I heard a rustling and looked over toward a group of trees off in the distance. A flash of something white filled my vision.

"What was that?" Raven abruptly stood to her feet.

"It's my stalker." I took a step forward, my feet crunching the dead leaves below me.

"You have a stalker?" Raven cracked a smile.

"Yeah. I think it's a squirrel from the squirrel mafia or something." I gave a chuckle. "I probably owe him money."

Raven shook her head at me, her eyes lighting up with amusement, momentarily forgetting her problems. "You owe everyone money."

"Come on. Let's see what it is." I nudged my head to the side.

I snuck closer to where the noise had come from, Raven following me. I got to the trees but saw nothing there. Another noise caught my attention, and Raven whispered, "Over there, Alex. I saw a tail."

I was just plain out curious now. Whatever it was, it wasn't too afraid of people, since it kept coming around me. I pressed myself up against a tree, like a ninja, making Raven smile again. I heard a strange noise and turned my head to the right.

"Raven, that's not a squirrel." I pressed my hands against my cheek dramatically. "What does the fox say?" I sang out in a whisper.

"Ding, ding, ding," Raven said in a chuckle. "A fox is stalking you?" Her face lit up, and I saw my real sister once again.

"It looked like a fox to me. I think we should follow it!" My old adventurous side kicked in, and for one moment I let all the weight and fear drop away. I grabbed her hand, making her laugh, and ran toward where I'd last seen the animal.

Every so often we'd hear another noise, see a flash of something, and follow behind it. We got further and further into the woods, but I figured we had a GPS on our phone in case we got totally lost.

"Maybe this fox is taking us to the pot of gold at the end of the rainbow." I lightly shoved Raven.

"He's not a leprechaun, duh." She giggled. I heard a noise again, and this time I got a look at the fox's face. I jerked backward. He looked highly intelligent, as if I was staring into the eyes of a person, not an animal.

"What?" Raven said. The fox jumped through some bushes, rustling the branches.

"This is freaking me out. What are we doing?" I took a step back. "We're following a fox, and I'm pretty sure we're lost." I looked around the woods, noticing that it had definitely gotten darker outside.

"Something is weird about that fox. Maybe we should get out of here." Raven wrapped her arms around herself as if suddenly cold.

We turned to leave, when I heard the leaves rustle again. I twisted around, and this time the fox was staring straight into my eyes. "Raven."

My sister turned around with a slow spin, and the fox glanced from her to me.

"Hello, I'm Grim." He stood on his hind feet, his red, white, and brown fur rippling in the wind. Golden eyes twinkled at us.

We both jumped backward a mile, tripped, and landed in the leaves with a *thud*. Raven was the first to scramble to her feet, and I followed suit.

"That thing just talked." She pointed at the fox, who looked at her with a curious expression.

"Of course I did." He dusted off the front of his fur, licked his paw, and rubbed his cheek.

I gripped the sides of my head. "Now we're going freaking crazy. You're hearing this too?" I turned to my sister.

"I just said that," Raven said with a roll of her eyes. She didn't look scared in the least bit, just shocked.

"Please, follow me," Grim said, and suddenly he was on the move again. Follow a talking fox—why the heck not? I ran after him, a strange sensation lighting up inside of me. Maybe I was a complete nutcase now, but Raven must have taken the same coo-coo pills because she also heard this "Grim" talk. We continued to follow him, running, tripping, and growing short of breath a few times. This thing was fast!

I swore we walked for hours, and more than once I worried that we'd been gone too long. The ground beneath me felt spongy, and the woods seemed to be thinning. Grim's red and white body bounced as he came upon an open field, where flowers of every color waved in the wind. The sky, above us seemed to be brighter than I'd ever seen, and the trees behind us seemed to whisper.

"Raven?" I turned and looked at her, and her eyes were wide with wonder. It was more of a feeling than anything else, but somehow, I knew we weren't in the same city anymore. Grim bounded over the waving grass, turned to look at us a few times, and continued to run. Raven and I both burst into a sprint, wanting to catch the fox. I nearly stumbled as I spotted a huge golden entrance, ornate swirls of floral and foreign designs etched deep into its surface. A giant, gray, stone castle stood off in the distance. It rested on the bank of a crystal blue lake, shimmering in the sun. Beyond the castle was a city of picture-perfect golden houses, winding white streets, and what looked like a well-functioning city, booming with tiny figures moving about.

Breathless, my chest ached from the run, but I finally caught up to the little creature.

"That's a castle."

Raven soon reached us, her own breathing labored. "Alex?" Her face was screwed into a confused, worried look. "Where are we? How did we get here?" She turned around, staring back at the direction we'd just come. "This is impossible. I'm pretty sure there isn't a field on the other side of the theater. We used to drive around town all the time with Mom and Dad."

"Raven," I said slowly. I pointed at the entrance first and then the castle.

"Whoa." She stumbled back a step. I had no idea how she hadn't seen that while we ran. "You sure we aren't dead?" She scanned the field, and I could tell she felt the majesty of this place like I did.

"I have no idea," I said, dragging air into my lungs.

"Welcome to Anxious." Grim smiled at the both of us, pointing to the words molded into the entrance above.

Chapter 14

Raven

I stood there like a dummy staring at this little fox, still not quite grasping the fact that a *fox* had just talked, let alone had taken us to a world called *Anxious*. Just the name of the world had me a bit freaked out. I turned to my brother.

"Alex, are you seeing this too?" I could feel the ground beneath me, see the castle and a beautiful city in the distance, and I was pretty sure there were no castles where we lived.

"No, it's all you, sis." Alex slapped me on the back, turning as if he was about to leave.

"Alexander Lance Dayton." I crossed my arms over my chest.

Alex started laughing. "Man, it's easy to make you go over the top. Yes, I see this. That thing is talking to us, and we somehow walked into another world without us even knowing it." He looked nervous, despite his sarcasm.

"Are we high or delusional right now? How is any of this possible?" I took a few steps forward, and I noticed everything looked really *normal*. I half expected another world to at least have something weird. If not for the huge golden entrance and a giant castle in the distance, I would have sworn we hadn't gone anywhere. *We've snapped that's what it is. We're both crazy people. Or maybe we are dead.* I turned to look at the little fox, who continued to stare at the both of us with an unbiased expression.

"Are you ready?" Grim moved his head from side to side.

"Ready?" Alex drew out the word, looking utterly lost.

"To meet him." Grim looked at us like we should know exactly what he was talking about. A shiver ran down my spine, and I thought about the life we'd left behind. *I don't know what this place is, but I'm sure it's better than there.*

"Who are we meeting?" Alex scratched his head. "Listen, Grim, we don't know anything about this place. This is a bit new to the both of us. It's not every day we encounter a talking fox who brings us to a medieval land."

"But you made this place." Grim turned his head to the side, making him look super cute.

"Yeah…about that…" Alex rose an eyebrow. "Pretty sure we didn't."

I wish Dad could see this place, I thought. The moment the thought passed through my mind, pain wrenched my heart, and I let out a soft gasp.

Grim let out a squeak, staring off into the distance.

"What?" I asked, wondering if he'd somehow read my mind.

A cold, prickling sensation swept over my skin, and I followed to where Grim looked. The ground rumbled, and far off in the distance, a swirling, black mass shot up from the ground, spewing clods of dirt.

"What was that?" I staggered backward, knocking into Alex, who caught me in his arms.

"That's why I had to find you two." Grim looked at the both of us, frowning. "You're destroying our world. The realms need your help."

"What do you mean?" I kept my eyes on the swirling black thing that flew off into the sky like a flock of wild birds. *Creepy.*

"Your ancestors created this place, a long time ago, and now the two of you are aiding in destroying this place." His eyes shimmered with tears. "You must come with me quickly. There is much to talk about." Grim jumped forward, bounding through the entrance, leaving us to run after him all over again.

* * * *

Between huffs of breath, Alex, I, and Grim ran toward the castle off in the distance. I tried to take in this place, but it was more of a feeling than anything else. I knew Anxious was different, even if it looked a lot like home. I saw birds flitting overhead, puffy clouds making their way lazily across the sky, but the air smelt cleaner, and of course there was a castle looming before us.

My eyes kept straying to the golden city, thinking of the city of Atlantis or El Dorado. It was pretty hard not to believe that Grim had taken us to another world. For the first time in a while, I wanted to draw what I was seeing. A herd of wild, multi-colored horses raced across the field, and my mind went to Colten. *He'd probably love this place. I'd love to ride with him here.*

"Grim…Grim…" Alex huffed, breathless. We were both obviously not marathon runners, and this fox could outrun anyone I knew—even if we were both in decent shape from gymnastics and Wing Chun. The little fox paused, turned and gazed at us, looking a little bit annoyed.

"We must hurry! There's no delaying!" He bounded off again, and Alex and I stared at one another.

"He's trying to kill us I think," Alex said, heaving in breaths.

"Pretty sure he doesn't understand that us humans can't run for miles like that—not unless we're trained to I guess. I haven't been practicing my gymnastics in a while, and I feel out of shape already." My side ached, my lungs were tight, and I was pretty sure I was going to pass out if we didn't stop running soon. We kept our eyes on the fox as he darted far ahead of us.

"He's not going to stop running, Raven, we need to catch up. I for one want to know what this is all about." Alex grabbed my hand, and I felt a surge of adrenaline hit me.

"Me too." We took off running again, and I found myself thinking about moving my feet faster and slowing my breathing down so that I didn't pass out. The moment I thought that, I felt a surge of warmth go through my body, and sure enough, my feet seemed to fly forward on their own.

"Whoa!" Alex's arm stretched out as I raced ahead of him.

ANXIOUS

"Alex, I know this sounds weird, but think about moving faster." I felt lighter, despite everything going on in my head.

"Sure," Alex said with a shrug, and soon he'd caught up to me. We finally reached the steps of the castle, where Grim waited with a calm expression. I got a closer view of the city and saw shapes moving along the roads and in-between little shops.

"Follow me." Grim walked on his two hind feet up the steps of the castle. When he reached the giant iron door, he simply rapped twice with his tiny fist. A glowing, golden light outlined the edges of the door, and it slowly slid open, making a sing-song sound as it did.

The moment the door opened, a great entryway with majestic, white pillars met my eyes. Wrapped around the pillars was vines of purple, blue, and pink flowers. The floor was sheen gold, looking like liquid, making me hesitant to step onto it. The very air was filled with pixie-like golden dust, and every so often I'd see something spark between the tiny specks—like a jolt of electricity. It was breathtakingly beautiful. Statues of tall, ethereal figures, wearing flowing robes were lined against the far walls—greeters to this strange place. My mind flashed to the pictures I'd been drawing lately.

I saw several entryways with golden arcs that were finely crafted with ornate flowers and designs. Whoever had made this place was amazing beyond words. Grim must have seen both Alex and I's hesitancy and jumped onto the floor. It rippled around him, dust rising into the air and swirling around like a mini tornado.

"It's all right, follow me. I'll explain everything soon." Golden dust coated Grim's fur as he bounded toward one of the archways. I saw the words Drite throne room etched into the door that Grim approached. *What's a Drite?* I exchanged a look with Alex, who looked like he either was going to pass out, pee his pants, or let out a whoop of joy. I couldn't quite figure out which at this point. I really didn't know what to think, so I followed behind Grim, feeling weird as I stepped into the swirling mass of golden dust. The moment my foot hit the liquid-looking floor, I felt it support me.

It was almost as if it *knew* me, which was insane to think that way, but it was the way I felt. The golden dust danced around me in a swirl—sparking a few times and making me jump. I reached Grim, where he waited at the entrance, and Alex followed close on my heels. He looked a bit disturbed but was trying not to let it show. It was weird to see Alex like this. He used to be beyond crazy adventurous, and to me this was a huge adventure. I was worried about him.

"What you see in here is not to be repeated to anyone outside of this castle. Understand?" Grim looked from me and Alex and back to me again. We both gave a serious nod to the fox.

"Good." He rapped twice on the door, and again the golden light rippled along the edges of the door, and slowly it opened with a sing-song noise. Grim bounced inside. A warm sensation swept over me, and I felt like I was snuggled deep in a blanket beside a fire. Wide steps led down to an open floor, a lot like a giant ballroom, and beyond that several more steps went back up to a long strip of floor where a pure white throne sat. Seated in that throne was a small boy—no older than seven. I threw a look at my brother, but he was already heading down the stairs after Grim. The room seemed to be buzzing with happy energy, and I found myself feeling a little bit like my old self. *I know that boy.*

"Welcome to Drite," the little boy said, standing to his feet. His hair was white-blond, and his eyes were golden in color, so that he reminded me of a wolf. *He looks like the boy from my poem. The one I saw in my room.* "My name is King Michael, or as some call me Archangel Michael, and this is the city of Drite—the realm of the angels." He ushered his small hands out, and I could instantly see that, though he looked young, he was indeed wise beyond his years. "You must be Raven and Alex."

I stared at this little boy. How did he know who we were? Alex, being Alex, broke the awkwardness.

"Question one. How do you know our names? Question two, where are your parents? And question three, where can I take a leak?" Alex looked back and forth, searching for a bathroom. My eyes swept the entire room, and I think my brother was probably out of luck.

Leave it to Alex to say something stupid like that. I slapped my hand against my face, hoping this little kid-king-angel didn't throw us into an eternal prison or something.

"Well, to answer your questions honestly I will try my best, but I am assuming the third question is the most important." King Michael let out a little laugh, and when he did, the air in the room filled with tiny sparks of gold. "The restroom is through that door and to the left."

My brother bolted out the door, and I was left to be standing with a talking fox and a kid for a king. This was getting weirder and weirder by the second.

"You must have a thousand questions, Raven," King Michael said. He snapped his fingers, and instantly a flood of white beings floated into the room. There was a flurry of robes, white hair, and fingers as these ethereal creatures set a table of food together.

I'd heard of angels, of course, but part of me had always thought they were just a fairytale. I'd never seen anything like this. I tried to get a good look at the beings who served us, but it was hard to put their appearance into words. If I had to describe them I'd say they were tall, lithe, and their body shimmered as if made of pure energy. Their faces seemed to be hard to distinguish one from the other. They wore long, golden robes that danced around their feet as if alive. Wings made of shimmery light and energy graced them like a cloak. I wasn't even sure if they were male or female by the looks of them. *Wow...I never would have imagined angels this way.*

"Please, come and eat. You must be famished." The little boy came to the head of the table and sat down. I noticed he sat on a thick cushion, so that he could reach everything. Without anything better to do, I hesitantly sat down near him. Once I was closer to him, I could feel a pure sense of love emanating from him, and it took me by surprise. I also noticed that his body seemed to be moving, as if he wasn't a solid thing, and for a minute it freaked me out.

"I know all this is strange to you, but please, let me explain what is going on in the world of Anxious. As soon as your brother returns, I will clarify everything I possibly can." King Michael's eyes locked onto mine, and I felt a surge of light ripple over me. His golden eyes swirled with love and a deep sense of mystery in them.

"How...are...you...doing that?" Euphoric feelings spiraled through my body.

"Doing what, Raven?" He turned his small head, and his golden eyes filled with compassion for me.

"You…I don't know…it feels—" I couldn't seem to put my words together in the right way. "Nice," I finished with a lame shrug. "What are you exactly?"

His small fingers reached out and grabbed a hunk of bread. "All will be explained."

A moment passed, and Alex came bolting back to the table. He let out a whoop at the sight of the extravagant meal laid out before us.

"Wow!" He sat down next to me and reached for the chicken, potatoes, and a half dozen biscuits. I started chuckling to myself as Alex went to work devouring as much food as humanly possible. My brother wasn't shy about anything. I loaded my own plate and started eating. King Michael watched us for a few seconds before he dug into the meal. We were silent for a few minutes, while we all consumed our food until Grim cleared his throat. I'd completely forgotten the little fox had existed.

"Sire, we are on a time crunch, please remember why I brought these two here." Grim bowed to the little boy.

"Oh, yes, Grim, thank you." King Michael stuffed another biscuit in his mouth and brushed his fingers off on a golden napkin.

"My world is dying"—he looked between the both of us—"and it's your fault."

Chapter 15

Alex

A piece of meat fell out of my mouth at King Michael's words. How was it our fault that his world was falling apart? I figured I'd give this punk kid the benefit of the doubt. He had just fed me an amazing dinner. I was stuffed like a pig, and I didn't think I could eat another bite.

"We're listening," I finally said. I felt something brush my back, and a beautiful, white-haired woman, with golden eyes leaned over and took my plate. Her wings brushed my cheek. Or at least I thought it was a woman; it was kind of hard to tell with these creatures who'd served us. She gave me a smile, and I nearly choked on my own spit at the sight of her. She shimmered like she was pure energy, and the moment her hand touched the plates, they also started to shimmer. *Wow, what is this place? Is it heaven?*

"Your ancient ancestors created Anxious." King Michael drew in a deep breath. "And now you're destroying it." He wiped his mouth off with his napkin.

"Please explain to us what you mean." Raven looked utterly stressed out by this kid's words. I still wondered if this whole thing wasn't a disillusion from stress. If not for Raven, I would have thought I'd gone off the deep end.

"The Dayton family bloodline carries the power to build or destroy the world of Anxious. Everything you believe comes to pass here. It passes on from generation to generation." He brushed his hands outward. "All of these golden orbs." He stared into my eyes. "I know they look like dust, but it is in fact every one of you and

Raven's loving, beautiful thoughts, as well as the ancient Dayton line's thoughts, holding this entire castle together. In fact, it holds all of Drite together."

One of the shimmering beings floated near him and took his plate, replacing it with a chocolate piece of cake. My mouth watered, and not only a second passed before another shimmering angel gave me a piece. She smiled at me, and warm, fuzzy feelings erupted in my chest. They reminded me of elves or fairies but not quite. *I guess this is what angels really look like. They're definitely not fat, chubby babies.*

"Wait, wait, wait, so this place is like our brain or something?" I reached out my hand and brushed a tiny gold speck. "What are these? Memories?"

"They are beliefs and thoughts you've felt since you were a child. And yes, memories." King Michael dug into his chocolate cake, smearing it on his face like most children his age would do. I chuckled under my breath.

"So these are my thoughts?" Raven hadn't touched her cake, and I could tell she was highly suspicious about this whole thing. Her brow scrunched, and her mouth twitched with unease.

"Yes. These are both your thoughts, as well as many from the ancient Dayton ancestors." King Michael brushed the crumbs off the front of him. "The realms are filled with worlds such as these… and us angels are responsible to protect them. This is your family's world."

"So you mean to tell me that this world my great, great, great, great, great grandparents created with their thoughts? And now Raven I are creating it?" I couldn't help but throw sarcasm into my voice. This was insane.

"Yes. I know this is hard to take in, Alexander, but you both have been greatly affecting Anxious. The demon horde has grown in the last few months beyond measure. We're having a hard time holding this place together."

"Why have we never heard of this place then?" Raven asked, still looking skeptical of this entire thing.

"The last Dayton to visit this world was your grandfather, Milton. Unfortunately, your father didn't understand his connection to Anxious. Milton used to visit multiple times, but I fear something happened to him, for his visits ceased."

"This is stupid," I said, standing to my feet. "This isn't reality. What I think doesn't affect anyone but myself." I felt annoyed. If my thoughts hurt Raven and other people, then I had to deal with the load of guilt weighing down on my shoulders. "Why didn't my parents know about this place then? If it's been in our family heritage for years, why didn't they tell us about it?"

"I know this is a lot to take in…but please, you must listen—" King Michael's voice sounded desperate. My mind swirled with tension, feelings of not being good enough overwhelmed me. For him to say I was destroying this place was too much for me at the moment. This whole thing was dumb, and I wanted to get out of here. A rumble shook the castle, and I stumbled backward. I fell with an *oomph.* Raven gripped the table, her face turning pale.

"What was that?" Her eyes grew huge.

"That is what I warned you about," King Michael said, sounding scared. "You're destroying this world."

"You mean, what I just thought did that?" I got back to my feet, feeling like an idiot.

"Yes. Your dark thoughts are creating more of them." His golden eyes bore into mine, and I could tell he wanted me to grasp what he said.

"More of what?" Raven sounded like a scared little girl.

"The Daegal, or the shadow ones…demons…"

A shiver ran over my skin at the name *shadow ones*. It was just like what my dad had been looking into—maybe he did know about Anxious but was too scared to share it. His father had ended up in a mental institution on account of his disillusions. *But King Michael just said Grandpa Milton used to come here.* I remembered when I was kid climbing up on my grandpa's lap and hearing him talk about a strange world of angels and demons. Dad always shooed me away when Grandpa would get too intense.

"There are two powers to the world of Anxious." King Michael gave a long pause.

"What do you mean?" Raven's full attention was on the little boy, her fingers interloped together.

"While our race is called the Endrita—the angels of the realms, living in the city of Drite, the Daegal have created their own city." He gazed between us, a disturbed look on his face. "The demon city—Dagmoth, and it's growing bigger every day." King Michael suddenly looked pale, leaning back in his chair. His fingers rubbed his forehead, and I could feel he bore a great weight on his small shoulders.

"One question," I said, leaning in. "Why is a kid ruling a city?" The question had been rolling around in my head since I spotted him. It really didn't make any sense. "Plus, I thought Archangel Michael was a warrior."

King Michael let out a laugh. "Oh, that's how you perceive me?" He continued to laugh. "Interesting. Well, I suppose everyone has their own internal view of who rules their kingdom." He straightened in his chair, and I saw a little less stress on his face.

"I'm not a child, Alex, but your perception of me has created that view. I could go into a much greater detailed explanation, but to put it simply I'll just say this one thing." His brow scrunched for a moment. "Your inward view of yourself or your hopeful side of life is how you view me. So if you view me as having the power of a small child, that is all I shall have in your internal world."

A rumble shook the castle, and King Michael's face filled with worry once again. He cast a look toward Grim, who's tail flickered back and forth.

"So the view of myself is that I am powerless to fight—these Daegal-demon things?" I was trying to get all of this straight in my head. An ache traveled up my neck, and I suddenly felt exhausted.

"You created all of this. The both of you. How you perceive us is by your design." King Michael leaned forward in his chair.

"So this whole thing is my fault—or our fault?" I stood to my feet, feeling annoyed. "This is bull." *It's your fault, Alex. Your parents' deaths are on your head.* The thought squirmed its way into my mind, until I felt tension building like a geyser about to blow. The castle rumbled again, and I saw several of the golden flecks spark and flicker like they were about to die.

"You're not getting this." King Michael's voice rose in pitch. "The more you let those black memories have their way, the more you'll destroy Drite." His small fists curled.

"This is all very…um…new to us, King Michael," Raven said, shooting me a glare. I knew she was annoyed at my responses to this entire thing. I really didn't need more guilt on my shoulders at the moment. My mind felt fogged, my body was heavy with the stress of being blamed for another thing. *I need to get out of here.*

"Raven, we're leaving." I crossed my arms over my chest.

"Alex, listen to him. He's just trying to help us." Her mouth went into a straight line, and her blue eyes narrowed.

"I don't care. Sounds like a guilt trip to me. His world is dying, and he's trying to cast blame on someone. We just happened to be the gullible ones he wants to pin it on." I started walking toward the door, my thoughts swirling with anger. *You're to blame for all of this… if you'd only been there. If you'd only gone home after work. You could have stopped him.*

Crack!

I nearly jumped a mile at the sound. I jerked my head upward to see a black crack traveling across the top of the golden ceiling.

"Please!" King Michael stood to his feet and bowed before me. "Please, I must teach you about the golden memories. Or this place will crumble!"

I stared up at the crack for a second, my stomach churning with unease. Raven's eyes swam with fear and confusion.

"I'm sorry. I can't help you. Raven, come on." I bolted out of there, picturing that crack in my mind. *This is my fault. Everything that's happened is my fault.* I ran out of the throne room into the entryway, where the golden dust sparked and danced, and out the front door. A weight hit me, and I couldn't shake the guilt of not only ruining my family's lives, but this beautiful world as well.

I didn't even know if Raven was going to follow me, but I had to get out of here. My feet hit the grass, and I noticed the sky looked a little grayer, but I didn't care. I wanted to go home. *I don't have a home. You're going back to a fake family, who doesn't even care about you.* The ground trembled. I saw, out of the corner of my eye, a black substance shoot up from the ground and swirl into the air.

    I made it to the edge of the woods and continued to run, my eyes burning with tears. The leaves crunched under my feet, and the tree branches scratched at my clothes. I did a quick glance behind me, and I spotted Raven running after me. I wanted to wait for her, but I had to get out of Anxious.

Chapter 16

Raven

"I'm so sorry," I told King Michael, standing to my feet. Alex had bolted from the throne room, and I had watched him flee. I knew all of this was too much for my brother. *He blames himself for everything.* He didn't need more guilt thrown on his shoulders.

"Please, Raven, you must let me explain about the golden memories. Please!" King Michael's eyes filled with unshed tears. He grabbed my hand, and a shock went through my body.

"I have to go to Alex. He needs me right now." I pulled my hand free and ran toward the door.

"Please, wait!" King Michael's voice echoed behind me as I went out the door, into the entryway, and out into the world of Anxious. I spotted Alex running, and a lump formed in my throat. The Alex I knew would never have done that. He'd have stayed and found out more. He'd laughed at the entire thing and shrugged off the feelings of guilt. Where had my happy brother gone? I pushed myself to run as fast as I could, to catch up to Alex, and pretty soon he was only a few feet in front of me.

"Alex! Stop!"

He nearly collided into a tree and came to an abrupt halt. His chest heaved up and down, and I saw sweat dripping down his face.

"Raven, I can't stay here. I need to go home. I need—" He pressed his hands over his face.

"Dad," I finished for him. I grabbed him in my arms and held him. I felt the tension in his body, and I wanted to help him, but my own guilt and fear made me feel heavy.

"How do we get out of here?" Alex pulled back from me, scanning the woods. "Do you recognize anything?"

"I don't know." What if we couldn't leave? Were we going to be stuck in a world that was slowly dying? The air felt muggy and hot, and my hair stuck to the back of my neck.

"I will take you home." A sudden voice came from behind us. Both Alex and I turned around to see Grim standing before us, looking solemn. He moved past us, and I could sense his great sorrow at our decision of leaving Anxious so suddenly. He walked on two feet for several minutes, before he turned and looked at the two of us.

"I am gravely sorry you found your world full of chaos."

"This isn't our world," Alex said. Stress lined his face. "This is your world, Grim. That…kid…wanting to blame this on us is insane. We have nothing to do with this place. We just got here."

Grim was silent for so long, I thought he'd turned into a statue. He finally let out a heavy sigh. "Alex, Raven, Anxious has always been here, but it was always ruled by King Michael. I fear if the both of you choose to keep going down the path you are, Anxious will be ruled by the Daegal forever."

A heaviness hit me, and I nearly started crying. What if Grim was right? What if Anxious was our world? What if all of this was true? I didn't want to be the one to destroy an entire world. I grabbed Alex's hand.

"No, Raven. I'm leaving."

Before I'd even asked the question, my brother had shut me down. I shook my head. There was no way I was going to stay here alone.

"It is settled. Follow me." Grim made his way slowly through the woods. All three of us walked in silence for what felt like a long time. Grim turned to us for the final time and nodded. He scurried away, his bushy tail bobbing as he bounced through the woods.

I felt the shift in the air. The heaviness of my life came back on me, and I nearly started crying again.

"Raven," Alex said, turning to me. He grabbed my cheeks in his hands and stared into my eyes. "We have to make the best of what we have now. I'm always here for you. Always." He slipped his hand in mine, and we made our way back toward the theater. I figured hours and hours had passed, and we probably needed to get back to our foster homes.

Alex pulled his phone out of his pocket. "Hmm…" He rose an eyebrow. "You're not going to believe me on this one, sis."

"What?" I pulled out my own phone. "How is that possible? It's only three thirty, but we've been gone for at least an hour." I looked up at the theater's board.

"Do you still want to see a movie?" Alex slipped his phone back in his pocket.

"Sure, I guess."

We walked toward the theater, the world of Anxious rolling around in my mind. I couldn't shake the terror on King Michael's face. What if all of it were true?

* * * * *

After the movie, Alex and I waited for Mark to pick us back up. I wanted to talk more about Anxious, but Alex seemed closed to the idea. Mark's car pulled up in front of the theater, and Alex and I both got into the backseat.

"How was the movie, guys?" Mark smiled at the both of us.

"It was kind of lame," Alex said with a shrug.

"That's too bad." Mark pulled out of the parking lot, and the car fell into silence. The ride back to my home was far too short, and pretty soon I was getting out, hugging my brother goodbye, and walking back into the lions' den. I pushed the creaky door open and came inside. The moment I did, a hand slapped across my face.

"Where have you been?" Jill screamed. I staggered back, my hand instantly going to my cheek.

"To a movie. I wrote a note." I pointed toward the table.

"You expect me to be okay with you gallivanting all around town with some boy?" Jill's eyes narrowed into slits.

"He's my brother." I took a step back from her.

"I don't care who he is. In this house, you need to make sure it's okay with us before you leave with anyone. You have chores to do." She shoved her fat finger in my chest. "If you ever leave again, without getting me or Nelson's permission, so help me, you'll get no supper for a week."

Fury went through me. There was no way she could do that to me. It was child abuse and negligence. I wondered if Amanda knew about this family's behavior. I buried my feelings and headed toward my room. I was still with Cody, and even though they'd told Amanda I'd be moving in with Jamie, it still hadn't happened yet. The moment I stepped into Cody's room, Jill was at my door again.

"Just wait until Nelson gets home. You'll think twice before ever disobeying again." She pulled a dirty list from her pocket and threw it at my feet. "Do those before he gets home, or you'll be facing a lot more than just a slap on the face."

After she left, I picked up the list and wanted to gag. It was covered in who knew what, and the chores on there was insanely outrageous. Who made a kid do this? I set my purse down, put my hair into a pony tail, and figured I might as well attempt them. I walked out into the kitchen to see another disaster, and with a frustrated groan started getting to work. I scrubbed every inch of the place, organizing and reorganizing things, until a couple hours had passed by.

The shuffle of feet caught my attention, and suddenly a hand gripped my arm. I could smell him before I even got a glimpse of who it was. *Nelson.* His beefy, round face glared down at me.

"I heard you nearly gave your mom a heart attack."

"I went to a movie. I left her a note."

"Well, in this house, you need to get permission and get your chores done." His grip tightened, and I stiffened. He yanked me forward. "Sit down." Nelson shoved me into one of the crappy kitchen chairs, which was covered in jelly.

I sat down, my fingers interwoven nervously in my lap. I'd never been a rebel, in the least bit, but these two brought out so much anger in me, I had a hard time biting my tongue.

"I want to have a conversation with you, girl." Nelson stood to the side of me and spun my chair toward him. "First of all, I don't know how your parents ran their household, but in this one, our children obey without question. You will have to earn your stay here. You can't just get something for nothing." His bad breath wafted down toward me. "Because of your disobedience today, there are consequences."

"I had no idea I couldn't go," I quickly said. My nerves grew taut.

"I don't care. There are still consequences. Doesn't matter if you didn't know. What would happen if I let my other children get away with stuff? Then this whole household would be chaos."

I heard the patter of feet and spotted Brandon in the doorway of the kitchen. He spotted Nelson and I, looked at me with fear, and bolted from the room. What was going to happen to me? Nelson reached down, grabbed both my arms, and yanked me to my feet. "You'll never disobey again after this." He threw me over his shoulder and made his way toward a chipped, white door. I'd noticed how the kids avoided going down there and had wondered about it.

Nelson threw open the door and brought me down a flight of steps. I feared fighting him, for falling and breaking my neck. The basement smelled like mold and like something had died. It reminded me of when a mouse croaked in our attic. My stomach clenched, and I feared I was going to puke right on Nelson's back. He finally got to the bottom of the staircase and sat me down in a rickety, old chair.

"This hurts me more than it hurts you." Nelson turned and grabbed a thick, black belt hanging from a nail. I jumped out of the chair, backing up.

"You can't do this to me. I'll call the authorities on you." My voice trembled, but there was no way this man was going to hit me with that. A slap was one thing, but this was too far.

"Sit, your skinny butt back in that chair. Do you really think anyone cares about you? They dumped you off and never looked back. Look at you. You're a waste of time to anyone. Now shut up and sit down. NOW." Nelson approached me, and I backed up, hitting the wall behind me.

"Please, I didn't know your rules."

"It doesn't matter." Nelson peered down at me, and I saw a sick smile twist his face. He grabbed me back in his arms, and this time I did fight. I kicked and screamed, trying to get his meaty paws off of me. He started laughing as he threw me back into the chair. Without hesitation, he pulled the belt back and let it fly. It struck my back, and I let out a painful scream. *Alex! Alex, please help me!*

Again and again Nelson let the belt fly and I tried to get away, but he kept cornering me.

"You're only making it worse on yourself, little girl." Nelson spit out of the corner of his mouth. "If you'd just sat still we'd be done by now. But now your defiance is just making me more upset." Nelson hovered over the top of me, whipping at my legs. I started to sob, curling into a ball on the basement floor.

* * * *

Nelson finally left, slamming the top of the basement stairs, leaving me in complete darkness. My entire body ached, and I could barely move. I'd crawled over to the corner, where a bunch of old coats had been thrown, and just lay there for what felt like hours. Were they going to keep me down here forever? *I did this. This is my fault. If I hadn't have fought him, he'd not have hurt me so bad.* The pressing thoughts circulated in my head again and again. A coldness swept over me, and I felt a presence in the room.

Raven, you are worthless. No one wants you. You are going to die down here, and no one cares. A finger brushed my skin, and a prickling sensation dug into my arm. I peered upward, and a red glow made me stifle a scream.

"What are you?" I whispered, trembling.

You know what I am, Raven…and you know what I'm saying is true. You're a piece of trash.

The words pressed into my mind. My body hurt so bad that I couldn't help but cry. My sobs shook me, until my nose was stuffed and my throat hurt. I wanted my brother. *There's no escaping my life now.*

Chapter 17

Alex

I stood in front of my old house, my mind a mess. After coming out of the world of Anxious, all I could think about was Mom and Dad. I'd gotten home, hung around the house until nightfall, and snuck out. Maybe there was some sort of connection or clue lingering about I could find. They had gathered evidence, supposedly, from the crime scene. I hadn't heard a peep from the local police about the thief, or any attempts to catch him for that matter. Our green doll house now looked like something from a horror movie. It was bathed in creepy moonlight, and the rustling of the trees nearby added to the effect.

I headed up the porch, trying to be as stealthily as possible, though I don't know why. No one was living here—at least not yet. I reached the front door and slipped my old key into the keyhole. I turned the door handle.

Squeak. I stepped into the entryway and headed into the living room. Even bathed in darkness, the sight of the room, my parents had been found, struck me in the chest like a physical blow. A wave of nausea hit my stomach, and I nearly vomited right then and there. I owed it to Mom and Dad to at least look around. It didn't make any sense what this man did to our family. Why would he murder them? My mind looped the scene in my head, and I had to leave the living room for a moment to take a breath.

After I recovered, I snooped around Dad's desk, looking for any clues as to what had happened. I hadn't searched very long when my hand rested on a file marked *Anxious*. My heart slugged in my chest, and I felt all the air leave my lungs for a moment. *How did Dad know about Anxious?* I grabbed the file, flipped my flashlight app on from my phone, and dragged the file over to the coffee table. My eyes quickly scanned the yellowed pages.

> *October 5*
> *I have recalled some strange sightings this month. After living in this house for the past twenty years, I have come to realize that all the stories grandfather used to tell me are true. Hazel thinks it's my old age getting to me, but I am sure that there is a world we cannot see or touch right under our noses. I've spotted several creatures coming and going, but always under the light of the new moon, and I wonder if I've finally gone loony like Grandpa Joe, who is holed up in that awful hospital.*
> *I visited my great-grandfather today, and when he looks at me I sense that he knows more than he can say. I wonder if he's seen the demon creatures the Daegal, and if he will ever recover. I have yet to visit the world of Anxious, but I know it's right there waiting for me. Though Grandpa used to call the world by some other name. But the Daegal they whisper the word Anxious when they speak of it. I wonder which is right?*
> *Milton Dayton*

My hand started to tremble, and I set the old document down. *Grandpa Milton saw the Daegal—the shadow men—demons.* My eyes scanned the pages again, but there wasn't a lot more to the old document. There was one sketch, but it wasn't very clear. A girl with huge eyes and long flowing hair was roughly drawn, but I found myself staring at her as if she was a real thing. There hadn't been anyone like that in Anxious, as far as I had seen.

I leaned back against the couch, letting out a loud sigh. "This doesn't help you, Alex," I said to myself. "Who cares if Grandpa knew about Anxious. Why did Mom and Dad get murdered? And does it have to do with this?" Sometimes talking out loud helped me piece together my crazy brain. Raven used to laugh at me about it, but I found it helpful to figure out detailed puzzles that way.

I wanted to look for more stuff, but I found myself suddenly exhausted. The stress of everything was getting to me. I kept the file, made my way out of my old house, and headed back to my foster home.

* * * * *

I laid in bed that night the image of the girl dancing in and out of my mind again and again. *Forget about her. She isn't real, plus who'd want you?* The thought was strong, and I winced at the feelings it arose inside of me. *Not even your own flesh and blood wanted you. He kicked you out like yesterday's trash.* An image of Uncle Jim pressed into my mind, and I felt a boiling over of anger. I pressed my fists into my eyes, willing the words to shut up.

Alex, you're never going to go anywhere in life. You're a screwup. You couldn't even be there for your parents. An oppressive feeling pressed down on my chest, and I sought to breathe but found it difficult.

A cold finger brushed my arm, and I nearly screamed right out loud. A collection of dark particles zigged and zagged in a figure-like form. I sent a glance in its direction and saw red eyes glowing.

It's hopeless to fight it, Alex.

He was right. I couldn't win. My life sucked now, and there was nothing I could do to force back the depressive, anxious thoughts that were now a part of my inner world. I curled up in a ball, trying to block out all the pain.

* * * * *

I stood before the entrance of where my grandfather was housed. It was a row of neat, picture-perfect homes, with well-manicured lawns, and you'd never know by looking at it that it was a place for those with mental challenges. I clutched in my hand the documents

Dad had put together. Part of me knew I needed to look through my old house to see if there was further information about Anxious. Instead, I'd forced myself to go visit Grandpa Milton. I hadn't seen him since I was a kid. I had a feeling Dad didn't want me to see his father as a crackpot who believed in fairies.

I knocked on the door, part of me hoping he wouldn't answer. After a couple seconds, the door flew open and Grandpa Milton stood there, his white hair standing on end.

"Come in, come in. Hurry, so they don't see you." His blue eyes stared at me. I walked over the threshold and inwardly gasped. Over every inch of the house was drawings of angel-like people and evil-looking creatures. When I looked at the creatures closer, I saw that they too were very humanlike. I spotted a fox, and my mouth almost hit the floor.

"You must be Ben's son—you look just like him." Grandpa Milton took my hand and patted it. "I must warn you I am a bit crazy."

His comment nearly made me laugh, but I held it inside. "Hi, Grandpa."

"Sit. Sit. Would you like some milk?" He wobbled over toward the kitchen.

"No, I'm okay." I was still trying to take in the endless amounts of pictures on his wall. I nearly choked when I spotted a man with a crown, with features nearly identical to King Michael.

"Ah, I see you recognize King Michael. He is a brilliant man, isn't he? If I can call him a man." Grandpa Milton sat down with a heavy sigh, patting down his flyaway hair.

"Grandpa," I started to say but stopped. I had no idea how to put any of this into words. So I just dove right in, wondering if he'd instantly know what I meant. "What is happening to me and Raven?"

Grandpa Milton rubbed his chin and stared over at the pictures. "Well, well, you must have been visited by Grim. Huh? You've been to Anxious, I can see it on your face. Though of course it's been called by many names over the years." His eyes bored into mine, making my stomach flip.

"None of this makes sense. We all thought you were crazy. Why didn't my dad know about Anxious, and why didn't anyone believe you if it runs in our family?"

"Ah, there's the million-dollar question, Alexander."

I didn't even realize Grandpa knew my name, so when he said it, something struck me. All the years we'd avoided Grandpa Milton made me sad.

"It's begun again, hasn't it?" Grandpa leaned forward, his wrinkled face falling serious.

"What has?" I still felt lost, despite the fact I'd witnessed Anxious for myself.

"The Daegal have returned. There must have been a breach—the mirror must have returned to the hands of a Dayton. It's the only way they can cross into our realm in a more solid form." Grandpa stood to his feet, pacing, his hands waving as he spoke. "Oh, if they'd only listened to me and destroyed the wretched thing. But of course I was the raving lunatic who believed in demons, ghosts, angels, and fairies." He stopped pacing and stared me dead in the eyes. "Have you found the mirror, Alexander?"

"Mirror?" I leaned forward, my head feeling lost and swarming with questions. "Grandpa, back up. I don't even know what's going on. What is Anxious? And is it actually real?"

"Oh, it's real all right. Back in sixty-two, your grandmother and I got into a huge fight because I started to experience what she called visions of Anxious. No one told me that the Dayton line was responsible for keeping Anxious in tip-top shape—and it wasn't always called Anxious, mind you. And of course, no one knew about the mirrors." He was rambling, and I still felt lost about what he was saying.

"What mirrors? Can you try to explain this from the start?" I rubbed my temples, feeling utterly confused.

"Oh, oh, sure. It all started roughly a hundred years ago, I suppose." Grandpa stroked his chin, looking off in the distance.

I leaned forward, open to hearing the story of how this crazy mess got started.

"It all began with your great-great-grandfather, William. He bought the property behind the movie theater. Of course, there was nothing there at the time, and he built the house your grandmother and I used to live in. One night, William was walking through the woods when he nearly stepped onto a rather peculiar mirror. He didn't think nothing of it and picked it up. The moment he did, he began to see into a strange world—right through the mirror."

Grandpa drew in a deep breath. "What he didn't know was the moment he held the mirror he bound our family to the world on the other side of it. Soon he noticed that anytime he fell into a depression or wrestled with his anxious thoughts, the mirror would swirl with blackness. It terrified him one day so bad that he hid the mirror from sight." Grandpa cleared his throat. "When he went for a walk in the forest the next night, a horde of shadow men met him. They pulled him through a door. Next time your great-great-grandmother saw him he was a changed man. He raved about the demon horde the Daegal and the world of Anxious, and continually spoke of this place where darkness and light fought."

I leaned back against the couch, finding it hard to take all of this seriously. Even though I'd been to the world of Anxious, everything inside of me wanted it to be a figment of my imagination.

"What William soon discovered was anytime he dealt with the darkness of his own mind, it built a greater army for the Daegal, and anytime he thought on the goodness of life he gave power to the angels of the realms called the Endrita. It was always a clash of the two people in the world." Grandpa sighed. "The one thing he didn't understand was that the mirror was letting the Daegal have access to our world. The opposite mirror—the one that could bring goodness—was missing on the other side. The balance of the mirrors needed to be obtained."

"Okay." I formed the word slowly, my mind spinning with the new information. What mirror was he talking about? Was that why I kept seeing this shadow?

"Ah, I can see you are a bit overwhelmed by this story. Let's take a break." Grandpa rose to his feet and shuffled into the kitchen. I watched as he made tea and then came back into the living room and sat down. He handed me a cup, even though I wasn't a tea drinker, I took it.

"This is all brand-new to me, Grandpa. Dad never talked about any of this, but he was studying your old letters and he'd been working on this story for months." My heart thumped loudly in my chest. "I wonder if whatever Dad looked into had something to do with my mom and dad's death."

Grandpa's eyes shimmered with tears. "I heard of their deaths. I am most sorry, son." He lifted his hands to me, and I awkwardly went into them. Despite not knowing Grandpa very well, I felt as if I had a family again. Once we broke our hug, Grandpa peered up at me. "You must find the mirrors. Have you crossed into the land of Anxious?"

I nodded my head. "Raven and I both have, and we've met King Michael. The world is falling apart, and he says it's our fault." I sat back down and took a sip of my tea, even though my stomach churned.

"Ah yes. You must learn about the golden memory. You must return to Anxious, Alexander. Find the mirrors. Wherever they are, they'll keep opening up portals for the Daegal to filter into our world if you don't learn to balance them. And you must find the Daegal mirror before he does."

"Who's he?" I held my cup out before me.

"Apollyon." Grandpa's eyes widened. "If he holds the power of the mirror, he will destroy Anxious, the Endrita, and this entire city."

"As in the devil?" I couldn't help but smirk a little bit. This was getting to be too much.

"Many people think demons have free reign over all of us, but that's not the case."

I found myself starting to zone out. I was never against religion, but neither was I into it. Some of my friends from school went to church, and I'd heard them talk about "the devil" from time to time.

"Yeah?"

Grandpa tapped the side of his head. "Our minds are the door, Alexander. Every time our mind dwells on evil or negative thoughts, a Daegal is born, but of course, the angels keep them contained in the other realms."

"Umm…" I nodded my head, although Grandpa was losing me fast. Angels, demons, this was all a bit out there for me. If I hadn't seen all this for myself I would have thought Grandpa really was nuts. It was still hard for me to wrap my head around all of it.

"Do you pray, Alex?" Grandpa suddenly grabbed my arm, startling me.

"Uh…"

"You better start. Apollyon isn't one to be taken lightly. Even King Michael has a limited amount of power over him—without your help."

"Wait, wait. Is King Michael God?"

Grandpa let out a chortle, slapping his thigh. "Of course not. Michael is an archangel of the realms. He keeps everything from falling into chaos. God himself doesn't live in those realms—He's much higher."

"Ah, I see."

"You don't know?" Grandpa stared at me with wide eyes.

"Don't know what?" I leaned forward, intrigued for a moment.

"God isn't just—somewhere else. He's in you, Alex."

"In me?" This was getting real churchy for me.

"Ah, you'll see in time, son." Grandpa slapped my knee again and stood up. "Find the mirror. Stop the Daegal. You'll be fine." Grandpa gave me a smile.

Right, because fighting a billion-year-old devil lord was easy-peasy-cheesy.

Chapter 18

Raven

A hand grabbed my arm and yanked me to my feet. My mind was fogged, and at first, I didn't even know where I was. Then it all hit me. Jill stood before me, her arms crossed and her greasy hair hanging around her face.

"Get upstairs, now." She turned and walked toward the steps, leaving me to follow her. I quickly did, still aching in places I didn't even know existed. I got to the top of the stairs and drew in a shaky breath. Jill turned and looked at me, scowling.

"You'll think twice before taking off again, won't you?" Her beady eyes narrowed at me, and she gave me a once over. "Now, get dressed, we're going to a family reunion."

Family reunion? I looked down at myself. I could smell my own odor, and it was making me feel sick. I ran to my bedroom, grabbed some clothes, and jumped into the shower before Jill could see me. I washed and rinsed as fast as I could and then got dressed. Luckily someone had finally bought some soap, but I still felt gross no matter what. I came out of the bathroom to see Jamie. She wore a blue dress, slightly out of style, but it still looked nice on her. She gave me a once over and smirked.

"Better look better than that or Jill and Nelson will have a fit."

"What's wrong with this?" I looked down at my jeans and hoodie.

"You need to wear a dress." She walked away from me, flipping her hair over her shoulder as she did. I ran to my room and found the only dress I had in my things—the one I'd worn to my parents' funeral. I felt sick putting it on, but I did it anyways. I didn't want any more punishment today. I already felt like a semi-truck had run me over. I stole a glance in a mirror in the hallway and headed into the living room. Most of the family was there, all except Brandon. A moment later he hurried into the room.

"Let's go," Nelson said and ushered all of us out the door. I got into their duct-taped minivan and tried to buckle up, but the buckles were busted. Nelson and Jill argued on the way, Jamie had headphones in, Brandon stared out the window, and Cody played some sort of gaming device. I stared into my lap.

We got to some sort of park, and Nelson parked amongst a row of other vehicles. Brandon slid the van door open, and we all piled out. The sky was overcast and gloomy, and it looked like it might rain. Jill limped toward a pavilion, a bowl of god knows what in her arms. Whatever it was she'd made, I was not eating it. I followed behind the family at a slower pace, taking in the park. It had a baseball field, a basketball court, a nice play place area for kids, and an area to eat under.

I reached the pavilion and felt my nerves rise. I'm not a people person to begin with, let alone people I didn't know at all. Jill wandered over to a group of women and started in on complaining about something. Nelson joined a table of men with a grin. The kids all scattered. I stopped where I was, unsure of what to do now. Instead of trying to interact with the group of old people, I wandered away toward where teenagers and kids were hanging out. I jumped on a swing and let it rock back and forth. My feet made lines in the sand. I got lost in my own thoughts when I heard a noise and jumped.

"Oops, sorry about that. I didn't mean to scare you."

I looked up to be staring into the eyes of a boy. His hair was mostly covered up by a gray hoodie, but I could see his dark locks sweeping upward. His eyes were blue, and he had a dimpled smile. My heart jumped at the sight of him. *Colten. Why is he here?* "It's okay. I'm pretty jumpy." Heat climbed my face.

"I had a lot of fun the other day." He pushed off on his swing and grinned at me.

"Me too." I wanted to hug him, but I felt it was weird at the moment. His eyes wandered to my arms and he frowned.

"Are those bruises?"

I felt embarrassed and looked away from him. "I'm kind of clumsy."

"Are you related?" He nudged his head toward the pavilion with a smirk.

"Um, not really. I was put into foster care with Jill and Nelson." My voice grew quiet as I said the words.

"Oh, I'm sorry to hear that." Colten looked genuinely sorry for me. "They're related to me somehow, but I don't like either of them much. My little sister screams whenever either of them try to hold her." He looked in the direction of the pavilion.

"Really?" I said. We swung back and forth on the swings.

"That's her right there." Colten pointed out toward the playground where a dark-haired man held what looked like a two-year-old little girl. She was smiling and clapping her hands.

"What's her name?" I watched the interaction for a few seconds.

"Hannah." He leaned back on the swing, letting it rock back and forth from his weight.

"She's really cute." I smiled.

"Yeah, for a monster." He gave a laugh. "She hides my phone all the time on me." He turned and looked at me with a smirk.

I giggled. "You probably deserved it."

"Oh, burn." He moved his hand up and down on the metal chain of the swing. "You stabbing me in the heart already?" He made a fist and tapped his heart twice. "I remember meeting you at the café once, and I think I saw you again at a store I went into."

"Yeah, that was my parents' antique store."

"Yeah, I was buying Mallory something," he said.

"Girlfriend?" I stared at him with a little bit of concern, remembering his comment at the store. How was he so open about giving me his number and then talking about his girlfriend?

"Oh, no, no. As in a girl as a friend. I've known her since kindergarten, but we'd kill each other." He bashed his fists together. "No chemistry there."

I breathed a sigh of relief, looking at my feet with a grin. I didn't want to show how much he affected me, but my heart was being crazy on me. He was really cute. We fell silent again, and even though we weren't talking, it felt nice.

"So, besides swinging and doing tricks on horses, what do you like to do?" Colten finally broke the silence.

"Umm…" I stared off toward the pavilion for a second. "I like a lot of stuff, or I used to. Drawing or writing poetry mostly."

"That's right, I heard you recite a poem one time. It was excellent." Colten perked up, his eyes sparking.

"Thank you." My cheeks flushed.

"So what do you draw?"

"All kinds of stuff. Whatever pops in my head."

"I'd love to see it sometime." He smiled at me, and I felt my body tingle with warmth.

"Okay." The wind picked up and blew my hair around my face, tickling me.

"Send me a picture of one sometime."

"Okay, I will." I gave him a smile.

"We should definitely hang out again soon. I think Mayfly already misses you."

"Jill and Nelson don't want me hanging out with you, so we'd have to be careful." My mouth went dry, and I forgot what he said. After a few seconds, he waved his hand.

"Raven?" He gave a laugh.

"I'm sorry, what did you ask?" I felt like an idiot.

"Why don't we grab a coffee sometime? Maybe tomorrow at three?" His eyebrow rose as he asked the question, making him look even cuter.

"Sure. Yeah. I'd love that." I tucked a lock of hair behind my ears. *I can't believe I just got a date.*

"Wanna grab some food? I'll tell you which ones to avoid." He gave a laugh, jumping off the swing.

"Sure." I found myself laughing with him, and we chatted a little more as we walked toward the food.

Colten got in line, and as secretly as possible, pointed out foods to avoid. I stifled a few giggles at his expressions he'd make when he pointed out the food. Our plates grew full, and Colten led me away from the crowd to a picnic table near the playground. We sat down, and he started to consume his food like he was dying. I picked at mine. After a couple minutes, he noticed.

"I swear none of that is poisoned. The other stuff had a high potential to be pretty toxic." He held his fork in his hand, watching my face.

"I'm having a lot of trouble eating lately." I couldn't believe I just told him that.

"Well, looking at Nelson's ugly mug would do that to anyone. That guy gives everyone the creeps." Colten shoved a hunk of chicken into his mouth. I continued to play with my food but managed to eat a little bit of it. Colten and I talked for a while longer, until suddenly it was time to go. Before I left, I gave Colten one final glance, a shimmer of happiness appearing inside of me.

* * * *

I stepped into the coffee shop the next day, nervous to meet up with Colten again. I'd tried to get all my chores done as fast as possible and told Jill I'd be back in a couple hours. She's surprisingly hadn't put up a fuss and had continued to watch her reality TV show. I smoothed the front of my hoodie and brushed a hand over my dark hair. I spotted Colten, sitting near a fake fireplace, and headed that direction. He saw me and smiled, giving a little wave. I sat down with a nervous smile.

"Ready to order?" He stood to his feet. I gave a nod, and we walked over to the counter. The last time I'd been here had been with Alex, and I tried my best not to think about that moment that changed my entire life. I got a mocha and Colten got a plain coffee. We made our way back toward our table and sat down.

"Did you bring me any pictures?" Colten took a sip of his coffee.

I fumbled inside of my purse and pulled out my notepad. I was usually painfully shy about showing anyone my art, but for some reason I wanted to with Colten.

"They're not that good." I handed them over. He took them gently, giving me a smile as he did.

"All artists think they suck. I'm sure they're amazing. Here, I'll show you mine too." He reached into a bag, I hadn't noticed sitting beside his chair, and pulled out a notepad as well.

"You didn't tell me you drew too." A ripple of surprise went over me.

"You didn't ask," he said with a wink. I flipped open his notepad, while he flipped open mine. I stared at the figurines, a lot like what I had been drawing lately, and felt a tingle go down my neck. When I flipped to the next page, I nearly jumped. A beautifully drawn fox was etched—Grim. It had to be him. I stared at the picture, for probably what seemed like a weird amount of time. Colten cleared his throat, and I jerked my head up.

"You like that?" He laughed.

"Well yeah, I—" How could I put into words why the picture of a fox had held my attention for probably a couple minutes straight.

"You should keep it." He tapped the table with his finger.

"No, it's yours. I can't do that."

"I think you should have it. I keep dreaming about foxes and these things lately. I noticed you kind of draw the same thing." He flipped open my notepad and reached across the table and flipped to a certain drawing of his own. "Look." He held them both side by side, and I couldn't deny that they looked almost identical.

"I...yeah...they do look alike." I felt suddenly nervous. What if I told Colten about Anxious? Would he think I was insane? I barely knew him, but there was something about him that felt familiar.

"Isn't that kind of freaky?" He set our notepads both down on the table, looking slightly disturbed. "I've told my mom about my dreams, and she tells me that there is a paranormal 'hotspot' in our city—at least that's the rumor. Have you ever been behind the theater?" He leaned back against his chair and took a sip of his coffee.

"Um, yes, actually. My brother and I wandered back there not too long ago." The back of my neck prickled.

"Well, supposedly there are shadows that people see from time to time—or least they did years ago. And my mom's great-aunt's best friend used to tell her about a little fox who she talked to when she was a kid, and supposedly it talked back." Colten took another drink of his coffee, raising an eyebrow at me. "Weird huh?"

"Not as weird as you think." I wanted to tell him so badly, but what if I did and he thought I was a freak. "Kids have pretty active imaginations."

"That's what I figured it was, but I wanted to go see for myself one day. My buddy Josh and I camped over there a few times, but nothing weird ever happened. Except, after that I started getting these dreams about the pictures I just showed you." He ran his fingers through his thick, dark hair and laughed. "You probably think I'm a crazy man."

"Not really," I said quietly.

"It's not normal for me to tell a girl this kind of crap on the first date. You probably think I'm nuts." He looked up at the ceiling for a second.

"No, I don't think you're nuts. My dad was looking into the paranormal activity in this town for months." I paused, because mentioning my dad brought up pain.

Colten leaned forward, interested.

"You'll find me nuts if I tell you more." I struggled inside, wanting to feel accepted, but also wanting to share the burden of the world of Anxious with someone other than just Alex.

"Hey, did you hear what I just said? I told you I'm dreaming of a talking fox and weird-looking people." He ran a hand down his face with a laugh.

"I've seen that fox." I took a deep breath. "And I've been to his world."

Chapter 19

Alex

I couldn't seem to get the documents I'd read out of my head. I woke up, ate breakfast, and did mostly nothing the entire day. Mark, Lynda, and the boys had gone out and done something without disturbing me. It was weird not being part of a normal family unit. Mom and Dad always told Raven and I where they were going. I'd ignored texts from my two friends for a long time, and they'd finally seemed to give up. I felt like a douchebag, but right now I didn't want to do much of anything. I scrolled through my phone, trying my best not to think about anything too depressing, even if the weight of everything still sat on top of me.

Ding. My phone went off, and I saw another text from Ian. I stared at it for a second and then forced myself to get out of bed. I needed to stop wallowing and actually do something. I sent a quick text back to Ian, telling him to meet me at the *hotspot*, where we'd first went camping awhile back. He sent a reply, and I headed toward the door.

As my feet ate up the sidewalk, the sky was gray up above me, the clouds masking all sight of blue. I passed by several picture-perfect houses, and I couldn't help but wonder if any of them had ever had their entire life thrown on its butt. I fought off the bitter feelings, my body shaking. It had been doing that a lot lately. I'd done several quick Google searches to uncover that I was experiencing high doses of anxiety. I knew I had a problem, but there wasn't anything I could do to fix it. No matter what King Michael or Grim told me.

Everything that had transpired since my parents died was creating a sucking hole on the inside of me.

Nothing mattered to me anymore. Even now, walking toward the woods to meet up with my friends seemed pointless. Part of me wanted to go back to bed, pull the covers up, and sleep until I was dead. I knew I battled depression, but I didn't care to fight it at this point. I'd always been a positive, uplifting person, and when I needed someone to uplift me there wasn't anyone. I had to deal with it.

I started to jog, my feet thudding against the pavement. After a good ten minutes, I reached the theater. Ian and Jack were there waiting for me.

"Dude! Where have you been?" Jack pounded me on the back, and I forced myself to smile.

"Around."

"It's like you died, bro," Ian said, and then slapped himself in the face. "Dang, I'm sorry. That was bad." He looked genuinely sorry about what he'd just said, so I let it go.

"It's fine. What did you guys want to do?" My nerves were tight in my stomach, but I didn't want to be lame and leave.

"There's been some weird crap going on lately. We wanted to do another campout tonight. Ian and I already set up camp for us." Jack looked at me with an eager expression.

"I don't know, guys." I looked away from them, my neck tensing.

"Come on, dude. We want to hang with you. Plus, last time it was pretty fun. Just for one night?"

"I guess." I sent off a quick text to my foster family, telling them I was spending the night at a friend's house.

All three of us headed toward the woods, Ian and Jack rambling about the latest tricks they'd been up to. Ian even talked about one of his latest girlfriends who'd ended up kicking his butt at videogames.

"She's a boss, dude. I can't believe it. I think I found my soulmate," Ian said.

"Anyone who can trash you at your own game has got to be the one," I said. It felt nice to joke around with them, and for one moment I could almost forget all the bull that had been going on in my life lately. We reached the tent, and Ian and Jack plopped into a couple chairs, letting me take the third.

"So come on, Alex, tell us what's going on? I hate being all sentimental, but you've been AWOL a while now," Ian said, prodding me with his gaze.

"It's sucked. What else can I say? My parents are dead, and I'm living with a new family. My sister is—" I couldn't even finish my sentence for fear of losing it in front of my friends.

"What's going on with Raven?" Jack asked, leaning forward. "Do I need to beat someone up?"

"Yeah, probably." I leaned back in my chair, staring up at the tops of the trees. "I can't get her out of there."

"What do you need us to do?" Jack asked.

"There isn't anything you can do, Jack. It's the system."

"I dunno, my mom would probably take her in." He glanced at Ian then me. "She's always loved Raven."

"Really?" I felt a tinge of hope at his words. "You really think she'd do that?"

"Maybe. I'll talk to her about it." Jack picked up a chunk of wood and tossed it up into the air, nearly slugging himself in the head with it as it came back down.

"Jack, stop trying to kill yourself. Hey, we got a few hours to burn before sundown, why don't we go visit the Mcdeen's farm?" Ian said, standing to his feet. "They've been talking to people about the shadow men."

I didn't have much enthusiasm for anything at the moment, but maybe this would help me keep my mind off Raven.

"Sure." I ran my fingers through my hair and let out a sigh.

* * * * *

We arrived at the Mcdeen's house, located on my family's property, in just a few minutes, and Ian and Jack went up to the door. Ian gave a few knocks, and we took a step back. A moment later, the door creaked open, and a tall, thin woman stood before us, her hair long and straight. She looked around thirty-five with bags under her eyes like she hadn't been sleeping for a while. I vaguely recognized her.

"Hi, can I help you?"

"Sorry to bother you. My friends and I were wondering if you could tell us about the shadow men encounters your family has been having lately. We've heard about them in the paper, and my friend Alex's dad, Mr. Dayton, was researching it. He passed away not too long ago. Alex wants to see if there are any clues about his father's death and these shadow men." Ian held his hands together as he explained everything quickly. The woman's eyes went from concern to empathy as she turned her gaze onto me.

"I recognize you. I think we met when my husband and I moved in a few years back." She nudged her head toward me.

"My parents own this property. It's been in our family for generations."

"Yes, the Daytons hold the keys." The woman's eyes grew wide. "Come right on in, kids. I'll get you some cookies." She held the door open, and all three of us entered. Her house was a bit rundown but felt cozy too. I noticed religious paraphernalia everywhere. I sat down on a threadbare couch as the woman headed into the kitchen. A few moments later, she came back out with a plate of cookies. She offered them to us and sat down on a cracked, leather chair.

"It's been getting much worse these days. Generally, the angels keep the shadow men at bay, but I fear something awful has happened lately." She gave each of us a stare. My stomach churned inside of me. Somehow, I knew all of this was my fault.

"Angels?" Ian said, and I could see him trying to suppress a laugh.

"Oh yes. They are usually wandering around outside in the woods, but lately, all I see is the shadow men, or as my husband calls them the Daegal demons." She shuddered, and I could tell she was disturbed greatly. "My husband has been sleeping for days on end. The shadow men release a very dark energy around our property. Joe has a hard time dealing with it." Fear crossed her features. "I pray the angels will return soon and remove the darkness."

Jack exchanged a look with me mouthing the word *crazy*, but I knew better. This woman wasn't crazy at all. The Daegal were entering our world at a much faster pace, and it was entirely my fault according to King Michael. If I didn't do something, would my whole city be overrun? Part of me wondered how this lady and her husband could even see them. I'd thought it was a curse put on my family. *Maybe because she's living in our ancestor's house and on our property?*

"Anyways, I like to try to think the best. This has happened in the past. You can read about it in the newspapers. We have had fluxes of deaths over the years on and off. I fear when the Daegal grow, they will bring death again on more than just a few." She threw me a pity-filled look. "I am so sorry about your parents. I heard about their death, and I knew deep in my soul who was responsible for it." She rose from where she sat, looking more stressed by the second. She stared out the window. "There has always been a Dayton to maintain the doors, but I fear the ones chosen to help the angels has fallen prey to the demons' evil influence."

Jack and Ian looked more weirded out by the second, but I hung onto this woman's every word. The pressure of trying to heal the world of Anxious was on me, and I didn't know what I was going to do to stop the Daegal from spreading here.

"It can't be helped," Kate said with a sigh. Her hand shook as she lifted it to her forehead. "The demons whisper lies to anyone who lets them. They break you down, until they grow more powerful in our realm." She suddenly shot me a wide-eyed look. "You must fight it, Alexander Dayton." Her eyes glazed over as she spoke. I felt a shudder go through my body, and the hair on the back of my neck stood up.

I felt uncomfortable, so I said nothing. She was right though. I was letting my mind rule over me. I'd never before had to deal with depression and anxiety the way it was attacking me now.

I've never had to deal with dead parents before, either.

"So you think these Daegal killed my parents?" I said the words in a small voice, because I didn't want to believe any of this was true.

ANXIOUS

Kate looked lost for a moment, her lips trembling and her eyes streaking to the window. "They're here." She stood abruptly, reaching for a little cross sitting on her end table.

I heard the woman whisper frantic prayers, holding the cross to her heart.

"Maybe we should go?" Ian whispered to me. I silently nodded, and the three of us rose to our feet.

"Thank you for your help, Kate," I said with a nod.

"Help the angels," she said in a near hiss.

Chapter 20

Raven

"Okay, now we're both crazy." Colten laughed.

I slapped a hand over my face. "I'm completely serious. I know it sounds nuts, but I've met that fox," I said in-between my fingers.

"I'm just insane enough to believe you." Colten grinned at me, placing his hand on my back. His touch sent a million tingles through my body, and I removed my hand from my face.

"Life is so weird." I let out a sigh and took a drink of my coffee.

"Around here, yes."

We both fell quiet for a few seconds, enjoying our coffees. After a moment, Colten leaned forward, his brows flexing. "You said that you've been to his world? What were you talking about?" He looked genuinely interested.

"My brother and I were wandering around the woods behind the theater when we spotted an animal. We chased after it for a little while, until we saw that it was a fox."

"Why did you chase it?" Colten looked amused.

"I have no idea. It felt like it was luring us. Anyways, it turned around and started talking to us. Almost gave us both a heart attack." I giggled at the memory.

"I'm pretty sure most people would have had themselves committed."

"We probably should have been." I smirked. "We kept walking what felt like an eternity until the fox led us to this big field, and off in the distance was a castle."

"As in a castle, castle?" Colten's eyes were glued onto mine, and he held his coffee aloft.

"Yup." I went on to explain the encounter with King Michael and everything in-between. Once I was finished, my chest felt lighter.

"Wow. This is crazy." Colten leaned back in his chair. "Can I ask you something?"

"Yeah, sure."

"Do you want to go to the beach?"

The question caught me off-guard, but I smiled at him. "Sure. Why?"

"I want to show you something." He stood to his feet, coffee in hand. I also stood, and he started to walk toward the door, turning and looking over his shoulder at me. "Come on. I think you'll love it." He reached for my hand, and a warm sensation pumped through my body. My fingers slipped in-between his as we walked out the door into the warm summer air. The beach wasn't a far walk, and I enjoyed the sunshine that caressed my face.

"It's beautiful outside," I said.

"Yeah, it is." He turned to look at me. "I'm just curious, but how can you wear a hoodie when it's eighty degrees outside?"

I laughed. I'd been asked that question dozens of times, but I never knew exactly how to answer it. As a younger kid, I'd been self-conscious of my body, and to hide it I'd always worn hoodies and jeans. I'd gotten so used to the feel of it that I felt weird not wearing them.

"As a kid it's all I would wear, and I guess it got to be so normal that now I don't even think about it."

"So you're not dying beneath that hoodie?" He squeezed my hand.

"No, not at all. I'm comfortable." We were fast approaching the beach, and I could see seagulls standing in the white sand. Instead of heading to the main beach, Colten pulled me into a jog, leading me toward a small path in the woods near the beach.

"I know a place," he said with a wink.

"You're not plotting to kill me and bury my body out here, right?" I said with a laugh.

"Of course I am." He suddenly turned and crushed me into a hug, passion lighting up in his eyes. I felt two feelings—terror and excitement—all mixed into one.

"I'm totally joking by the way. You're too pretty to murder." He stared down into my eyes, and something popped open in my chest. Hope furled out, and a joyful feeling rippled all the way through me. I had never experienced this feeling before, but from what I'd heard my friends tell me, it was the feeling you get when you were falling in love.

"That's good to know." I blushed. We maneuvered around trees, his hand still holding mine. We walked for a little while, until we came upon a secluded section of the beach.

"Come on." He flashed me a smile and led us down to the shore. I slipped my shoes off and let the sand squish between my toes.

"This is beautiful." The lake stretched out before me, crystal clear, blue, and sparkling beneath the sunshine. A pang struck my chest, and my eyes lowered to my feet. *We used to go out on the lake all the time. All that's gone now.* I felt bad about letting a past memory ruin this moment, and I tried to shake off the depressive thoughts.

"You okay?" Colten noticed my sad expression and held my hand up and kissed it. His gentle affection made my heart squeeze tight in my chest.

"Yeah. Yeah, I'm okay."

"I know this sounds crazy, Raven. I know we don't know each other well yet, but I feel like I already know you." He turned his eyes onto mine. I didn't know what to say, so I just stayed silent.

"It sounds corny, right? My friends are always telling me I'm a romantic sap." He laughed at himself, breaking our handhold. I felt strangely empty without the feeling of his fingers looped through mine.

"No, it's not corny. I'm the girl who writes hopeless poems about love at first sight." I let my eyes rest on the sparkling water. *He won't actually stay. This will never work.* The dark thoughts swirled in my head, and I felt my pain arise all over again.

"You look like you're going to be sick. You sure you're okay?" Colten put a hand on my back.

"I don't know." *This can't be real. There is no such thing as love at first sight. Nothing good lasts.* Colten stared at me, looking concerned.

A dark ripple formed just behind Colten's head. I let out a soft gasp as tiny black particles swirled through the air, wrapping around Colten and then me. A face formed, a grin, and a finger coaxing me to step forward. *I'm going crazy. What is going on?* My heart sped up, my hands grew clammy, and my chest tightened. Was I having a panic attack?

"Raven?"

I stared at the black form, the red glowing eyes, and something in me glazed over. *Love is impossible. Who would want me? Look at me.*

"Raven!" Colten's voice broke me out of my daze, and the image of the dark man disappeared into a vapor.

"I'm sorry." I stared at my feet again.

"You looked like you were going to pass out. Should I take you home?" His fingers brushed my cheek.

"No, I'm fine. Let's have some fun." I gave him my best attempt at a smile, though it was hard to shake the heavy feeling that hovered over me like a cloud.

"Okay." He grinned at me, scooped me right off my feet, and started to run straight toward the water. I let out a squeal, half-heartedly kicking my feet to get him to let me down, but he kept running. We hit the water, and he dove straight in. The water was cool, but not freezing, and I came up laughing, slapping at him.

"You dork!"

"But you said the water looked nice. I thought you'd want to see for yourself." Droplets dripped down his face, a crooked grin on his lips.

I sent a splash toward him, which started a splashing war. After a few minutes, we were both breathless and laughing. He reached for my hand again and pulled me to his chest.

"Raven, I like you, a lot." With that, he pulled me into a passionate kiss. Joy erupted all the way through me. Even though I was soaked, I'd never felt happier in my entire life. When he pulled back, he searched my eyes. "I'm not freaking you out, right?"

I laughed. "No. Not at all." I wrapped my arms back around his neck and kissed him again, and then pulled him straight into the water.

* * * * *

I wasn't sure how long Colten and I talked after we climbed out of the water and laid on the beach to dry. The sun warmed my face, and I'd shed my hoodie and hung it up to dry. Being in wet jeans wasn't the most comfortable, but today had been amazing. My mind drifted to my mom. *I wish she was here. She'd love to hear about this.* Colten and I's head rested in the sand, and his hand was looped through mine. Call me a hopeless romantic, but I'd always dreamed of a relationship like this—instant love and attraction. To believe I could have all of that with Colten made me feel amazed and in awe.

"Has this ever happened to you before?" Colten asked, turning his head to look at me. His blue eyes danced with affection.

"Being thrown in a lake?" I winked at him.

"Yup."

"Alex did it to me before." I patted the sand beneath my feet.

"You know what I meant," Colten said with a light-hearted laugh.

"This?" I shook my head. "No. I've never even had a boyfriend before."

"Oh, so I'm your boyfriend, huh?" Colten turned on his side, getting sand all over his bare chest. I couldn't help but stare at it.

"I don't know. Maybe."

"I'm just messing with you. I don't just kiss a girl and run away. I've only kissed two girls in my life. A girl I met a couple years ago. I thought she loved me, but it turned out I was dead wrong. And you." He leaned forward and brushed my lips with his. The same warm sensation pulsed through me again, and I let my lips linger on his for a long time.

"You're not just doing this because you feel sorry for me, right?" Fear climbed over me.

"Raven, why would I do that?" He looked straight into my eyes.

"I don't know. It seems too good to be true." My insecurities rose all over again, and I felt the heaviness I'd felt earlier come back over me.

"You're still healing. Your parents just died, Raven. Give yourself a break. You went through a huge crisis." He reached his hand out and brushed my hair back from my face. He leaned down and kissed me again, his fingers intertwining into my hair as he did. I wanted to trust what he said. I really did. But we barely knew one another—despite him saying he felt he knew me. *You feel like he knows you too,* I told myself.

"You're right." I leaned my head back into the sand with a sigh.

"Give yourself time. Don't destroy a good thing before it even begins." He gave my hand a gentle squeeze.

* * * * *

"Where have you been?" Jill's sharp voice came at me the moment I walked into the house. I was still soaked but happy.

"Outside." I shrugged. I didn't want to get into it with her today.

"You're soaking wet." Her face twisted with disgust.

"I know." I went to go move past her when she shoved me back.

"Don't give me that sass, young lady." She gave my arm a sharp pinch. I winced but didn't make a sound. "Jamie said she saw you with my cousin's son, Colten, at the family reunion."

"Yeah," I said the word quietly, wondering what her deal was.

"He's off-limits. That family is bad news." Jill's eyes narrowed at me.

"Why?" I felt intimidated, but also annoyed that she was ruining my feelings of happiness.

"His dad is a cheat, and his mom is a gossip. She spreads rumors about Nelson and me all the time. Stay away from their son." Jill shoved her chubby finger in my chest.

"Whatever," I mumbled, and tried to move past her again. She shoved me back again.

"You're not listening to me, young lady."

A pair of strong arms were suddenly around me and pulled me backward. I could smell alcohol.

"Why aren't you listening to your mother?" Nelson's voice came behind me. "I think you need to learn some manners." He pulled me backward, and panic started to make me shake.

"Let go of me! I didn't do anything wrong!" I struggled to get out of his arms, which only made him get rougher with me. He pulled me, struggling and kicking, down the stairs and shoved me into the same chair as before. He hovered over me, a sneer on his face. Jill came wobbling down the stairs and stood before me.

"Show her how to be respectful, Nelson." Jill crossed her arms over her chest.

Nelson grinned at me, a malicious look in his eye. He walked over to the basement sink and started to fill up a bucket of water. I jumped out of the chair and ran toward the door. Jill was too slow, and her fingers only grazed me, but I could hear Nelson's thudding footsteps chasing me. I had barely reached the bottom of the stairs when he grabbed me and threw me to the ground.

"Little girls who disobey must be punished." He gave me a wicked grin and threw me over his shoulder. He dragged me back down the stairs and shoved me back down into it. This time he grabbed some rope and tied me tight. I started to cry. I couldn't help it. I'd had such an amazing day, and to come home to this was a slap in the face. What was wrong with these people? Before I could hold my breath, a bucket of cold water was dumped on my head. Next came the belt against my back, the cold and wet feeling made the strike hurt worse than the first time he'd done it. Jill proceeded to fill the bucket again, and together they continued to punish me, until I slumped over in the chair.

"Enough, Nelson," Jill finally said and dropped the bucket. "I'm tired and hungry. Let's go upstairs. Let the little brat sit here and think about what she did."

My eyes were squeezed shut, but I heard them walk up the stairs and shut the door. They left me in utter darkness. I tried to grasp the happy feeling from earlier today, but I couldn't. This was my life now. This was my reality. I didn't get a happy ending.

You are mine... a cold voice hissed. I tried to lift my head up but didn't have much willpower at this point. I felt a presence hovering around me, and a clammy finger lifted my chin. I managed to get my swollen eyes open, and a pair of red eyes glared down at me. *You don't deserve happiness, Raven. You aren't worth it.*

I started sobbing.

* * * * *

The next morning, I woke up, my entire body aching. I'd somehow managed to fall asleep in the chair. I'd wiggled enough to get the ropes to slack, until I could untie the sloppy knots Nelson had tied. *I have to get out of here.* My mind replayed their abuse, and I found myself sobbing all over again. I finally managed to get the ropes off and stood to my feet.

I nearly passed out at the pain that swept my body. I was freezing, and every bone and muscle screamed at me for relief. *I can't take this anymore.* I struggled to climb the stairs, praying that Nelson and Jill were out of the house. I got to the top and pressed my ear to the wooden door. Nothing came to my ears, so I tried the handle. It was luckily open. They had probably figured since I was tied up, there was no point to lock it.

I slipped through the door, trying to be as quiet as possible, and went to my room. I threw my clothes in one bag as best as possible, scooped up the little money I had, and headed toward the front door. The house was completely silent.

The moment I was outside, I ran. I ran until my lungs burned and my throat was dry. I didn't even realize I was sobbing again until I felt the wetness drip onto my neck. I fumbled for my phone and called Colten. I had no idea why I wanted to call him instead of my brother. He answered on the second ring.

"Hi, Raven!" He sounded so happy. I was about to shatter his world.

"I can't be with you." I got the words out as fast as I could, shivering and wanting to vomit.

"What's wrong?" His voice filled with deep concern. "What happened?"

"I...I can't be with you."

"You can't? What do you mean? Who's telling you that you can't be with me?" he said.

"I...I just can't. You need to find someone better. You deserve a really nice girl, someone who's happy. I can't do happy right now, Colten." Tears streamed down my face as I ran.

"No one is forcing you to do anything, Raven. I'm willing to be patient. I know you're going through a hard time."

"Colten, it's better if we end it now." My hand trembled.

"Remember what I told you? Don't end a good thing before it even has a chance. Please, can we meet? I want to talk."

I hung up the phone. Something sucked me down, and I felt a hand wrapping around my head, draining the life out of me in an instant.

You will never be happy...

A dark figure loomed before me, long fingers reaching for me. *Give us the key...no one will ever want you, Raven.*

The dark figure swirled, growing bigger with each breath. I could make out vague features of sharp, jagged teeth, bulging red eyes, black armor, and the stench of a dead animal.

Please, God, if you are there, help me. Please help me.

Something shimmered in my peripheral vision, and I panicked, scampering backward on my hands and knees.

"Do not be afraid, Raven." Glowing golden light emanated from a figure to the side of the shadow. I could make out golden and white armor, plastered with beautiful symbols I didn't understand, white flowing hair adorned the man's head, and a purple fiery sword was gripped in his hand. Stretched around him was enormous wings that looked alive with pure white energy.

You have no place here...archangel of the realms. The girl is mine. The shadow flicked in and out, and where the light of the angel touched, the demon seemed to shrink. A snarl ripped across his face. *She has chosen the path of darkness.*

"She called on the light. Be gone!" A purple shimmer flashed, and I saw the angelic being use his glimmering sword. The demon shied away in fright, and in a moment vaporized back to wherever he'd come from.

I laid on the ground for several seconds before looking up at the angel.

"Umm…" I tried to find words to say, but nothing came to mind. "Thank you."

"You're welcome." His smile spread across his face, and I instantly felt at peace. "We have much work to do." He took my hand and helped me to my feet.

Chapter 21

Alex

"She was a loony, huh?" Ian said, as we left the woman's house and headed back to our campsite. I simply shrugged, knowing that everything she'd said was true. Jack bounded ahead of us, his pent-up energy obvious.

"Come on, let's do something. Do you guys want to go jump in the lake? I'm hot." Jack fanned his face, scrunching his mouth.

"Sure." It would be nice to get my mind off of the world of Anxious and the Daegal that were running amuck in our city. We hurried back to camp and got into our swimming trunks. As we walked toward the beach, Ian kept looking at me. I finally turned to him, stopping in my tracks.

I threw up my hands. "What?"

"Nothing, man. You just seem weird is all." He scratched the back of his head, casting his gaze to the ground.

I shrugged, forcing all I felt into a hard ball in my stomach.

"Come on, Alex, what did you think of all that? I know your dad was into all that stuff." He stopped walking, waiting for me to answer. Jack looked half-bored but still waited for us.

"You guys wouldn't believe me if I told you anyway," I said with a shoulder shrug.

That got both of their attention right away.

"What are you talking about? Spill it," Jack said. His attention was now on high alert.

"It's nothing." I tried to keep walking, but Ian stopped me.

"I know this has all been hard on you. You're like another person. What is going on?" Ian looked right into my eyes, and I found myself breaking inside.

"It's stupid. Come one." I tried again to move forward, but now both Jack and Ian blocked the path.

"Alex, come on, man." Jack folded his arms over his chest. "You need to talk to someone. If you don't, all that will blow up. Or at least that's what my therapist says." Jack rose an eyebrow.

"You got a therapist?" Ian chuckled.

"You don't?" Jack's eyebrow rose with exaggeration.

I shook my head at the both of them. "You guys will think I'm a freak."

"That's nothing new," Ian said with a smirk. They didn't move. I finally let out an annoyed sigh.

"All that stuff, the woman said earlier…" I drew in a deep breath. "It's real."

Jack and Ian stared at me with blank expressions on their faces.

"I've been to Anxious. I've seen the angels and the Daegal. It's my fault the Daegal are here, and I have no idea how to stop it."

Both of my friends stared at me in utter silence. Then suddenly they both started laughing.

"You're nuts, man! You really had me!" Ian slapped my back.

"I'm not making this up." I shoved him. "I told you that you wouldn't believe me."

"You're serious?" Jack scratched his head.

"Of course I am. Raven and I have both been there. And their world is falling apart." I didn't want to talk about it anymore, so I pushed past them and ran to the beach.

* * * *

Ian and Jack didn't bring the subject up again. They knew when I didn't want to be pushed anymore, so they thankfully left it alone. I saw Ian give me a few worried glances, but other than that, the time at the beach was well-needed. But it still didn't feel like it used to. *I used to be so carefree about life. Nothing ever got me down.* I looked back on the old me and felt envious. I wish I could go back and be him again, but I couldn't. No matter how hard I tried. I was someone else now. We messed around for another hour, before going back to our campsite and starting a fire.

Ian and Jack joked about all the usual stuff, but I had a hard time joining in on their conversation like I used to. I knew I needed some sort of psychotic help, but I didn't want to admit it to myself.

* * * * *

I had just closed my eyes, later that night, wanting to ignore the jittery feeling in my body, when I heard the scuffling of small feet. My eyes flew open, and I turned my head to the corner of the tent. A small shadow stood there, wringing its small hands.

"Alex, you must come with me now." I could barely make out Grim's worried face in the dim light. "Anxious is in a dire state."

Ian and Jack were out cold, and I found it weird that they didn't wake up from the sound of the fox's voice.

"What's wrong with them?" I pointed at my two friends.

"Please, come with me. King Michael needs your help." Grim made his way over to me, his golden eyes glowing. My body stiffened.

"I already told you—it's not my fault your world is falling apart. Stop trying to pin that on me." My anger started to build, and I wanted to throw the fox out the door.

"Listen to me!" Grim jumped up on my stomach and stared me straight in the eyes. "I know you're in pain, and I know you blame yourself for your parents' death, but if I told you that only you can stop the Daegal from hurting more people in your world, would you follow me?" His small paws pressed into my chest.

"What do you mean? How can I stop the Daegal from coming here?" I looked around the tent, suddenly feeling cold.

"I will teach you how. The Daegal murdered your parents, and unless you want more death, you must come quickly." He turned his head to the side, like I should have known that vital piece of information. Shock swept over me.

"You mean to tell me those demons will keep killing?" The thought so disturbed me that my mouth fell open.

"The portals have been opened somehow, and those who invite them by mental invitation will suffer." Grim scowled at me.

I climbed out of my sleeping bag and ran my fingers through my hair. "So these creatures can come over on our side and murder people? This is insane. How can they do that? Who's letting them through?" I turned and stared at the little fox. My mind went back to the woman Ian, Jack, and I had talked to yesterday.

"I am the gatekeeper, yes, but there are two ancient mirrors, which have been lost for ages. With them, one can gain access to the world of Anxious, and sadly, the Daegal can also use these portals to bring trouble into your world." Grim rubbed his chin, looking sad. "There hasn't been sight of either mirror in many years, but if the Daegal are gaining a foothold in your world, then the Dagmoth Mirror has been found again."

I had never heard the little fox talk so much, but I tried my best to listen to everything he said.

"Find the thought that brings you out of the darkness, Alexander. Find that thought and bust through your agonized patterns of defeat. If you do so, you will overcome the Daegal and so will Raven." Grim reached his hand out and touched my hand. I bent down to him and looked into his golden eyes.

"I'm not a warrior, and I'm no savior." My heart churned in my chest at the words I spoke. I couldn't even save my own sister.

"You don't need to be either." Grim lifted my hand slightly. "All you need to do is lead yourself. The rest will follow." He put his paw against my heart. "It's all inside of you." He looked gravely serious as he said the next words, "If you don't return, all will be lost and the Daegal will continue to slip through the open portals. You must lead others, Alexander, to the truth of who they really are."

The weight of Grim's words struck me. How could I lead others when I was a mess myself?

"You must learn to find the golden memory. Please, you must let King Michael teach you, so you can teach others in your town. If not, more pain and destruction are coming. The Daegal are finding more portals by the second, and they are attacking Drite." The little fox danced back and forth, his voice rising in pitch. "Please, follow me."

I considered every world Grim said to me. *How can I lead anyone? I couldn't even save Mom and Dad.* A rumble shook the ground and a look of terror passed over Grim's face.

"Please come!" Grim grabbed my hand and gave it a hard tug. I found myself following and then running. We made our way outside and toward the house Raven was holed up in. Grim darted around to the back of the house, so I followed behind him. He came to a window and easily jumped in. A moment later, he came back out.

"She's gone. Call her phone."

I pulled my phone from my pocket and hit recent calls. After a few rings, she finally picked up.

"Raven? Where are you? I'm at your house." I was instantly worried about her.

"I'm headed toward the woods. Alex, I can't be there anymore. I have to go. I have to go somewhere." I heard the pain in her voice, and anger roared through me. What had those people done to my little sister?

"Meet me behind the theater. I'll be right there." I hung up the phone, giving Grim a stressed look. "Something is wrong with her."

"Yes." Grim's eyes filled with deep concern. "Hurry now."

It didn't take long before I saw Raven's figure standing in the woods, a backpack flung over her shoulder. She dropped her bag with a *thud* and ran toward me, wrapping her arms around me. She kissed my cheek, surprising me. She buried her face in my neck for a long time, and I felt her shuddering.

"We must go," Grim said, looking first at me and then at Raven. "Please."

Raven gave a nod, and I saw that she'd been crying hard. Anytime she cried hard her face would get red splotches.

I grabbed her hand and gave it a squeeze, silently telling her I was here for her. Grim took off running, his tail bobbing.

I pulled her forward. "Talk to me."

"I got a boyfriend." She tried to smile at me, but it ended up being a grimace. "And then I broke up with him already."

"When did that happen?" Our feet pounded the ground, spraying dead leaves and crunching sticks as we ran.

"Just yesterday. His name is Colten." Her face filled with brief hope, followed by devastation. "He must think I'm crazy. We got along amazing, and then today I told him I couldn't be with him." Tears dripped down her face. "He dreamed about Anxious, and he's drawn Grim and the Endrita in his sketchbook." Her dark hair whipped behind her as we ran.

"Raven, why'd you break up with him?"

"I got home, and—" She turned her face away, and I saw the flow of tears falling again.

"It's okay." I squeezed her hand again.

Grim came to an abrupt stop, nearly making Raven and I fall on top of him.

"Here." He sniffed the air, and his eyebrow raised as if he questioned something. "The quick access door is here." He sniffed again. He raised his paw upward and pressed it up against the air. Energy rippled making Raven and me both gasp. A golden door appeared, and Grim opened it up, revealing the steps of the castle. I grabbed Raven's hand and we both stepped through.

The moment I stepped into Anxious, I could feel the difference in the air. The door of the castle looked as if it had been burned. The air felt tight and cold, and I had a hard time breathing it in.

"Follow me quickly." Grim put his paw against the door, and it opened with a groan. From the last time we'd been here I noticed the immediate differences. The entryway was no longer filled with golden specks but felt empty of life. The floor was marred in spots with black smudges, and the once ornate décor seemed to be neglected and crumbling. Grim hurried us to the door for the throne room. He pushed it open.

I heard Raven gasp at the sight. Inside, the throne room looked bleak and rundown. The table sitting in the center was broken, and I felt the oppression crushing down on me.

"Sire? They're here!" Grim said.

A shuffling resounded, and I peered into the semi-darkness to see a figure making its way toward us. I spotted the form of King Michael, but he looked much older, and his once white hair was filled with ashes. His face was smeared with dirt, and his robe was torn in several spots. *What did we do?* Raven ran ahead of me and crouched before the young king. She gave him a hug. She turned her head and looked at me with an expression of deep concern.

This is my fault. I squeezed my eyes shut, feeling even heavier at the sight of this once beautiful place in such disarray.

"Come, come quickly. I have much to teach you." King Michael waved me forward. He turned and hurried as fast as he could out the door, down a long hall, and to another door. He paused for a moment, looking weary, and then hurried out a backdoor into a garden. Tree branches dipped over us, golden leaves swaying in the light breeze, and colorful flowers were dotted along the sides of the path. At least this place was still beautiful.

King Michael drew in a deep breath, drawing energy from the beautiful environment. "I must teach you about the golden memory." He looked at each of us in turn. "In order to save your world, you must fight the darkness of your pain. Don't run away from it; embrace your pain and fight back with the light." He turned back around and kept walking, the path broadening the further he went. We walked through an archway, vines and white flowers twisted into the metal. He stopped walking and faced the both of us. Behind him stood an enormous tree, with long branches, which dipped down a lot like a willow tree. On each branch was tiny golden orbs that swirled with surges of light. Instantly captivated, I stared at the strange sight.

"These are the golden memories." King Michael lifted his hand, and I noticed how it looked like an old man's hand now. "These are your golden memories." He stared at first me and then Raven.

"What are they?" Raven asked, her eyes round and full of awe. I could tell she was just as captivated by these things as I was. I felt warmth spread through me, reminding me of Mom's cookies and snuggling under the blankets as Dad read a bedtime story to me.

"Each orb is a happy memory from when you were young. From age zero to six you are receiving these golden memories. They soak straight into your subconscious mind and create your belief about the world. As you grew older, more and more golden memories were formed from those core beliefs." King Michael hovered his hand just below a memory, and I felt a surge of happiness go through my body.

"You are the keeper of this garden, and the seeds your parents planted into you have not gone away. Despite your inner world being destroyed by the Daegal. They cannot touch this place." He withdrew his hand suddenly as if bit and jerked his head to stare at me. "Not yet anyways. But if you continue down this destructive path, even that which was light will be remembered as darkness."

"You mean to tell me that these are our memories?" Raven approached the tree, her blue eyes growing rounder by the second. The tree's light illuminated her face with a golden glow, making her look angelic. She reached out and touched one of the orbs, and I heard the sound of laughter fill the garden. *That's Raven. I remember that moment!* I had been upside down on a pair of monkey bars, and Raven had found my hair hilarious as I swung there. She'd been five at the time. The memory made me chuckle, because when Raven laughed it made others laugh to. Her laugh was loud and infectious, despite her quiet demeanor.

"Wow," she whispered. "What do we do with these?"

"Remember them. Feel the moments of happiness you've had in the past. Let your mind absorb joy again; if you don't, the Daegal will continue to grow rampant through the world of Anxious."

I approached the tree next, and one by one began to touch the golden globes on the ends of each branch. I could feel the joy I'd felt as a child, and I tried to hang onto the feeling as long as I could. I saw Raven doing the same thing, until we were both laughing at some of the things we used to do together.

"The love you two share between each other is strong. While, yes, you have golden memories with your parents, I'd advise you to hold onto the ones with each other tighter."

His words sent an ache straight through my heart. *Because Mom and Dad are dead.* This brought back a sense of dread, and a cold sensation replaced the once warm pulse that had started to return inside of me.

"Alex and Raven, you must hold onto the golden memory to learn how to overcome the darkness. If you don't, you'll fail. This tree and these orbs are what hold Drite together, if the golden memories disappear, so does Drite." King Michael's face looked ashen, his hands trembling. "Please hold onto the golden memories." He slumped onto the ground.

Chapter 22

Raven

"King Michael!" The sound of my voice was lost as a rumble shook the ground beneath my feet. I watched the young king slump onto the ground. The air around me shifted from gold to gray, and the temperature dropped twenty degrees. I shivered, wrapping my arms around myself, trying to get warm.

A deep-throated laugh cut into the peacefulness of the garden. "It's too late for the both of you. You'll never save Drite."

The tree shook, the golden orbs clinging and clanging as they struck each other. I saw several fall and split open, leaving a liquid pool on the ground. My mind went back to the pool of blood beneath my parents, and I relived the moment all over again. I wrapped my arms around myself tighter, my sobs threatening to spill over.

"King Michael has no power here anymore." The disembodied voice grew stronger, and I heard a powerful *thud* hit the ground. I looked skyward to see a host of black particles buzzing around one another, creating horrific shapes in the sky. Where the *thud* had struck, the ground split open into a black void. Several of the golden orbs from the tree were sucked inside it, tumbling over top of one another.

"Alex!" I pointed up to first the sky then the giant void. My brother jerked his head upward, his dark hair blowing in the turbulent wind.

"Daegal," he said. "What do we do?" He looked at the wilted figure of King Michael, all color drained from his face.

"King Michael said we had to fight with our golden memories. Alex, we need to get to the tree, now!" I grabbed his hand and yanked him forward. We stumbled toward the tree, but it was waving and clanging so loudly that the instant my hand came close to one of the branches, it struck it hard.

"Ouch!" I yanked my hand back, sucking on my throbbing fingers. "I can't touch them."

"King Michael, wake up!" Alex ran back over to the slumped king and started to shake him. Grim bounded toward the king and slipped his hands beneath him.

"I must take him away from this place," the fox screamed above the noise.

"Please tell us what to do." I couldn't tear my eyes away from the black void sucking in the golden memories.

"The golden memories are inside of you. You must learn to find them and create more angels to fight for you." Grim looked shaken as he held the king in his arms. For such a small fox, I'd never imagined he was so strong as to hold a child.

"Raven! Grab my hand!" Alex shouted above the noise of the tree clanging and the rumbling. The ground continued to shiver and groan, flowers turning into ashes right before my eyes.

"I thought he said this was our garden! Our world! Why is this happening?" I screamed above the noise. I spotted Grim scurrying away, and I saw that in his arms he had a very small infant-sized boy. *Is that King Michael? He's getting younger.*

"We need to get out of here." Alex pulled me into a hard run, the ground cracking beneath our feet, nearly tripping me several times. I looked behind me at the tree to see it still shivering, but still very much alive. The golden orbs broke off, flying into the air, scattering all over the place.

Oh no! I knew that had to be bad. The words Grim said came back to me. *The golden memories are inside of you. You must learn to find them and create more angels to fight for you.*

I tried to reach back into my mind and find one of the memories the tree had shown me, but all I could feel was terror that Anxious was being ripped apart. I tripped and fell, skidding my knees and the palms of my hand. Blood beaded on my skin.

"Come on, Raven! Get up." Alex grabbed me and yanked me back to my feet, and we continued to run toward the forest, praying we could get back to our world. I hated the thought that we were leaving Grim and King Michael behind. What would happen to them if we didn't try to fight?

"Alex! We need to find our golden memories. They disappeared from the garden," I called to my brother as our feet thudded against the ground. The sky above us turned a chalky gray; black streaks of lightning intermixed.

"Look at this place, Raven. It's too late. We're too late. The golden memories are lost—you saw what happened to them." A tree branch nearly slapped Alex in the face. He pushed past it, pulling me forward. My chest grew tighter the further we ran.

"No! We can't be too late. We have to work on our golden memories. Help me, Alex, please." I tried to reach inside of me and find a happy moment—anything. A warmth spread through my heart at the thought of Alex and I building a tree fort behind our house. Alex had found some logs, which had ended up being infested with big bugs. I let out a giggle at the memory.

The sound seemed foreign and out of place with all the chaos going on around us. A golden light shot through the forest; a beacon in the impending darkness. I let out a gasp as several glowing figures, with white hair, draped in golden armor and giant wings, appeared out of thin air. They turned and looked at me with smiles on their faces.

"Alex, look! It worked!" I pointed at them, my heart thrumming with excitement. My brother struggled to turn around and look, concentrating on running through the dense forest. Another branch nearly slapped him.

"Where did they come from?" Alex managed to turn around, staring at the angelic soldiers, who stood there as if awaiting orders from the both of us.

A golden globe appeared in front of me, hovering, sparking. In the shiny surface I saw the memory I had recalled in my mind.

I watched it unfold before me, a smile on my face. I grasped it and tucked it into my purse.

"I remembered a golden memory." My eyes darted to the brand-new Endrita. "Please go help King Michael!"

They took off into the air, bypassing the swirling darkness which spread at a rapid pace. "Alex, we can't leave. This place will be destroyed." I stopped running. Alex nearly fell onto his back at my sudden stop.

"Raven, we don't have a choice. It's too late. This place is overrun with Daegal." A hopelessness filled his eyes. "I want to save King Michael, too, but I can't."

"Alexander, yes, you can. Fight. Fight for your golden memories to come back." My fists clenched, and I pulled my shoulders back. I wanted to shake my brother. I looked on the inside for another golden memory I could pull out, but the negative energy around me was starting to drain me and fast. "You have to do it with me. I can't do this by myself." I yanked on his sleeve, staring straight into his eyes.

"It's pointless. I'm no leader." He looked at everything but my face.

I grabbed his chin gently and caught his attention. I tried to find the brave brother I'd always known. "The only one you have to lead is yourself."

A malicious laugh filled the air around us.

"Wise words, little bride." A massive, swirling shape landed before the two of us. A pair of red eyes stared at me, unblinking. A form of a man, roughly eight-feet-tall, with black armor encrusted with a large deformed *D* and demon-like faces imbedded into the surface of it, grinned at the both of us. Despite never seeing him before, his presence felt familiar. Far, far too familiar.

D for Dagmoth. He's the leader of the Daegal. My stomach curled with nausea. My skin prickled with unease, every muscle in my body tense, ready to spring into action.

His black helmet covered over half his face, the top of it protruding with red horns, which curled downward, and his legs looked like giant tree trunks. "I'm Apollyon." His grin grew wider at the sight of both of us. "And I'm your new leader."

"Raven, get behind me, now!" Alex went into a fighting stance, shoving me behind him.

I stared up at Apollyon, and I knew there was no way Alex would be able to take this thing down. I tried to conjure up another golden memory, but in the presence of this monster all I could feel was every ounce of pain, hopelessness, and depression I'd felt since my parents died.

"Ah, little Alex. Such a brave, stupid boy. It was too bad about your parents. Too late. Too slow. All those years of training for what?" Apollyon circled around the two of us, still grinning as if knowing a secret we didn't know.

"Shut up." Alex stood at ready, waiting for Apollyon to make the first move.

"You're a waste of space. Everything you thought you were good at ended in a puff of smoke. Daddy and Mommy are looking down at you right now, and you know what they see?" Apollyon's armor-coated hand reached for the handle of his sword. A lump formed in my throat. I didn't care what this thing did to me, but he was not hurting my brother. I couldn't bear to see the only close family I had left die at the hands of this demon—I didn't care if he was the devil himself.

Alex grabbed a branch from the ground with a smooth swipe. Apollyon let out a fit of laughter, his entire body rippling with black energy.

"Oh, Alex, you are amusing, if not a bit dense. I think Mommy and Daddy see that their little boy is nothing but a failure and a coward." At those words, Apollyon's hand pulled out his giant sword. It sparked with darkness, the energy around it swirling, making me feel dizzy. I leapt backward, nearly hitting a tree as Apollyon and Alex started to battle. My brother was excellent with any weapon in his hand, and I could see, even though Alex was the underdog, he would fight to the death for me. The ground rumbled as the two of them swung, dodged, and danced with quick, smooth steps.

"I just want a couple things out of life." Apollyon's voice dripped with feigned sadness. Alex took several steps back, shooing me to run. I wasn't going anywhere though. Not without my brother.

"A breath mint and plastic surgery?" Alex said, gripping his branch so tight I could see his knuckles turning white.

Apollyon raised a finger, laughing. "You have quite a tongue on you. It's one reason why I don't want to actually kill you. Besides, who would be my best man at my wedding?" Apollyon's eyes locked onto mine, and a cold sensation pumped down my spine.

"You're not going near Raven." Alex's body went into fight mode again, and for a moment I felt hopeful. Maybe Alex could defeat this creepy guy. I'd seen him do some amazing things with a stick.

"Oh, I don't have to do a thing." Apollyon tucked his sword away, crossing his arms smugly over his chest. "That's why I have them." He nudged his head beyond Alex and me. Before I even saw them, I felt the presence of them. I heard my brother say something under his breath as he turned around to face hundreds of demons. Their red eyes, dark forms, and shifting bodies filled the entire woods behind us.

"They do whatever I want, you see. And if I say I want Raven as my bride, so that we can rule over Anxious together, well, they like me to have what I want." Apollyon lifted his hands to the sky, and I saw clutched in his hand a black mirror. A dark vortex formed above his head. Daegal started to spill out from the mirror, landing all around my brother and me.

No. Something cold gripped the back of my neck. I saw Alex reach out his hand, letting out a scream from the bottom of his feet. A wave of fear held me steadfast. A swirling, black mass formed into the shapes of men gripped my body, dragging me down to the ground. I screamed and kicked, trying to fight them off.

"No need to fear, little bride, they won't hurt you. They only want you to sleep." Apollyon pushed the shapes aside, bending down to my face, a sneer on his lips. "So sleep, dear." His hand covered my face, and darkness swept over my body.

Sleep.

* * * *

I awoke to be lying on a king-sized bed, a comforter tucked up around me with care. *Where am I? How did I get here?* I tried to recall what had happened. Images swirled on the inside of my head, a big blur mixing together. I could see a tree, and for some reason that tree was important, but I couldn't remember why it was important. I looked beneath the covers to see a black gown covering my body.

It was sleek and smooth, and for some reason it felt familiar. *I've been here before.* I looked around the open room. The windows were covered in a gray film, and black curtains hung like rags. A candle flickered to the side of me, but the flame, for some weird reason, was red. I stared at it for a few seconds before I heard footsteps. I looked up, and a smile lit my face.

"Hello, Raven," a man with black hair, dressed in a black robe, said. I couldn't seem to get a good look at his face for some reason. He bent over me and touched my cheek with affection. The sensations that pumped through me was like a drug. "Did you sleep well, dearest?"

The man's voice made me feel sleepy. "Yes, yes, I did."

"The only man who will ever love you is I, Raven. I will give you whatever you so desire if you commit to me alone." His mouth tipped into a smile, and sensations of love pumped through me. His words almost made me laugh. Of course, I'd commit to him. I loved him. Didn't I? The image of a golden orb danced in front of my eyes again, before being snuffed out. My head felt foggy.

"I suppose you'd like to get something to eat?" His fingers brushed back my hair from my face. My emotions felt confusing—love and fear. He ran his fingertips down my cheek and touched my lips. The feel of his finger on my lips made me jerk backward as if an electric shock had gone through me.

"Who are you?" I sat up in bed, and a shooting pain went through my heart. *Colten. What about Colten?* The memory of a dark-haired boy with a beautiful smile came back to me. The warmth of a hand—the genuine hug of someone who cared about me. My heart pounded in my chest, and I felt the air leaving my lungs.

"Where is Colten?" I said without thinking, brushing him away from me.

"Colten?" The tall man jerked backward, looking annoyed. "Colten is no one. I, Apollyon, am the man you love. Do you not remember me, sweetest?" The man's eyes bore into mine, and I felt a strange wave washing over my head. A flicker of red, in the center of his eyes, made me wince. *How come I can't think clearly?*

"Apollyon…" I said the word like I was tasting it on my tongue for the first time. "Oh, yes, I remember you now." A dreamy smile came over my face.

"We shall be wed soon, darling, and you and I will rule Anxious forever. Now, arise out of bed and follow me." Apollyon lifted me from the bed and set me onto my feet. "We have a lot to do to prepare for tomorrow."

Chapter 23

Alex

Something hard dug into my back, every one of my muscles screaming at me. *Ugh, I feel like I slept on a bed of nails.* My body was drenched in cold sweat, making me feel even worse.

"Gross. I need a hot shower," I mumbled to myself. I tried to move, but I found myself restricted, chained to the floor like a dog. An ache traveled from the back of my neck, down my spine, and spread into my lower back. How long had I been out? What happened? My mind felt muddied, and I couldn't seem to remember what had happened to get me to this point.

"I see our little sleeping beauty has decided to arise. Just in time too." A voice like rocks scraping over glass resounded in the darkness. I jerked, startled by the sound, sending a rippling ache deeper into my bones.

"Where's Raven?" My throat was dry, and my eyes felt like someone had poured sand in them.

"Oh, she's having a grand old time with me," the disembodied voice said. I could hear a slight slithering sound, and my skin crawled, picturing snakes sliding around on the floor near me.

"This is our world, not yours." I pulled against the chains, and a ripple of agony spread through my limbs, reminding me that I'd more in likely *had* slept on a bed of nails. Obviously, I had been down here far longer than I thought. My mind traveled backward, trying to recall *how* I ended up in this thing's prison. I remembered running from the castle, being in the woods with Raven, and then nothing. It was like part of my memory was simply erased.

"The battle is over, Alex, and the city of Drite is no more." A crackle bounced around the room, until I felt sick with the sound. *Drite… Drite… I know that name.*

"Where's my sister?" I pulled against the restraints again, and a surge of anger made the chains groan.

"Raven, oh dearest, come here." One single dim green light lit the space I was in, and I heard the shuffle of feet against the floor. I strained my neck up to try and get a look at who approached. A fist punched my chest at the sight of Raven. She was coated in moving shadows, which swirled all around her like a swarm of flies. Her dark hair was curled and covered by a thin veil, a blood red tiara resting on her head. She wore what looked like a black wedding gown, tiny red flowers etched into the front of it. Her blue eyes looked completely void of all life.

"Raven!" I pulled against the chains again, my chest straining upward. I had to get her out of here. What had that monster done to her? There was no way I was going to let him marry my sister.

"Oh, she's perfectly content. Aren't you, dearest?" The giant of a man leaned over and planted a kiss on my sister's cheek. She didn't flinch at all. "Today is our wedding day. She's awfully excited."

Raven, Raven, what has he done to you? Spikes of fear went through me at the thought of that slimy demon touching my sister—let alone marrying her. Raven's desperate words about helping her with the golden memories came back to my mind. *This is my fault! I should have listened to King Michael.*

"Let her go. Do whatever you want to me, but please, let Raven go." My fists clenched at my side, my entire body longing to spring into a fight.

"I suppose you think ill of me," the creature said with feigned sadness. "That's no way to treat your future brother-in-law. Raven loves me, don't you, dear?" Apollyon, coated in thick black armor, a helmet with red horns, and a face to make a child wet his pants, leaned over and kissed my sister's lips. A shudder swept over my skin.

"Let her go!" A rush of power went through my entire body, but a crushing darkness had already begun to take root in the corners of my mind. It was hopeless. I'd never get out of here. I'd never save my sister in time. What was the point of even trying? I knew those thoughts were the demons' mind-sets imprinting deeper into my subconscious. *He's going to marry Raven, and there's nothing I can do about it. Just like I was a helpless baby to fight for my parents' lives—it's happening all over again.*

I felt myself falling deeper into a void in my own mind. I struggled to fight the emotions arising, trying to find an ounce of the old me. I was the dumb kid who'd fall down and try and try again. My friends used to laugh at me, because I'd do something stupid until it worked.

Believe, Alex. Believe against the odds. It may be idiotic to believe you can beat this thing but do it anyways. I pulled on the deepest parts of myself, forcing faith to arise inside of me.

Please, God, help me. After what King Michael had taught me, I couldn't let this dummy win. I'd been an idiot, letting the world of Anxious fall apart like I did. This was all my fault. Everything that happened was entirely my fault. I'd been the idiot to not believe any of this stuff was true—and now Raven was going to be this evil demon thing's bride. I had to put a stop to him—no matter what.

"Alex, you too will be a part of my kingdom. There is no use fighting my power. I suppose being my best man is out of the question, huh?" The dim light evaporated, and I was left in complete darkness again. An echo of a laugh bounced off the walls.

"Raven!" I hurled myself against my restraints again, and only managed to cut the chains deeper into my skin. I had to do something. I couldn't let this demon marry Raven. I had to try. I had to. King Michael's words filtered back into my mind, *In order to save your world, you must fight the darkness of your pain. Don't run away from it; embrace your pain and fight back with the light.* I had no idea where King Michael was now, or if Apollyon had snuffed him out forever. *Find the thought that brings you out of the darkness, Alexander. Find that thought and bust through your agonized patterns of defeat.* I heard Grim's words all over again.

I felt a breeze on my face and the sunshine warming my skin, and I smiled. I pictured in my mind Mom and Dad out on jet skis with Raven and I, laughing, and splashing us with the wake from the water. I held the picture tightly in my head, and I let the emotions of love flood my chest. *There is hope in the world. Mom and Dad may be gone, but I'm here. Raven's here, and we can push through the darkness.*

I got down on my knees, clasping my hands like they'd taught me in Sunday school. My family had never been very religious, but Grandma had taken me to Sunday school until I was ten.

"God, if you are there. Give me strength to overcome this. I need your help." Bible stories flooded my mind. *Daniel in the lions' den, Jonah in the whale, the three Hebrew children in the fire.* Without an ounce of doubt, I knew my prayer was heard. "Thank you." I looked up to the ceiling. Every encouraging word Dad had ever spoken to me came back to my mind, and I nearly jumped.

Alexander, you have the makings of a leader. Your mom and I are so proud of you. We know you can do anything you set your mind to. Dad's words looped through my mind. He'd told me that when I was thirteen, had completely failed at a science project, and had nearly blown up the gym. Somehow Dad could always see past my stupid mistakes into something far greater.

"I have to be him," I told myself. "I have to be Alexander. I can't be Alex anymore." My mind spun with images of myself going out to battle the demons, armies of angels behind me. A warmth spread over my chest, traveled down my neck and seeped into my very veins. A deeper strength erupted inside of me, and I pulled hard against the chains again. I let out a scream, using every ounce of inner energy I could muster. The image of Raven's blank face drove my belief deeper. *I have to do this for her. I'm not losing Raven too. Please, God, give me the power I need.*

The sound of glass shattering tinkled, and I shot upward, off the ground, and landed on my feet with a burst of energy. *Whoa!* Tiny golden flecks filled the air, dancing and swirling, sparking at me. A large golden orb circled the room, spinning at a high speed, sucking in the darkness around it. I inhaled the light, drinking in the energy the golden orb gave me.

"Give me back my sister!" The door to the prison cell let out a scream as it flung open, darkness shattering like a black mirror all over the ground. The walls illuminated—the floor filled with the tiny golden specks. I looked down at myself and saw my entire chest was coated in light. My body shifted, a golden and white armor spreading over my skin—alive with power. I reached up and touched my head and let out a whoop of joy. A helmet had formed all on its own accord. A vague memory of a scripture came to my mind, *Put on the whole armor of God, that you may be able to stand against the wiles of the devil.*

"Let's kick some demon butt!" I reached down to my sides and felt the scabbards of two butterfly knives. Pulling them out, I examined them both for a brief second. The golden knives shifted and moved, the energy of my belief pulsing through them, swirling. I bolted forward, my feet hitting the ground beneath me.

Sparks of light exploded. Long, dark fingers tried to grasp me, but the moment they made contact with my skin, they screamed in agony, my flesh burning them. I swiped my knives, letting out several whoops. One of the Daegal loomed over me, his red eyes sizzling with hatred.

"Stop!" It moved in front of me with a *boom*, its massive body dancing with shifting shadows.

"All right," I said with a smirk. I stopped in my tracks and faced the creature, feeling my confidence build by the second. "Want a piece of this? I'm not shy." I swung my glowing knives at him, the light around me splattering everything in sight. Mr. Ugly let out a horrified screech as the light smacked him in the face. He clawed at his eyes, stumbling backward. He landed with a *boom*. His body evaporated into a thousand dark particles. I moved past him, brushing the walls with my fingertips and leaving golden smears that sparkled. *Ooh pretty.* It was like watching fireworks.

I ran past room after room, the golden specks sticking to everything. I approached a decaying door and shoved it open with a screech. The room was bathed in a sickly green light, casting shadows on the pews of dark figures sitting in them.

Their faces turned to me, making my stomach drop for a moment. A long aisle stretched before me with a black strip of carpet, coated in blood-red flower petals. At the end of the aisle I saw Raven and Apollyon, facing one another. A flickering image of what looked like a priest was standing behind them, his hands raised as if about to pronounce something.

"You may now kiss—" the priest's croaky voice said. Apollyon leaned in toward my sister, his long fingers latching onto her face.

I launched myself down the aisle, running toward the two of them. "Raven, stop!" I waved my hands like a mad man, making the Daegal in the aisles stir with unease. They were unsure what to do, seeing my flickering golden knives and the waves of light circling around me. As if the living dead, Raven pulled away from Apollyon, her face slowly turning to look at me. Her blue eyes barely flickered at the sight of me.

"Hello, Alex." Apollyon sounded amused. "I see you found some toothpicks to fight with. You're far too late I'm afraid."

"Alex." The calmness of Raven's voice made me stop in my tracks. "I'm happy." The creepiness of my sister's voice sent a cold chill through me. Raven walked toward me, coated in thick shadows, her face a complete mask of nothingness.

"Raven," I whispered her name.

"You mustn't fight him. He is my love. This is what I want. Please be happy for me." She sounded like a total robot, her body stiff.

"Raven, he's got a hold of your mind. You're not thinking clearly. Please, you need to think of a golden memory. Remember when we used to go swimming with Mom and Dad? Or remember when we'd spend hours laughing in my bedroom at stupid videos? Think, Raven! Create a new world again." I was nearly trembling at the intensity of my words. "And, Raven"—I gulped down my emotions—"God's not just a fairytale. He's real. I know He's real. I prayed…and it worked." I lifted my hands upward, and spitballs of light lit the room with brilliancy. The demons in the aisle screeched.

"There is no point to the golden memories. They are all gone now." Raven gave a cold smile beneath her veil, and pinpricks traveled over my skin.

"No, they aren't! I just created—this." I held my knives up. Raven shied back, shielding her eyes. A tremor went over her body, and I knew Apollyon had her mind deeply inflamed with his beliefs.

"You must create your own beliefs, Raven. Don't let him control who you really truly are. Ask God for help."

"God…God left us a long time ago, Alex. Grandma lied to us." She turned to look at Apollyon for a moment. "It's my fault." Raven's voice was still unemotional as she stared at me. "My abuse is my fault. I was a bad girl. I defied him, and I paid for it. I need to be submissive to those over me." Her mouth moved, but I saw no ounce of my sister as she spoke the words.

"Raven, listen to me. Nothing that happened—none of it is your fault. Mom and Dad were murdered, and you got put in a bad home. You are the most amazing person I've ever met. Please, please, give me back my sister." I felt my anxiety building, and I fought it as hard as I could. If I gave Apollyon any hold, we'd both be lost forever.

"I will be free with Apollyon. He promised me that I would be happy with him. God can't help me." She cast a glance at her waiting groom, who stood with a cocky smile on his face.

"No, Raven, you like Colten, and he's waiting for you back home. Please, listen to me. Remember what you shared with your boyfriend—remember the love you felt." I wanted to reach out and touch her. *Please, God, help me.*

"I'm so glad the family's all here. Now we can finish our ceremony," Apollyon suddenly said with a grin. A heavy oppression filled the air, making me want to choke. The lithe, dark forms, sitting in the pews, shifted to their feet, and I felt all my gusto starting to drain.

"Colten left me. He doesn't love me," Raven said, and I saw a shimmer of sadness in her eyes. Somewhere, buried deep beneath the darkness, was my little sister, and I was determined to find her.

"No, Raven. You left him. You were scared what your foster mom and dad would do to you. Apollyon is lying to you. He doesn't know what love even is. God is love." I wished I could shake my little sister and make her see what was happening, but I knew she was under the heaviness of her own depressive, anxious thoughts, and I couldn't be the one to save her. She had to save herself. She had to make her own thoughts and choices for her life. Raven looked confused for a moment and turned her head to look at Apollyon.

"Is this true? Did I leave Colten?" Her face flickered with brief emotion, before smoothing back to her stony face.

"Oh, darling, no one loves you. The only way you'll ever be accepted and loved is to marry me. We will rule the world of Anxious together." Apollyon took several steps toward the both of us, looking rather annoyed that I'd stopped the procession of the wedding. Raven shook her head, rubbing her temples as if trying to clear away her confusion.

"I thought you told me Colten left me? I left him? Why would my brother lie to me? Alex doesn't ever lie to me." She examined my face, reaching a hand out.

"Yes, darling, you are a terrible person, and you left your boyfriend. That is why you are mine now." Apollyon gave her a chilling grin, and Raven shuddered.

"So I left him." Lost in a daze, it seemed Raven was trying to fight her way out of it. "God is love?" Her face twisted in pain. "How is God love? Look what He did to us."

"Raven, Colten would take you back. I'm sure of it. Don't listen to dirt face over there. He's lying to you. Fight it. Find your golden memory. Yes, God is love. Hold onto that, and like Grandpa told me…God is in you." I took another step toward her. "This isn't you. Find the real Raven. Come back to me." The pews stirred, and I felt a momentary burst of fear. I smothered it quickly with the feeling I clung to deep inside. *I'm not giving up on you. Come back, Raven, please. God show her your love.*

Chapter 24

Raven

I stared down the dark tunnel—my lungs tight—feeling suffocated. I vaguely heard my brother's words, and a dim light swayed before my vision. *Colten wants me?* I thought about my amazing boyfriend, who I had fallen head over heels for in such a short time. He'd been kind, handsome, and had always treated me like a princess.

Colten's blue eyes, filled with love, popped in my head, and a surge of light shot through my veins. *Colten...I need you.* I had to go back. I had to find my boyfriend and beg for his forgiveness. I'd been unable to handle the pain of my life, and I had forced Colten away from me because of it. Swirling images of black creatures crawling all over me filled my mind, and I let out a scream.

"Get off me!" I held the memory of Colten in my head, and I fought through the heaviness dragging at my chest.

"Fight, Raven. Fight." Alex's voice broke through my confusion. "Find your golden memory. Ask God for help." My brother's body shimmered with golden light.

The image of Colten sent a wave of good feelings right through me, and I looked down at myself. *What am I wearing?* Golden flecks sparked over my skin, spinning around my body, burning up the black gown fitted to me. As if caught aflame, the black veil disintegrated right before my eyes. *God, please help me fight this darkness that's trying to consume me.*

"Raven, you are mine." Apollyon let out a screech of rage, jumping from the stage toward Alex and me. With a loud *boom*, he landed in the aisle, scattering several Daegal in his wake. They scrambled before him, streaks of black particles circling around them. Apollyon bounded toward me, his fingers in the shape of claws, a roar coming from his lips.

I held Colten in my mind and ducked. The big dope flew over top of me and landed in a heap on the ground. The floor shifted and moved, cracking and groaning beneath his fall. Golden light burst upward, sizzling the flesh of several demons.

"This is my world." Apollyon slowly stood to his feet, growing in size by the minute, wincing at the sight of the golden energy starting to filter into the room. "This war has just begun." With a burst of spiraling black particles, Apollyon disappeared.

* * * * *

"Come on, let's get out of here." Alex grabbed my hand and pulled me forward. We broke out into a run, the Daegal running the opposite direction for some reason.

"Why didn't he stop us? And why are they running away?" It didn't make any sense that Apollyon had disappeared instead of trying to come after Alex and me.

"Nothing he does is ill planned. I think he's preparing for war." Alex kept pulling me, winding his way past corridors like he knew the way.

"Are you going the right way?" I still felt weird—like I'd been sleeping for a hundred years. *God, thank you for rescuing Alex and I both.* I glanced down at myself to see the black wedding gown was gone, and I now wore a white flowing dress.

"No idea." Alex shrugged, grinned, and we continued to run. "It just feels like it's this way."

Our feet continued to pound the black, swirling ground below us, until we reached a huge door. The moment we got close, the door flung open, and we ran out, back into the world of Anxious. The ground beneath us was black, the grass ashy, wilted, and dying. The sky above was a charcoal color, swirling with black clouds.

"Alex, what happened?" My throat was raw. I still felt as if I was in a fog. Had I really been about to marry that monster? The thought chilled me to the bone.

"I'll explain when we get to Drite—it has to still exist. It has to." The anxiety in my brother's voice piqued for a moment. The forest to our left looked like it had been caught on fire, the leaves black and wilted, breaking off into black particles.

"This place…it's…it's dying." I choked out the last word.

"No, Raven. We can still save it. We have to fight. We have to get to Drite. No matter what." I'd never heard my brother so determined about anything in his life. A giant roar resounded behind us, and I turned and looked over my shoulder. Hundreds and hundreds of demons flew up into the air, and I saw several of them absorb right into Apollyon's body.

"He's trying to use the past thoughts and beliefs. Alex, what if I screw up again? What if I let him in again?" Fear tingled through me.

"Don't think like that. It's going to be fine. We just have to get to Drite." Alex's hand squeezed mine.

The pounding of hundreds of feet filled the air, and I peered up ahead to see a herd of golden-colored horses galloping toward us, their white manes billowing in the breeze.

"Look!" I pointed at them, feeling a swell of hope.

"Come on, we need to catch one." Alex ran toward the horses, his golden knives slapping his legs as he ran. One of the horses, with a golden and white mane and tail, approached Alex, nodding his head up and down. Without hesitating, Alex flung himself up onto the horse, reached his hand out, and pulled me up behind him.

"YAH!" Alex got the horse moving. The wind whipped my hair back behind me, but I could feel the oppressive cloud building in the city of Dagmoth. The landscape became a blur as the horse cantered across the black fields, the sky rumbling above us.

"Alex, wait, slow down." I spotted a white horse, its hooves pawing at the air as if trying to signal the both of us.

"We need to get to Drite."

"I know, I know, but we have to get that horse." I pointed to the stallion, and a sense of determination struck me. Every moment I'd trained for finally made sense. This. This was my chance to use all my years of horseback riding and gymnastics. That horse was my weapon. I don't know how I knew that, but I just did. Somehow Alex managed to slow our ride down, and I slid off the side of the horse. I ran as hard as I could toward the white stallion. The moment he spotted me, he started running toward me, his white mane fluttering behind him like a stream of light.

He got within a few feet of me and stopped suddenly, spraying chunks of dirt. He dipped his nose to me, and his eyes glowed with golden energy.

Hello, Raven. I've waited for you. The words made me stagger for a moment, but my hand reached for the horse's long mane, and I pulled myself up onto his back. I heard Alex let out a gasp as a spiral of golden light started at the base of my toes and went all the way up my body, creating a white and golden armor. It was light and comfortable, but I knew it was strong. My eyes dipped down to see a curved, dual-edged blade resting before me. A golden saddle had also formed with a long handle at its front for doing my gymnastic tricks. I picked up the weapon, holding the handle in the center, and lightly squeezed my horse's side.

"Come on," I shouted to Alex, and we rode hard toward the direction of Drite. I allowed my mind to expand, and I pulled out as many happy memories as I could. With each memory, I heard a loud *pop* noise; angels formed from the earth, glowing and golden, weapons in their hands. Some of them jumped onto the backs of more horses and started to ride with us.

A loud *thud* shook the ground beneath our feet, and my horse reared up, shaking his head back and forth.

"Whoa, whoa, boy." I held on tight to his mane. His feet hit the ground again.

"It's over. The Endrita can't save your world now." A voice made my chest rumble. I couldn't see where he was, but I could feel the oppressive darkness.

"Yes, they can," Alex said in a growl. He squeezed his eyes shut, and I heard more *pop, pop, pop* noises, as more Endrita were formed from the ground, swirling with golden light.

"Drite is dead." Apollyon's body shimmered into view, and a wicked grin crossed over his face.

"Raven, we need to get around him." Alex threw me a glance, and I nodded.

"Yah!" I got my horse moving, standing up on his back, one hand grasping my double-edged knife. My breathing slowed down, my heart sounding like a faraway drum. When we got closer, I launched off the back of my horse, did a double flip, and ran my blade down the front of Apollyon. He let out a horrific scream, curdling my blood.

"You wish to betray me?" He threw me off, and I flipped through the air, landing on my feet like a cat. I back flipped three times and held a fighting stance. Then like that, Apollyon was gone again in a burst of black particles. I cast a look at Alex, and he nodded.

"We need to get to Drite. He'll be back, and with an army."

I swung myself back up onto the back of my horse. He seemed to naturally know the direction we needed to go, so I let him run as fast as he wanted. Alex was quick on our heels. A cold shudder ran over me as my eyes caught sight of the castle in the city of Drite. *Maybe Apollyon is right.* My horse let out a scream beneath me, and I barely had enough time to cling to his mane as he bucked at a demon, which had popped out of the ground. The Daegal creature swung a black spear, nearly catching my horse in the chest.

"Raven!" Alex flew off his horse, his butterfly knives spinning with expertise. I'd seen Alex use those for years, but never like this. His movements looked like a dance as he fought off the demon. The creature screamed and disappeared into a black vapor. Alex's chest moved up and down.

"We have to find King Michael." Alex's jaw clenched with determination.

"Come on." I nudged my horse to get going, and he obliged without question. Alex slid back onto the back of his horse, and within a few minutes we'd reached the remains of the castle.

For a moment, the two of us stared up at it, feeling a mixture of hope and hopelessness.

"Alexander, Raven, come with me. There is much to do." Grim suddenly appeared, his nose twitching, his golden eyes glowing.

Chapter 25

Alex

Raven and I hurried after Grim, our horses kicking up clods of dirt behind us. Grim led us past the castle and to a lake beyond it. The city of Drite was covered in a thick fog, making it hard to pick out the once beautiful little homes. When Grim stopped, he turned to face us with a concerned look, his small hands wringing together.

"King Michael suspects it's in your world. It hasn't been seen in our world for ages." Grim looked between the two of us.

"What is, Grim?" I said, sliding off my horse. I kept my hand on the creature's neck, feeling its warmth.

"The Drite Mirror." Grim stood with his feet apart, his hands on his hips.

"What is that?" Raven said, still sitting on the back of her white horse.

"There are two mirrors forged from the ancient days of our world. One they call Dagmoth and the other is called Drite. This is what our cities were named after. The two mirrors are tools which the Daegal and the Endrita have used long ago to open portals, build armies, and many other things which has been lost to our legends." Grim paced back and forth, rubbing his chin as he did.

"Where is King Michael? Is he okay?" Raven clutched her double-edged knife, looking ready for a fight. Grim's head dipped down sadly.

"He is in the sleeping chamber, beneath the waters." Grim's paw motioned toward the lake before us. I peered beneath the surface to see a clear, long tube, and when I squinted, I could make out a pale face beneath the glass.

"He's under there?" Raven climbed off her horse and came to the edge of the water. "How are we supposed to know what to do now?"

"You must restore the tree to rebuild the city of Drite. The mirror is a tool to formulate it quicker." Grim put his hand on her hand and pulled her down to meet his gaze. "You must gather all the golden memories back in order for the world of Anxious to be saved."

"Won't Apollyon come for us right now?" I asked, remembering our encounter just a little while ago with the big demon.

"As long as a golden memory exists, Apollyon doesn't have complete control. His skin burns when he gets too close. Unfortunately, Apollyon has linked others from your world with the mirror so that his Daegal army continues to grow in numbers. In order to defeat him, you too must grow the Endrita to battle the army of darkness." Grim's paw brushed the lake, and a golden vein ran all the way to the bottom. "In order to awake King Michael, you must restore the golden memory tree. It is the key. You must find the Drite Mirror."

"I thought you said the mirror has been lost for ages," Raven said, her voice full of deep concern.

"It has. But I believe the two of you together can uncover where it hides itself. Your ancestors have always been the one to use it." He nodded his head up and down.

My mind shifted suddenly to the family who lived in our old house. Mom and Dad had left a lot of old antiques there as decorations. *How did the people who lived there see the Endrita? Unless...* I thought back to when I'd visited their home, mentally examining the contents around me. *Oh my god.* I locked eyes with Raven.

"What? What is it?" She came to my side and grabbed my hands.

"I think I know who has the Drite Mirror." A thrill went through me. If I was right, we stood a fighting chance.

"Who?" Raven said.

"They live on our property, and they can see the Endrita and the Daegal." I jumped back onto my horse. "I have to go back to our world again. I know who has the mirror."

"You must restore the tree first." Grim's paws clasped together.

"But you said the mirrors would speed up the process, right?" I looked at first Grim then Raven.

"Yes." Grim nodded. "But leaving now could be deadly. The Daegal are all over those woods." Grim pointed beyond me.

"Where is the gate you led us through straight into the castle?" My horse danced beneath me, feeling my anxiousness to get moving.

"It has been destroyed. The Daegal are trying to close all portals to trap you both here."

Grim's words sent a shiver through me. We could be stuck here forever? *God, please help us.*

"What about the door in the woods? Is that one destroyed too?" I gazed beyond, a flicker of hope arising.

"I don't know. Alexander, you must stay. It isn't worth dying for. Focus on the golden memories, they will help." Grim jumped on top of a log, pacing back and forth.

"But will it be enough?" I stressed.

"Let him try. I will work on rebuilding the tree here." Raven rested her hand on her horse, determination burning in her gaze.

"This could be costly." Grim wrung his hands together. "But go. Go and find the Drite Mirror. It may be our only shot at winning this war. Meanwhile, Raven, I will teach you how to restore the tree." Grim's tail flickered back and forth.

I jumped off my horse, hugged my sister and Grim tight, and climbed back on my ride. I sent out a happy thought, praying that I would make it back before those things destroyed everything. With a streak of light behind me, I allowed my horse full control, and we headed into the woods.

* * * * *

As my horse ran into the woods, black particles circled around the trunks of the trees and the branches looked marred and burnt. A heaviness hit my chest, and I lost my breath. In the woods, dark forms darted in and out, swirling around anything living and choking the life out of it.

A sob stuck in my throat, and I tried not to breathe in the oppression, focusing in on what I needed to do. The portal wasn't too far; I could feel it drawing me to it. The Daegal didn't seem to notice me for a few minutes, until my horse let out a screech.

"Whoa, boy, it's okay." I patted the horse. Flickering, red eyes locked onto me, and like a black haze, the figures started approaching me. My armor still glowed, and my butterfly knives were warm against my thighs.

"It's too late, Dayton," a voice said in a hiss. One of the Daegal was within a few feet of me, his black hair slithering like an endless number of snakes. "Give it up."

"Let me pass." My hands reached for my knives, and I felt a thrill go through me. I looked forward to using my Wing Chun on these losers.

"There are many more of us than there are of your precious angels. Anxious is our master's world now." Ugly Face moved forward, a long red tongue snaking out of his mouth.

"That'll make the victory so much sweeter. Now get out of my way, Ugly."

The demon's mouth curled back into a sneer, and a dripping black sword was suddenly in his hand. "Why don't you make me?" The creature roared, his body twisting through the air, black particles exploding around him. I flipped off the back of my horse, landing on my feet, my butterfly knives ready.

I swiped upward, one butterfly knife tucked against my arm, the other thrusting. I switched, and in a liquid motion, all my years of training flooded my body. The Daegal let out a screech of surprise as my golden knives swiped at him. My knee lifting, I brought my arms up, pulling my knives downward, slicing into the creature's neck and shoulders. With a burst of black vapor, the demon screamed.

The other Daegal rushed toward me at the sound. I hopped back onto the back of my horse, urging him to move toward the location of the portal. I cut at the creatures all around me, balancing as I did so, trying to remain on my horse's back. I wasn't nearly as good at balancing as Raven, but I could hold my own. I spotted a glowing spot in the woods and vaulted off the back of my horse, tumbling, and then going into a full run again. I felt the breath of a demon on my neck, and pulled my arm down and then upward in a firm strike. It recoiled, screeching at me. With a tumble, I made my way into the portal.

I landed in the woods, behind the theater, my body taut and ready for more fights. Several Daegal followed me, and I danced with them, my butterfly knives moving so quickly they were simply a blur of golden energy. As soon as I could, I bolted toward the Mcdeen's place, praying they were home and that they had the mirror like I thought.

My feet pounded the ground, and I glanced several times behind my back to see demons following me. Once I had the mirror, I would deal with them, but time was of the essence right now.

It didn't take all that long before the Mcdeen's old house rose before me. I stopped in my tracks, my heart speeding up instantly. *Oh my god.* The house was swarming with Daegal. Like vaporous ghosts they went through the walls, their long fingers digging into the structure of the house. *It's too late. They got the mirror.* Dark thoughts tried to force themselves into my mind, but I made myself think of a golden memory to ward them off. A warm, glowing orb formed around me, lighting up the ground beneath my feet.

"I have to get inside," I told myself. I ran toward the house, letting out a warrior cry as I did, slicing, spinning, and doing the delicate dance of Wing Chun as I did so. The Daegal let out screams of distress as my glowing blade met their black flesh.

Warmth flooded over me, as I held a golden memory in my mind, challenging the dark creatures with my blades. They spat and hissed at me; their long claw-like fingers tried to touch me but burned when they did. I managed to get to the door and flung it open. Inside was a mess. Furniture was shredded, glass lay scattered, with torn pictures inside of them. The image of my parents' house came back to me, and for a moment I stood there in stunned silence.

Keep going, Alex. I thought of Raven left behind in Anxious and managed to pull myself together, focusing on the moment. Black forms dove toward me, long spears swiping. Their faces shifted and danced, a swirling amount of energy, their mouths bared with dripping, sharp yellow fangs. My knives met their flesh with a *sizzle*, sending them into a screeching fit as the light of my knives hit them. The more I held onto my golden memories, the stronger I felt, until the dark forms fled the house with loud screams.

I heard a whimper, and something moved in the far corner of the living room. Buried beneath what looked like dirty laundry I saw a pale hand stretch out.

"Hello?" I called, making my way toward the figure. Beyond the walls I could still hear the angry screeches of the demons, but they didn't seem to want to brave going against my knives again.

"You're the Dayton's boy, aren't you?" the voice said, still trembling in fear.

"Yes, I'm Alexander Dayton. This house belongs to my family."

"Please, please, they want it. Please take it." A woman's voice trembled. "It's in the trunk, locked tight. I wouldn't let them have it." The hand held a key out to me, and I grasped it. Without even asking what *it* was, I rushed around the house, looking for the trunk she spoke of. Finally, I spotted a small trunk, sitting atop a dresser. I shoved the key into the small hole and turned. A warm energy filled me when I peered inside. An antique, handcrafted mirror was inside. It curved with an ornate flower design, reminding me of the Drite castle. Imbedded into the top of it was a fancy A.

My hands trembled as I picked it up. As soon as my fingers touched the handle, a surge of hot energy went through my blood. I nearly set the artifact back down but managed to hang onto it. I didn't want to waste another minute and rushed out of the room and toward the door.

"Please stop them," the woman said from the pile of laundry.

"I'm going to try. Stay hidden." I bolted out the door, fighting off more demons as I did. Black vapor exploded into the atmosphere at the touch of my knives. I ran as fast as I could toward the portal, clutching the mirror to my chest. This was our only chance; I had to get back to Raven and Grim.

I neared the portal when I heard a gagging scream. A black creature held a dark-haired boy in his grasp. I recognized him from the café, and I knew it had to be Colten.

"Let him go." I pulled out my knives, my muscles ready to fight.

"Give it up, Dayton, or the boy will go crazy," the Daegal said in a growl. His dark fingers curled around Colten's throat, and I watched my sister's ex-boyfriend's eyes roll back into his head. He convulsed as if having a seizure, and a momentary fear shot through me.

"She left me…why? All I did was love her." Colten started to shake, and I saw the imprint of the demon reaching into his mind.

"She still loves you, Colten. Fight it. She still wants to be with you." I took a step forward, my knives aching to dive into the flesh of the Daegal in front of me.

"I thought she was the one, but I was wrong." The words came from the Daegal, clutching Colten, but Colten said them, as if a puppet on a string. I had to get through to him, or I'd never get back to Raven and Grim.

"Colten, Raven loves you. She barely knows you, and she loves you anyways. Fight it. Reach for those memories inside of you." I took another step forward, and the Daegal clutched Colten's neck tighter. He convulsed, his fingers reaching up to the creature's hands around his neck, trying to pry them off.

"Fight it. I can't do it for you. Listen to me. Raven still loves you." My knives tremored, aching to fight. Colten closed his eyes, and I heard a *pop* sound. A glowing light pulsed in the center of his chest, and the Daegal let out a loud screech. The moment the creature released him, my knives flew toward him, carving into his black flesh. Colten tumbled to the ground, his shoulders trembling.

"Get out of here. Now."

Colten bolted, his feet spitting up leaves and dirt as he ran. I faced the portal and stepped through it.

"I'm coming, Raven."

Chapter 26

Raven

I had no idea what I was doing. Alex had taken off, and I stood at the edge of the lake, trembling with fear and anticipation. I cast a glance at the gray sky, swirling with black lightning.

"Is this going to work?" I cast a glance at Grim, who stood patiently waiting for me.

"You can do this, Raven. You must restore the tree. Begin by thinking and holding as many golden memories in your mind as you can. Next, picture the tree coming back together." Grim waved his paws in the air as he explained. I could feel the buildup of negative energy in the atmosphere and feared that I would fall back into its power once more. I didn't know if I could do this.

"Hold the strongest golden memory first," Grim continued to explain. My mind instantly went to my memories with Colten; even though they were few, I'd never felt such a strong connection with anyone in my life. I pulled the feelings into my thoughts and body, holding it tight against me. I could see his smile in my head and smiled back at the image I saw.

"Good." Grim's face turned toward where the garden had once been. A flicker of golden light danced around me, swirling in a vortex of flickering mini lightning bolts. Slowly more small golden globes began to formulate, circling around me as if fairies dancing beneath the moon.

"I'm doing it," I whispered to myself, grinning. I continued to hold the powerful feelings I'd had with Colten, and slowly integrated more thoughts of my family and Alex. I pictured the tree growing from the air, the branches stretching out, and the golden globes swinging from each branch.

Crack.

I looked over to the garden and saw something shoot out of the ground. It wove its way upward, dancing like a reed in the wind.

"That's it, Raven, you're growing it." Grim's eyes were filled with excitement at the sight beyond us. I held the images tighter, picturing the tree as I'd seen it not too long ago. The beautiful orbs. The branches strong and sturdy. All of it began to formulate stronger in my head. I heard Grim gasp with delight, clapping his little hands together. His mouth opened in a happy grin.

"Good, good." His head bobbed up and down. As the tree began to grow, I noticed the castle walls starting to shimmer with golden energy.

"I'm doing it. Oh my gosh. I'm doing it." I got so excited that for a moment I forgot to hold the memories in my head. The tree stopped growing.

Grim turned his head in a jerk toward me. "Keep going, Raven. Don't stop. We must rebuild Drite in order to save Anxious."

I let myself loose, filling my heart, soul, and mind with as much positive feelings and thoughts as I could. I closed my eyes, focusing on the tree, the orbs, and most of all Colten. I started giggling as I thought of his playfulness, the way he looked at me, and the touch of his hand in mine. I could hear stuff shifting and growing, the ground beneath my feet shaking.

"Raven," Grim whispered in awe. "Look."

My eyes fluttered open and before me stood the tree, covered in golden orbs, and a host of angels, cloaked in armor, holding swords in their hands.

"Oh my gosh," I said, startled that I had done all that. I reached out my hand, wanting to touch the creations I'd made.

"Drite may have a fighting chance now." Grim's eyes went beyond to where Dagmoth was located. "We must put Apollyon's reign to an end. We must find the Dagmoth Mirror."

"We'll get it." I crossed my arms over my chest, feeling the warmth of all the happy memories I'd flooded myself with. "What do we do now, Grim?"

"We go find Alex." Grim bolted toward the tree, his tail swishing.

I climbed onto my horse's back, fitted myself in the comfortable saddle, and grabbed his mane. "Follow Grim." I ran my fingers over the horse's neck. "What is your name, boy?"

Barloc. I heard the name in my head and smiled.

"I like it."

It means strong warrior filled with love and hope. Barloc nodded his head up and down, his white mane fluttering in the light breeze.

"Come on, boy, let's go find Alex." I lightly squeezed the horse's sides, and he took off after Grim. The sky above us swirled with dark particles, spitting and sparking, but my mind and heart held onto my golden memories, fighting off the darkness around me. I barely saw Grim ahead of me, his swift movements looking like an orange blur at times. He came to a sudden stop as we both watched Alex launch through the portal, butterfly knives swinging as he did. He tumbled, ready to fight more. He spotted the two of us and gave us a grin.

"I got it. Come on."

I pulled him onto the back of Barloc, and we cantered toward the rundown castle.

"We may have a fighting chance now, Raven," Alex said, hugging me from behind.

"The tree is back, but the Daegal keep getting stronger. We have to hurry and use the mirror." I clutched Barloc's mane. "Come on, boy, hurry." The stallion picked up even more speed, making me feel as if we were flying.

"I don't even know how to use this thing," Alex said.

Grim led us back to the tree, still looking worried, despite what we'd already overcome in the last couple hours.

"Not a moment to lose. Alex, I shall teach you what the mirror does." Grim wrung his paws together, looking at the tree, his ears twitching back and forth.

"I'm all ears," my brother said, holding up the mirror. We both slid off the back of Barloc, running toward Grim. The golden tree shimmered with an electric current, and I resisted the urge to reach out and touch its surface.

"The mirror contacts those who have strong golden memories. You must use it to contact them so that the Endrita army can grow larger. Just as the Dagmoth Mirror pulls from the minds of those lost in darkness, so you must pull from the minds who have the light." Grim touched a golden memory, his face illuminated with the essence. The tree sparked, tiny little flecks of gold drifting down onto Grim's fur.

"How do I do that?" Alex looked slightly worried at the suggestion.

"The mirror is a portal." Grim looked first at Alex and then me. "You can draw on the golden memories of those the mirror finds. With those golden memories, more Endrita will be born."

Alex went into a fighting stance, rubbing his hands together. "Let's do this." A slow grin passed over his face.

Chapter 27

Alex

Grim paced before me, wringing his small hands, his ears twitching back and forth.

"You must first look into the mirror. Find those with strong golden memories." Grim stopped pacing and stared straight into my eyes. "Because you are a Dayton, the mirror will communicate with you easily." He waved his hand at me, urging me to start.

I gripped the mirror, wanting to close my eyes for some reason. The energy of this thing was almost more than I could handle. I could see why it had drawn so much activity from Anxious to inhabit the property owned by my family.

"You can do it, Alex," Raven said from beside me. I could see the nervousness on her face, her dark hair pulled back into a messy ponytail. She put her hand on my back, looking over toward the tree. It was gaining more golden memories by the second, but I could still see the hordes of demons forming near Dagmoth off in the distance.

"Okay, here goes." I looked deep into the mirror. The instant my eyes found the glass, a feeling like warm butter slid over me, incasing every inch of my skin. Inside the glass I saw face after face—laughing, carefree—most of them little children. I started chuckling under my breath at the sight. As the feelings transferred to me, I heard Raven gasp with delight.

"Alex, look!" She pointed to the ground a few feet in front of us. Beams of light shot out of the earth, giving way to tall, ethereal figures, bathed in golden, shimmering light. Their hair flowed as if drifting underwater, and their faces were plain but extremely beautiful. I noticed that most of them appeared male, but a few were definitely female. Energetic, shifting wings flowed from their back and cupped around them like a shield.

As they were born, their eyes were directed over toward me and Raven—as if awaiting orders. I continued finding the golden memories through the people in the mirror, until my body felt as if it were buzzing with high amounts of energy. The mirror shook in my hand—alive.

"This is trippy," I said out loud as more and more angels were formed. Raven laughed as one of the Endrita nudged toward her dual, curved blade as if saying, *Fight?* He pulled out his longsword and the two of them began to have a friendly match. Out of the corner of my eye I could see Raven weaving in her gymnastic skills with what I'd taught her over the years with Wing Chun. The more Endrita I helped bring to life, the more I saw them sparring with one another, training for the upcoming battle against the Daegal.

"What about King Michael?" I suddenly stopped looking in the mirror to catch Grim's attention. "What's wrong with him? Where is he?"

Grim looked over at the lake with a serious expression. "King Michael will come back when he is ready."

Beams and more beams of energetic light shot up from the earth, creating angels bathed in golden armor, their swords at ready as they were born. For men, these things were darn pretty. I smirked at the thought.

"Alex! Look!" Raven laughed, swinging her dual blade like she was born using it. She flipped several times, and I had to admit I was pretty impressed with my little sister.

"You've got the whole Xena warrior princess going on, sis. I'm liking it." I grinned at her. She continued her spare with the Endrita, and I continued to pull on the golden memories of the mirror. I felt my muscles growing taxed, and I had a feeling that I couldn't keep doing this for too much longer. It felt as if I'd been looking in the mirror for hours and hours, but in all reality, it was probably only thirty minutes. After that amount of time, Grim put his paw on my arm.

"It is enough for now. The mirror, despite it's good feelings, is also draining on the one who uses it." His ear twitched, and he lowered my hand with the mirror.

I looked at the hundreds of Endrita I had produced from the mirror, and still wondered if it was enough. From what I'd seen of the Daegal army, they were far into the thousands.

"We will not stop here, but this is a fine start." Grim finally smiled at me, bounding away. He wove in-between the angels. I could hear him instructing as he ran through the crowd—a blur of orange, black, and white.

I pulled out my butterfly knives and grinned at the closest Endrita near me. He gave a grin back, and we started to fight. I overcame him after a few minutes, and I could see the look of surprise on his face.

"I'm Illis," he said in a sing-song voice. It was weird talking to a shimmering, energy-looking man.

"Alex." I raised my butterfly knives up as a greeting.

"The Daegal do not give in easily. Keep fighting until they have been turned into the vapor they should be," Illis said.

"I noticed. Those things are like wild dogs." I held my fighting stance again, and the two of us went at it again. I lifted my leg, bringing my knives down, twisting out of the way as Illis's sword came at me. The clash of swords and the scuffle of feet continued as the Endrita practiced on one another.

Raven came over to me with a smile, barely breathing hard from the exertion of the training. "How's it going?"

"Finally feeling useful again. You?"

She flipped three times and landed smack in front of me with her curved knife. "I don't think the Daegal will stand a chance." Her confident attitude was catchy.

"Not with your mad skills." I kissed the top of her head.

"Did you see them fight?" Raven pointed with her knife.

"Yeah. They're amazing." I stopped and stared at the ongoing sparring between the warriors.

"Alex, Drite is still suffering—look at it." Raven pointed toward the city, where I could see a black fog running between the streets.

"We'll get it back on its feet. I promise."

"I know we will." Raven smiled at me.

Chapter 28

Raven

My dual blade flew, leaving golden streaks in its wake. I struck at the nearest Endrita, and he struck my blade back with a long sword. His feet moved fluidly, so that I barely saw them, but I held my ground as we went back and forth.

"You're pretty good, human." The man tilted his head to the side, making him look like a bird.

"Yeah?" I struck at him again and ducked as he tried a strike back.

"I can tell Dayton blood runs through your veins," the Endrita said with a proud look in his eye.

A rumble shook the ground beneath my feet, making me stumble forward into the angel I'd been practicing with. As if one fluid mind, the army around me went into a fighting stance. Grim launched himself onto an Endrita's shoulders and gave a loud barky cry.

"Our world is under attack, and it is up to each and every one of you to take back what belongs to us. The Daegal will not go quietly, and it is up to you to fight back their darkness." His gaze swept back and forth. "I know we are still few in number, but you have the power of ten demons. Most of all remember who you are, and that God is on your side!" Grim's voice boomed through the air. My chest swelled with pride. Alex's shoulders went back, and he lifted his head at the powerful words Grim spoke. We hadn't practiced very long, but Grim knew it was vital we fought back the Daegal now.

The more we waited, the more the Daegal would grow in strength. I threw my brother a glance, and he gripped the mirror with determination glinting in his eyes. I'd heard what Grim said about the mirror, and part of me was still wary about launching ourselves into battle without more Endrita to back us up.

God, we need your help now more than ever.

The ground rumbled again. The sky zigzagged with black lightning and a loud *crack* of thunder made the hair on the back of my neck prickle. I heard the ring of swords coming out of their sheaths. Some of the angels pulled their helmets down, their stances ready to jump into the upcoming battle.

"They're coming," I said. I could sense the growing darkness just beyond the Drite castle. Like a lurking predator, it waited for us to be vulnerable to its grasp.

"Do you think we're ready?" Alex said beside me, flitting his butterfly knives back and forth. His eyes narrowed.

"We have to be." I gripped my dual blade, looking for my horse. Once I spotted him, I ran over and launched myself onto his back. I gripped his mane, got myself comfortable in the saddle, and spotted Alex climbing onto his horse as well.

"Alex?" I motioned my brother over. He slid off his horse and jogged toward me. He looked up at me with inquiring eyes.

"Yeah?"

"I feel like we should pray together over this. I've been asking God for help since…well…since my near wedding."

"Yeah…sounds good." My brother reached up and grabbed my hand, his eyes shimmering with determination. "You want to start, sis? I still feel I suck at this."

I giggled under my breath. "You can't suck at prayer, Alex. I'm pretty sure God hears you no matter what. But sure…I'll start." My fingers tightened slightly around my brother's hand, and a warm ball filled my chest. Every time I thought about what we'd learned here in Anxious, I felt emotional. How many others suffered, because they didn't know about the golden memories? Was there any way we could help them?

"God, we're both new to this, so I'll make it short." I peeked one eye open to see Alex grinning at me. "Anxious needs your help. Alex and I both know you're powerful, and we need your help to win this battle. Please give us strength, courage, and light to overcome the darkness. Send us and your angels help today. Amen." I peeked my eye back open, and my brother this time started clapping.

"Stop. You dork." I took a mini bow to entertain him, and he laughed.

"You're flat out the best, Raven." He kissed my hand and ran back over to his horse. "Now, let's kick some demon butt!"

The ground shook and rumbled. But instead of being afraid, I noticed what was starting to happen all around me. The once dark ground beneath our feet was starting to shimmer with golden dust. *Wow!* Waves of warm light flowed like an electric current between the Endrita, sparking and flowing in-between their legs.

"Look, Alex, look." I pointed at the beauty of the light. It continued to build until it reached the outer rims of the castle. The light started to gather, growing taller and taller as it circled around the walls. It swept back and forth, as if a giant ocean wave, dancing and growing taller by the second. With a burst of light, the golden energy traveled up the walls of the castle and created a giant canopy of light.

The once ruined walls, soaked in the energy, and yet gave back to it at the same time.

"Wow," Alex whispered. "That prayer worked fast."

The moment the energy swept over the castle, I started to notice the angels gaining more confidence. It was as if the energy not only fed their castle—it fed them as well.

"Trippy," I said under my breath. The Endrita's armor gleamed brighter, even though the sky above was still rumbling with dark clouds.

"What's going on?" I called to Grim.

He jumped onto the back of Barloc and clasped his hands. "The golden memories Alex brought into this world are restoring Drite. The first structure to be rebuilt is the castle, and after that the city will formulate. When Alex gains more strength, he must bring in more golden memories. Plus—" Grim stared at me for a moment. "Did you pray?"

I gave a smiling nod. "Yeah. We did."

Grim let out a happy yip. "That adds energy to the golden memories."

Suddenly something clicked in my head. "Are the angels golden memories?" Why hadn't I thought of this before. They appeared like forms of massive amounts of energy, and their faces weren't distinguishable from another.

"Yes, yes, they are, Raven. Some would call angels thoughts of God or thoughts of light."

"And the Daegal are dark thoughts?" My mind lit up. That's why every time Alex or I thought negative things more demons were formed.

"Yes." Grim gave me a patient smile. I should have figured this out long ago, but I'd felt as if I was in a fog about the world of Anxious.

"Which memories are mine?" I looked over the army of Endrita.

"The ones which glow with an *R* and the golden bird on their chest." Grim pointed at several nearby, and I noticed the emblem molded onto their breastplate. There had to be at least twenty of them that I could see.

"All those came from me?" Barloc shifted beneath me, and I could tell he wanted to ride.

"Barloc is also one of your golden memories." Grim patted the horse, and Barloc turned and looked at him with his kind eyes. "You must stay in tune with your golden memories, or those angels will vanish from Anxious." Grim's face turned serious, and he reached out his small paw and put it against my chest. "The true battle is within you. Hold fast to your true self and you'll conquer anything. Plus, a little prayer never hurts." He gave me a wink.

"I'll try," I said wanting to hug the fox. "I promise, I'll try."

He gave a nod and jumped off the back of my horse and headed toward Alex. I figured he was going to give him the same pep talk he'd given me. The Endrita seemed to grow restless, their eyes were directed toward where Dagmoth was located. I could sense that the ones I'd created wanted to rid this place of the darkness once and for all.

"Grim?" I slid off from Barloc and rushed over to the fox. He paused and looked at me.

"Who is Apollyon then? Whose negative thought is he?"

Grim's tail twitched back and forth. He closed his eyes, deep in thought. "Apollyon and King Michael are two sides of everyone on the planet. He is not one person's negative thoughts, but a collection of many. The Dayton line has held him at bay for ages, but he gained much power over the last fifty years. But…even he has a greater master." Grim's eyes filled with sadness. "Your grandfather was called a fool, belittled, and put into a facility where he couldn't fight Apollyon anymore. The Daytons have been protectors of this world since they were born, and their thoughts are highly linked to King Michael and Apollyon."

"So this really is our family's fault?" I shivered, feeling the weight of his words. I looked at the deteriorated castle, the host of angels waiting battle, and my mind went to King Michael, sleeping beneath the waters.

"The Dayton line has been keepers and protectors of this world, but do not worry, dear, all is not lost." Grim gave me a warm smile. "I have faith in you both."

"Grim, you told me Apollyon has a greater master. Who is it?"

"You know him by many names—one of which is Lucifer."

Having been to Sunday school as a kid, I knew who that was. My face blanched for a minute. A cry echoed across the valley we stood in, and my skin instantly broke out in nervous sweat.

"Quickly, climb aboard your horse," Grim said with a wave. I ran over to Barloc and mounted him. He turned his head and nodded to me twice. His coat shimmered with a white, energetic light, illuminating my face and arms.

Hold on tight.

I gripped Barloc's mane as he reared his feet into the air, letting out a loud whinny. Alex let out a loud whoop near me, and the Endrita army followed it with a cheer of their own. Golden, shimmering waves of energy flowed through the air, and golden sparks flew in-between each member of the army.

Almost like they're syncing up. A thrill raced through me, and I pulled out my double-bladed knife. Grim stood atop a tall angel again, his small hands raising.

"People of Drite! The enemy is fast approaching and will soon pound upon our doors. Are you ready?"

A loud cheer arose from the midst of the army.

"Hold fast to the light. Don't allow the darkness to penetrate your heart. Fight for our great and beautiful city. Fight for Drite!" Grim pounded the air with his fist.

Another roar filled the valley, and I felt an excitement building in my chest.

Crack!

The sound startled me, and I cast a glance over at my brother.

"Ready, sis?"

"I hope so." I mustered up the most confident smile I could.

Crack!

"I think that's our lovely neighbors." Alex threw me a smirk.

"They're sucky neighbors. They didn't even bring us a pie." I gripped my knife tighter, grinning.

"Dang, Raven, now I want pie." Alex pulled out his butterfly knives.

I laughed at my brother as another sharp crack resounded.

"Let's take the fight to them." Grim pointed toward the sky, which was churning with a million black particles. "Endrita, forward!"

Barloc didn't need to be encouraged to move forward; he followed the fox's instruction without me doing a thing. The host of angels turned, golden light shimmering between them, helmets covering their flowing hair. Grim, on the back of a horse, let out a roar so loud that it shook me down to my toes. *I didn't know foxes could make that sound.*

Grim's golden horse lurched forward, followed by the great army of Endrita. Alex and I quickly came to the front, beside Grim, our weapons drawn and ready. *I should be scared, but I'm not.* The thought drifted through my mind. *I know this is you, God, helping me feel brave. Thank you.* As I thought the prayer, a spark of light shot up from the ground and swirled around me. I laughed in delight.

The pounding of hooves and feet made a *thud, thud, thud* sound in my head. As if one entity, the angels of Drite ran forward, their shields and swords linked together. Several Endrita rode golden horses; the horses themselves covered in a sheen of white, energetic armor.

When we went beyond the castle, the cries of the angels ringing in my ears, I got a good look at what we were about to face. The air was suddenly knocked from my lungs at the sight of thousands and thousands of Daegal. They stirred together like flies around a carcass; their black faces shifted and moved with living energy.

Wow! I couldn't formulate anymore words than that at the sight of them. A loud, malicious laughter resounded from the midst of the swarm of demons. As if oil in water, the Daegal moved aside as Apollyon walked through the midst of them. His red eyes locked onto me first and then my brother. I couldn't help but shiver—thinking about the near wedding. I gripped my knife tighter, fighting the urge to run back the other way.

"I see you came out to play." Apollyon scoffed. "I came to make you another offer." He gave a mocking bow, and the Daegal army laughed—sounding like rocks scraping glass.

"Dang, you're ugly." Alex shook his head back and forth. "We don't accept offers from little girls."

"Ah, Alex, the boy who thinks he's brave, smart, and wise. I know your true flaws. I know how selfish and weak you truly are deep inside. I am you, Alexander Dayton." Apollyon's face rippled with darkness, and I felt as if I was staring into an abyss.

"This is my fault. I should have been there. I'm to blame. My parents are dead because I wasn't there." Apollyon's voice sounded exactly like my brothers. The giant of a man leapt into the air and landed in front of Alex. A malicious laugh came from his throat, sounding like a choking animal. "That's right, Alex, it is your fault. You couldn't save them, and you certainly can't save anyone now. You think you're so brave and tough with your little toothpicks. Look all around you. This is a battle that is already over. And that little mirror is not going to save you."

Chapter 29

Alex

Apollyon's nasty breath was in my face, breathing in and out. His words struck me straight in the heart, and I felt my courage starting to dissolve. My gaze fell on the huge army of demons, and my stomach clenched. I felt like I was about to puke. *Maybe he's right. I am a loser.* A dark vapor danced around my face.

"You're just as weak as your father and his father before." Apollyon leaned forward, his red eyes glimmering with mockery. "These people will never see you as a true leader. You're nothing but a failure." Apollyon leaned up, rocking on his heels. "Give it up, Alex. Anxious is mine." Apollyon pulled out his long, black, ragged sword, his lips tilting into a half smile.

"You know what, Apollyon?" I pulled out my two butterfly knives. "Shut your ugly pie hole." I leapt off my horse, the air rushing around me as I flipped and sliced at the dark monster. Apollyon let out a roar of surprise, jumping backward. Instead of facing me like a man, he vanished into the horde of demons.

"Get rid of them!" Apollyon's voice echoed, sounding angry.

My sister let out a cry from her belly, the host of Daegal rushing forward. The clash and clang of sword against sword sang; darkness swirled like flies in my face. I held in my mind the strongest golden memory I could, my sister and I's strong love for one another, and started to fight the darkness all around me.

A Daegal rushed me, his sword slicing through the air, cutting the dark particles that danced and swirled. I did my Wing Chun moves, waving my knives back and forth, striking the creature in the chest. He let out a scream, part of his body disintegrating into black particles.

You are a failure, Alex.

The words seemed to come from my left, so I turned, bringing my knives down into the chest of a demon. It looked at me with wide red eyes, screeching as it turned into vapor. As I fought, I noticed more negative words trying to get into my headspace. I held fast my golden memory as tight as I could.

This was the Daegal's greatest weapon—trying to gain a foothold once again in my head. I quickly realized that the Daegal were far under-matched compared to an Endrita, but there was way more of them.

The battle around me raged and hummed, like a living thing. Angels and demons fought, bursts of dark particles or explosions of light going up into the air. I cast a glance at my horse to see how he fared. He fought with his two front legs, smacking a Daegal in the face. I let out a chuckle as one hit the ground with a funny, twisted expression. I ducked down, a Daegal rolling over my back and face-planting. I brought my knives down and struck his neck. He burst into black particles with a gassy smell.

Gross. These things stink. Out of the corner of my eye, as I swiped and sliced, I spotted Grim on the back of a horse kicking major butt. The little fox held two small swords, and he wasn't shy with them. Anytime a demon would try to climb onto the back of his horse, Grim would jump and cut at anything within range. Bursts of black vapor *popped* all around me as Endrita struck the enemy.

"Yah!" The cry came from my left, and Raven flipped off the back of her horse and kicked a demon straight in the face. Her double-blade struck again and again. She bent backward, flipping in-between the enemy. For a moment, I just watched her in awe, until a Daegal came at me, bringing me back. I easily avoided him and struck him down in mere seconds. Watching Raven fight was like watching a dancer. She combined her gymnastics with the fighting style I had taught her growing up.

"Dang girl," I said under my breath. Something whizzed over my head, and I barely ducked in time. A blade, the size of Texas came at me, trying to cut out my heart. "We could have been best friends," I told the creature.

The Daegal opened his ugly mouth and growled at me, showing his yellowed teeth. His sword was half the size of him, and I wondered how this dude even held it without falling over.

"Ever heard of a toothbrush?" I curved my blades together, struck him in the chest, and shoved him back into another Daegal. They both fell on their backs like turtles, and I finished them off with another stab. The more I fought, the more I realized that it seemed like the Daegal weren't growing any smaller in number. Though our army was holding their own, I could see weariness quickly forming on their faces. *God, we need a boost here.*

"You are all so pathetic." Apollyon stood atop an incline, shaking his head. He held up a black mirror and looked deep into its surface. "There are far more dark memories than light on this piteous planet." With a grin, he lifted the mirror upward, gazing steadfastly into it like a vain school girl.

The earth rumbled beneath my feet, and the Daegal started whooping and cheering. The ground split open and black forms clawed their way out, dirt crumbling from their heads.

They're like freaking zombies.

"The more we defeat, the more he'll use the mirror," I said to myself and threw Raven a look.

We need to get that mirror, her eyes told me. I reached into my sack and pulled out the Drite Mirror. I had to create more Endrita, or we weren't going to make it. My fingers wrapped around the base of the mirror. A warmth spread through me.

"Come on, where are you?" I gazed deep into the surface of the mirror and spotted several kids glowing with golden memories. I pulled on them mentally and felt the joy of their young hearts. Several shafts of light shot up from the ground, scattering several Daegal in the process. I chuckled under my breath as the Endrita, which had just arrived, went in swinging their golden swords, shattering the darkness. I continued to pull on the golden memories, bringing more and more Endrita into the battle. Apollyon let out a frustrated scream. I was getting the hang of this mirror thing.

"You must get his mirror," a voice beside me said. Grim was suddenly there, his brow lowered. "If we do not stop him, he'll continue to draw on the darkness to overcome us."

"Why me?" I didn't mean to sound like a whiner, but I was still pretty amateurish at this whole mirror thing. Plus, Apollyon was about twice the size of me.

"You're the Dayton's firstborn. You're the heir of this world." Grim spun up into the air and kicked a Daegal in the face. He wiped his paws together, spinning and striking another demon. My knives sung. Several Daegal erupted into vapor, screaming as they disappeared.

"What if I lose?" My eyes went up to the giant of a man, wielding the mirror, creating more and more Daegal. I looked into the Drite Mirror again, drawing on more golden memories. We were still far outmatched, but I continued to notice that the angels were much stronger than a demon.

Light always dispels darkness. It made me think of a single candle in a room—light always won. A scripture my grandma used to say came to mind. *The light shines in the darkness, and the darkness has not overcome it.* The ground erupted with beams of light all over the field, throwing Daegal back as the Endrita were born from the golden memories.

"Whoa," I whispered. It was beautiful—like shooting stars across the sky.

"Use the mirror—defeat Apollyon. You can do this, Alexander." Grim spun through the air, leaping over a Daegal and bringing his sword down into the neck of another one. He was like watching a mini *Yoda*.

Dang, I need to step up my game. I weaved between the demons, striking, spinning, and slicing. Using my Wing Chun, my feet fell into sync with my movements. I silently thanked my Wing Chun teachers who had pushed me as hard as they could. If I had decided to be into video games instead of fighting, I'd been a puddle on the ground by now.

Raven backflipped, twisting out of the way of several demons' weapons and striking them unexpectedly in the face. Their long fingers clawed at her, but she was an unstoppable force.

Remind me not to make her angry, I told myself.

I pushed through the Daegal, cutting them down, weaving and dodging to get to Apollyon, who stood at the top of an incline. The big, ugly brute spotted me and pointed his mirror in my direction.

"Come to die?" Several Daegal crawled out of the ground, their black faces swarming with tiny particles. It reminded me of walking corpses—flies all over their faces. I shuddered with disgust.

"Meh, maybe later." I shrugged, holding out my own mirror and drawing on the golden memories. Endrita beamed out of the earth, their swords coming out swinging at the Daegal. The little, dark wimps started to run, screaming and clawing at anything in their way.

"Wow. That's the best you got? Think you better rethink your strategy, cupcake." I pulled more and more from the mirror, formulating a nice group of angels around me, ready to kick some major butt.

"It's far easy for you to hide behind the skirts of the Endrita. It's another thing to face me man to man." Apollyon pulled out his giant sword, smirking at me.

"And who was the one who ran like a little girl earlier? You're one to talk, Ugly Face." My knives itched for a fight.

"Tsk, tsk, Alex, you and I are not so different. The darkness inside of you is just as powerful as it is inside of me. I've just tapped into its power." Apollyon curled his hands into fists, darkness swarming his gloves.

"I'm nothing like you. You feed on people's suffering—and you create more." I stood my ground, keeping my eyes locked onto my enemy. *Don't let him in your head,* I told myself. *God, please help me.*

"But haven't you created suffering in others as well? Where were you when your father and mother needed you?" Apollyon smirked down at me.

His words tried to crawl into my chest, but I fought against them. "There was nothing I could have done to save them. They weren't supposed to be home yet."

"You're a lot like your father." Apollyon picked his teeth with the end of his sword. He spat something black and slimy out of his mouth. "You're just as pathetic at trying to protect the ones you love." Apollyon took a step forward, the ground cracking and rumbling beneath his feet. "Ah, please don't hurt us. What do you want? I'll do anything! Please!" Apollyon's voice sounded just like my father's.

Pain shot through me, and I stumbled backward.

Apollyon let out a low laugh, seeing the agony on my face. "Pathetic. It was over before it had even begun. Your father just handed himself and your mother on a platter for me to slaughter."

My heart churned in my chest, my mind flickering to the image of my dead parents. *Fight him, Alex. He's trying to get to you. God, please, I don't know if I'm strong enough for this.* I felt a warm energy swirl through me.

"They really should have been more careful about antiques they didn't know anything about." Apollyon flipped the mirror around in his hand for a moment and grinned at me.

"Mom and Dad had that mirror?" The pieces were starting to come together in my mind. Apollyon had gotten into our world with that thing.

"Of course they did. Your father had no idea that his own father was right all along. But enough talking." Apollyon snarled at me, lurching forward, his sword swinging. His words made me stagger back, my heart clenching with pain.

He murdered them? Fear, pain, and finally rage filled my chest. "Why don't you fight *me* then?" Strength coursed through me. I could feel the power of my prayer starting to gain strength.

Apollyon's sword sang—the black particles dancing around it. My butterfly knives shimmered, and we both dodged out of each other's way, the air around us turning gold and black. My feet slid, and I pulled myself back into a fighting stance. Apollyon's sword came at me again. I tucked the Drite Mirror into my pouch, and with a series of fast moves, danced with him. Gold and black swirled around us—cries of the Endrita and Daegal echoing in the back of my head. Apollyon's mouth pulled back and a row of yellow teeth flashed.

"Those little sticks aren't going to do a thing. You're worthless. All those years of practicing, and you couldn't even save your mother or father. What a waste of flesh you are." A black cloud boiled in front of Apollyon, sparking with energy, swirling around him like a tornado. I knew exactly what he was trying to do. He wanted to feed into my negativity and draw strength from it.

"You're as dumb as you are ugly." I allowed my mind to think of every golden memory possible, building up my own energy. I pulled on my inner strength—who I really was, who Raven and Grim believed I truly was, who God inside of me was. I was a leader. I just had to believe it. I cast a quick look toward the army and noticed that the Daegal were being forced backward, most of them trying to tuck tail and run away. It made me laugh as I saw the Endrita filtering into the darkness and dispersing it.

"You don't have what it takes to be a real leader. You'll fail them like you failed your parents." Despite Apollyon's words, I could tell that something was hurting him.

He's full of bull. He knows the only way I'll back down is if he gets into my head. A new resolve came over me. "The only one I need to lead is me, the rest will follow." I jumped into the air, drawing my knives upward and bringing them down into Apollyon's chest. He let out a roar, shaking me off. I tumbled, nearly hitting my head on a rock, and jumped back to my feet.

"You think it'll be that easy?" Apollyon let out a crackling laugh. "I have years of negative energy pumping through me." He took a step forward, his shoulders shaking as he continued to laugh. The grass beneath him wilted at the touch of his feet.

"Probably why you so ugly," I said, approaching him. "You know, happy thoughts take years off your face. You should try it sometime." I spun, slicing upward, then down, my feet moving in a blur of motion. Apollyon's eyes tried to follow my movements, but I could tell he was having a hard time. His big sword struck downward and nearly nicked my armor.

"You quick, Ugly Face, but too slow for your own good." I pulled my knives up again, striking his side. He let out a bellow, hissing. He stumbled sideways for a moment. Tapping into some kind of inner strength, Apollyon jumped at me, his giant sword swinging again and again. I dodged, my body fluently moving. I calculated wrong, and his sword struck my armor, jarring me backward. A cold feeling went through me, and all my negative thoughts bombarded me.

I'm a failure. I can't help anyone. No one will listen to me. I wasn't there to help them. I'm useless.

Black particles swarmed my helmet, creeping underneath it. Cold fingers dug into my scalp, driving deep into my mind.

I'm never going to save anyone. I can't even save myself. I might as well give up. This world doesn't belong to me anymore.

"No!" Something snapped inside of me. Anger boiled over in my eyes, and I gripped my knives tighter. It didn't matter what this giant pig face said, I was going to win this thing. I stumbled backward as Apollyon's sword came at me again, hitting me in the arm. Black energy crisscrossed over my shoulder, down my arm, and into my hand, wrapping around one of my knives. The dark feelings shook me to the core, and I fought to remain positive—to think of my golden memory.

"Raven," I whispered to myself again and again, trying to conjure up the good feelings to ward off the darkness. I stumbled to my knees, my left knife thudding to the ground.

"Ah, little Alex, what a waste of flesh you are. You could have been such entertainment for my court. Now, I grow tired of you and your little acts of bravery. It is a shame really." Apollyon stepped closer to me, his sword poking into my chest. "First, I will take Raven as my wife, and I will remind her how worthless she truly is." Apollyon twisted his sword. A shooting pain swept through me. "Her screams will echo throughout all of Anxious." He leaned closer to my face. "And Drite will be no more."

My chest burned. My throat ached. All the pain of my parents' death washed over me again and again. But the moment he mentioned Raven, my eyes snapped with fury. *No one touches my sister.* I let out a ferocious animalistic scream, twisting my body in a way I've never twisted. Golden light shot from my chest.

"Ahh!" Apollyon jumped back, white and gold light traveling down his dark blade and wrapping around his hand. He slapped at his skin, the light traveling up his arm. I got to my feet, gripping my knives once more, my chest heaving in and out.

"No one messes with Raven."

Our weapons clashed again, and with renewed fever, I fought him back, spinning and turning, bringing my knives down then up, using all the resources I'd learned over the years in fighting. My knife dug into his chest, and Apollyon let out a horrified scream.

"You were supposed to be easy," he said with a grunt. "You are weak." He fell to his knees.

"And you're just plain stupid," I said, pressing my knife to his throat. The golden energy pulsed through my knife, wrapping around his neck like a snake.

"I'll be back for you, Alexander Dayton," Apollyon said with a growl. I watched pain cross his features as the light continued to wrap around him.

Sizzle.

The light burned into his flesh, and he let out a scream of pain. I pulled my second blade out and jabbed it deep into his chest.

"I'll be waiting."

Apollyon's dark form rippled and snapped, sizzling and roaring. Dark particles exploded into the air with one final scream of pain. The dark mirror clattered to the ground. I turned to face the army of Daegal. Every one of them stared at me, frozen in time.

"Get them!" With a force like no other, the Endrita attacked the Daegal, dispersing them into black particles and vaporous smoke. I pulled out the Drite Mirror, drawing on more golden memories, until the Endrita army far outweighed the Daegal. The clash and clang of swords continued. I jumped off the incline and joined the fight, grinning at Raven.

She backflipped, slicing with her dual blade, making demons scream in terror. It didn't take long before each shadow man was nothing but a memory, the air stinking of their vaporous flesh.

A beam of light shot down from the sky, and I craned my neck upward to see the gray clouds dispersing and the sun starting to shine through. I heard the footfalls of someone and brought my attention back downward.

"I am so proud of you, Alexander Dayton." Raven's arms wrapped around my neck, and she buried her face in my neck. I could feel her either laughing or crying; I wasn't sure which. "Mom and Dad would be so proud of you too."

We held each other for a long time, until I heard someone clear their throat. Grim looked up at us, his arms crossed.

"You did well, Alexander." He gave a nod.

"Where did you get moves like that?" I gave a nod back. "I mean, dude, you were kicking butt out there, Grim." I grinned at him, keeping one arm around my sister.

"*Karate Kid* movies." He grinned back at me. Raven and I both started laughing.

Chapter 30

Raven

"Now what?" I asked, looking between Grim and my brother. Despite having fought like a mad woman, I wasn't all that tired. I felt rejuvenated.

"The golden memories are already at work," Grim said, pointing toward the Drite castle. Before my very eyes I watched as each stone of the castle shimmered and danced, reconnecting by itself. The Endrita turned to both Alex and I, their lithe figures bowing before us.

"Why are they bowing?" I asked Grim.

He smiled at me. "They honor those who rule well."

"Rule? As in?" I exchanged a look with Alex. I pointed at him then me.

"No, no, no. I can't be their king. That's King Michael's job." Alex took a few steps back, running his fingers through his dark hair.

"Not a king, Alexander. You are the one who holds the mirror. You are now the negotiator of our kingdom. You hold the key to our world in your hands." Grim jumped atop of an angel, so that he was eye level with me and my brother. The Endrita stood still, but I could see him smiling.

"I'm not quite following you," Alex said. He pulled out the Drite Mirror and looked at it for a moment. He ran his finger over the ornate surface.

"You must collect the Dagmoth Mirror as well. There is much work to be done." Grim pointed to where Alex had defeated Apollyon. A wave of excitement went through me, followed by something that tugged on my heart, hard. *Colten.* My mind drifted back to our world, to the boy I'd left behind. *You have to let him go. Do you really want to live with Jill and Nelson?* My stomach clenched into knots, and tears pricked my eyes.

"Alex, go get it," I said. My brother rushed off, collecting the Dagmoth Mirror and tucking it into his pouch he carried.

Once he returned, Grim continued his speech. "This world is about balance. The Dagmoth Mirror will help you identify where the problems lie, and you can help teach others about the golden memory." He waved his hands as he talked.

"I'm game." Alex crossed his arms, smiling. "If I can help other people not go through what I did, it'd be awesome."

My heart tugged at me again. *Colten.* I saw my boyfriend's face in my mind, and the feeling wasn't going away. *Ex-boyfriend, Raven, you broke up with him, remember?*

"Why do I get the feeling that you're not into this, Raven?" Alex said. My brother knew me far too well. He'd always been able to read me like a book.

"It's not that—" How did I put my words together so that I made sense? He'd think I was just being a girlie girl for wanting to try to fix it with Colten.

"Colten." Alex supplied for me so that I didn't have to embarrass myself.

"Yeah." I covered my face with my hands, heat traveling up my neck and into my cheeks.

"Hey, you don't have to be embarrassed about it. I get it. You like the guy." Alex sounded slightly amused.

I took my hands away from my face and looked into my brother's eyes. He understood me better than anyone else on the planet. He also knew when my heart was set, there was nothing that could change my mind.

"You're not mad?" I squinted.

"Why would I be mad? You're falling in love with someone. If he makes you happy then I'm happy." Alex wrapped me up in a huge hug, burying his face in my hair. "I love you, Raven."

Tears sprang to my eyes, and I nearly started sobbing. After all the pain we'd both been through, I didn't want to leave him alone, but I also felt that if I didn't leave, I'd always have Colten in the back of my mind. Regret would eat me alive. I felt like something beyond me was happening, tugging me back toward the boy I'd started to love.

"I don't even know if he'll take me back. Where will I live? I can't live with those horrible people." I felt nervous, but something bloomed in my chest. I recognized it—hope.

"Ian's mom," Alex shouted the words, making me jump. "Ian told me his mom would take you in. I'll come back with you and we'll get you settled, and after that I'll come back here." He caught Grim's attention to see if he approved of what he said. The fox nodded.

"I will help you both arrange Raven's situation, and I will lead you back. Though, as the holder of the mirrors, you can open any portal in both worlds. You don't need me any longer." Grim clasped his hands together.

I bent down to the fox, hugging him gently. "We will always need you, Grim. Thank you for everything. You saved our lives." I wiped tears from my eyes as I pulled away.

"You are most welcome." Grim wiped a few tears from his own eyes, clearing his throat.

"Ready?" Alex wrapped his arm around my shoulder.

"Yeah. I'm ready." I suddenly turned to Grim. "What about King Michael? What happened to him?"

Grim let out a little happy yelp. "That's right! Let's go check the lake." The little fox bounded toward the castle, a streak of orange and white.

With a chuckle, Alex and I jumped on our horses, riding after him. The angelic army dispersed to the city nearby, streams of gold light trailing behind them. We quickly came to the backside of the castle, where the lake resided, and slid off our horses. Grim stood on the edge of the lake and dipped his paw into the clear water. A shaft of light shot like lightning through the water, zigzagging like a vein. It went deeper and deeper until it struck something at the very bottom.

ANXIOUS

Who;Osh!

A rush of water shot up out of the middle of the lake—looking like an explosion. Gold and white light circled around and around the tornado of water, and in the center a clear casket rose.

"Holy crap." Alex's eyes were fixated. It was like watching the Fourth of July—light sparking and shooting, and the water filled with energy. The casket burst open, and a beautiful sing-song tune filled the air around us. A man stood up with white hair, a flowing golden robe, and the brightest eyes I'd ever seen. Giant, gold, and pearl-like wings unfurled from his muscled back.

"King Michael?" I gulped. Oh my gosh. He was a man—well, an angel—but not a child! King Michael laughed, jumped from the casket, and floated down to the earth. The sound of his laugh sent me into a giggling fit.

"Hello, Alexander. Hello, Raven." His eyes locked onto Alex's then mine. He bowed to the both of us and took each one of our hands. "You saved Amora."

"Amora?" I turned my head slightly. "What's Amora?" I knew the word, but I wasn't sure why King Michael had said it.

"This is Amora." King Michael stood back up, sweeping his hands outward with a laugh. "This world was never to be called Anxious, but the more the Daegal ruled, the more Anxious was created."

"The world's name is different?" Alex looked utterly lost, but I think I understood what King Michael was trying to tell us.

"Alex, look." My finger pointed to the beautiful entrance far off that I had first noticed when we got to Anxious. The beautifully crafted, golden words started to shimmer and shift. As we both peered at it, before our eyes, the words started to change.

"That's the gate to Anxious." Watching the letters shimmer and dance made joy erupt in my chest. "We changed everything."

"Yes, you did." King Michael's arms were suddenly around the both of us, and his genuine love filled my every pore. I had never felt such kindness, love, or affection in my entire life. I soaked it in as tears sprang to my eyes. Once the hugging was complete, King Michael held us at arm's length, his face warm and full of love. "So someone else wants to say something too." Michael took a small step backward, and behind him I noticed a brilliant portal of light.

Something akin to fear and complete awe swept over my entire body. I found myself naturally wanting to bow from the weight of the pressure of the light. As I peered toward it, I could make out a figure—it wasn't a portal after all. Like diamonds, the person sparkled beyond comprehension and his face glowed so brightly, I could barely look at it. As if a wheel within a wheel, another figure stepped out of the light and approached us. He was dressed in a plain, loose-fitting white shirt, and a pair of jeans. His light brown hair was longer, and his eyes seemed to dance with a variety of color.

God wears jeans? I started to giggle at the thought, as the figure stopped before Alex and me.

"Hi, guys." He grinned at the both of us, and I found myself grinning in return. He touched the top of my head and gently lifted my chin to him. "I am so proud of you both. Thank you. Everything you did here will ripple out into the realms as well as your world."

Alex stood in shock, his mouth slightly open.

"Just so I know I'm not tripping. Are you?" For some reason Alex couldn't get the word *God* out of his mouth.

"Yes. The big guy in the sky?" He laughed at his own joke, and waves of joy swept over me in an instant. His laugh was like the sound of tinkling bells, and a mixture of feelings like warm cookies and a puppy snuggle. This felt unreal. All of it.

"So, um…" Alex looked at King Michael and then back at the figure known as *God,* and suddenly burst into tears. He fell into God's arms, his face burying in His chest, his arms wrapped around Him in a tight embrace. God embraced him back, His face tucked up close to my brother's cheek.

"Alexander, you've always been worthy. You've always been loved. Your parents are so proud of you. And so am I." God kissed my brother's head, holding him tighter than anyone had ever done before. After several long moments, they pulled away, and Alex wiped his face.

"Um, okay, so…" Alex looked awkwardly at his feet. I wanted to laugh. Boys were so funny about this type of thing.

"Alex, just admit it. You cried—it's fine." I lightly shoved my brother, who shoved me back.

God gave one more grin to my brother and opened His arms for me next. I fell into His embrace, and love like I'd never experienced it overcame me. He was like sunshine, filling my every cell with light and love, until I felt I'd burst.

"Raven, you are beautiful beyond measure. Thank you for being my daughter and stepping into the light. You will lead many to embrace the light within them. Don't be afraid. Much is coming, but you can handle it all. Remember, I'm with you both."

Instead of tears, I felt uncontrollable laughter arising. I started to giggle, and the more I did, the more God grinned at me, until we were both laughing without restraint. After our laughing fit, my brother was wiping happy tears away from his eyes this time.

"Are you turning into mush, bro?" I teased him.

"Shut up." He smiled at me, and I caught him staring at God again. "How is this possible?"

God took both our hands and looked at first Alex and then me. "Don't forget what you've learned here. Share it with others. Share the light. Share with them my love." With one final kiss on each of our foreheads, God walked back to the giant man-shaped portal of light, disappearing into a burst of golden sparkles.

"Well, wow!" Alex let out a long breath, rubbing a hand down his face.

"Yeah…wow is right." I started to giggle again, until Alex and I were both laughing our heads off. After we'd slightly composed ourselves, Alex turned to the beautiful angel before us.

"King Michael, Grim told me about being a negotiator for Amora." Alex cleared his throat, trying to regain his composure.

"And Raven wants to return home. Yes, I know." King Michael squeezed my arm.

"Yeah, I'm sorry…I…just—" I looked at my feet.

"No need to apologize, dear. You have a separate path than your brother does. You will always be able to access Amora—at all times. There is no need to fret." King Michael rubbed my arm.

"Thank you." I let out a breath I didn't know I'd been holding.

"Both of you have played your role here. And now it's time to discover even more about who you are. Raven, you will need not worry about a home. Alex, you will protect and love this world, and forever the Endrita will thrive with you at our side." His golden eyes danced with affection.

I pulled the king into a giant hug, wanting to hug him forever. He'd taught us about the golden memories, and I'd forever be thankful to him.

"Ready?" Grim said to both Alex and me.

"Yes." I gave King Michael one more hug, and all three of us headed for the woods, me leading Barloc along. "One question." I stopped for a moment.

"Yes?" Grim looked up at me.

"Can I keep my horse?" I'd fallen in love with the white stallion already.

"Of course you may." Grim smiled at me, patting my horse's leg. "He's part of you now."

"Thank you." I wrapped my arms around Barloc and kissed his nose.

Have any sugar? I heard him say in my head. I laughed. Even if he was a golden memory horse, he still acted like any other horse. We approached a door, and I knew the moment I stepped through it, all of this would feel like a dream.

"Ready?" Alex put a hand on my back.

"Yeah."

We walked through, Grim following behind us. The woods were nearly identical to that of Amora, but I knew we were home. A warm chuckle came beside me, and I felt the presence of another person.

"This will be the quickest way to get your situation under control," a deeper voice said. I nearly jumped out of my skin. A tall, red-haired man stood beside Alex and me, wearing a business suit and tie. In his hand was a suitcase. "I will arrange your stay with Ian's mother. Before I go, step back into Amora for a few minutes." With a golden flash, Grim was gone.

"He doesn't look bad as a ginger." Alex rubbed his chin. Alex looked up at the trees, putting his hands on his hips. "Even though it looks like Amora, I can tell it's not."

I shook my head, looping my arm around my brother's waste. "I'm going to miss you like crazy." Tears came to my eyes again. I buried my face in his chest.

"I'll visit all the time. Or you can visit. The mirrors give me full access. I can keep an eye on you through them. If you need me, simply ask." He wrapped his arms around me, holding me tight against his chest once again. "I love you, Raven. I'm really proud of you."

"I'm proud of you too." I felt like we were being cheesy, but I didn't care. I let him hold me for a long time.

"I wanted to tell you, Raven," Alex started to say. He cleared his throat. "Apollyon killed Mom and Dad." He paused for a moment. "Mom must have found the Dagmoth Mirror, and because Dad was a Dayton, his touch was a portal for Apollyon to come through." Alex closed his eyes.

"They didn't know any better." I let out a sigh.

"Grandpa tried to warn all of us. It sucks." Alex let out a huff, pacing back and forth.

"Hey." I touched my brother's arm. "Now we know. We'll teach our kids and tell them the truth. I just wonder why Grandpa didn't show Dad, instead of just trying to tell him about it."

"Maybe he was scared to."

I shrugged. "Amora is so beautiful. Maybe Grandpa was scared Dad wouldn't want to come back."

Alex scratched the back of his head. "That's possible. I just wanted to tell you, so you knew the truth."

"Thanks, Alex." I hugged him tight. "You better visit me a ton."

"I will." He pulled back from me and smiled. "I guess we should step back into Amora like Grim said."

We stepped through the portal.

Not more than a few minutes later, I heard the rustle of leaves, and pretty soon we saw Grim bounding toward us, a grin on his face. I wasn't sure how much time had passed, but it seemed as if it'd been mere minutes since he'd left.

"It's arranged. I'm having your stuff moved as we speak." His body shifted from fox and into the form of the red-haired man. He brushed off the front of his suit.

"How did you do that so fast?" I said.

"Time doesn't exist with Amora. It was weeks, rather than minutes, that passed by." He winked at the both of us.

"Wait, just now?" Alex's eyes widened.

"Yes. Weeks have passed." Grim smiled at us.

"That's still really trippy," my brother whispered. He shook his head and grabbed my hand. "You're going to love Ian's mom. She's awesome."

"I remember her. She was always nice to me, plus I think she boards horses like Colten's family does." My excitement grew at the thought of settling down into a new home.

"She's willing to take Barloc as well." Grim nodded toward my horse, who waited beside me patiently. Barloc nudged my back.

"You are amazing." I wrapped my arms around Grim, hugging him tight.

"Come on, they're all waiting for you." He urged us both forward through the portal once again.

* * * * *

Alex, Grim, and I walked down the long road toward Ian's house. I led Barloc along, feeling content and happy.

"Why don't you two ride Barloc, and I'll meet you there," Grim said. We nodded and climbed aboard my white horse. Without being asked, Barloc seemed to know the way to my new home. Alex wrapped his arms around my waist, sighing softly under his breath.

"I miss them," I said. The warm breeze tickled my cheek.

"Me too." We both knew what we were talking about, so we didn't need to explain anything about our parents.

"Dad would have freaked out. He would have loved Anxious—or Amora." Alex chuckled. "All the legends and myths he looked into over the years was right in front of his eyes."

"Mom would have loved those mirrors and the castle with all its beautiful decorations." Something filtered into my mind suddenly. "Alex?"

"Yeah?"

"I found a mirror in our old house." I turned toward my brother. "If you have the Drite and Dagmoth Mirror. What mirror is that?"

"Maybe it's just a mirror?" Alex shrugged. "Not every mirror is magic." He winked at me.

"But now that I think about it, it looked like the mirrors you have. It had a fancy letter on it like those did."

"Hmm, I don't know. Maybe somebody just created a similar design." Alex rubbed my back.

"Yeah, you're probably right." The scenery around us started to change, and I saw an inviting farm house coming into view. Rolling hills were beyond it, and even further beyond that was a cluster of tall trees. It was beautiful.

"That's it, right?" I leaned forward, my fingers intertwining into Barloc's mane.

"Yeah." Alex nodded.

"Come on, Barloc, let's go home." Excitement shivered in my voice. My horse didn't need to be asked twice, and he took off a bit faster. When we got closer to the house, I spotted a brown-haired woman standing there waiting for us. She spotted the both of us and gave a friendly wave. Alex and I slid off Barloc and approached her. She wore jean shorts, a blue tank top, and her hair was pulled up into a messy bun. Her brown eyes sparkled at us.

"How are you both doing?" she asked. She pulled us both into her arms and gave us a long, motherly hug.

"Good," I said. "Thank you for taking me and Barloc in. I really, really appreciate it." I smiled at her. I remembered her from school. Always baking cookies and doing nice things for other people.

"I'm Mary. Of course, Alex knows that." She lightly touched my brother's arm.

"Thank you for everything." Alex hugged her. "You're awesome."

"And I heard that you are living with a great-uncle? Why aren't the two of you sticking together?" Mary looked between us, curious.

"Raven wants to stay here and work on a relationship she has. I wanted to start over, but I'll be back to visit a lot," Alex said.

"Ian and Jack are going to miss you like crazy," Mary said. At the mention of Alex's two friends' names they burst out the front door, nearly tripping on each other.

"I hear you're leaving us?" Ian punched Alex in the arm.

"Got to follow my dreams, man," Alex said in a fake choked voice.

"I heard your great-uncle is going to help you keep up on your moves?" Ian did a karate chop.

"I'm going to be a Wing Chun master." Alex overemphasized the word *master*, making me laugh. Obviously Grim had woven a great story to convince everyone. It was true to a degree. Grim was going to help Alex keep up on his skills. I loved how my brother just went with the flow as if he knew the whole time.

"You're going to be the little sister I never wanted." Ian play-punched me, but I knew he was happy I was going to be living with them. Ian was an only child, and Alex had told me he had always thought it was boring.

"Thanks, Ian. And you're going to be the weird cousin I wish I didn't have." I giggled under my breath.

"Glad to supply that role for anyone." Ian grinned. As if suddenly noticing my horse, Ian and Jack both took a step back.

"Dang, that's a big horse." Jack pointed like a little kid at Barloc.

"His name is Barloc." I stroked my horse's neck, loving the feel of him beneath my fingers.

"Can he do any tricks like Mayfly?" Ian asked.

I grinned at the both of them. "Wanna see?"

My mini crowd nodded at me. Alex grinned up at me as I climbed back on top of the white horse.

"Let's show them what we got," I whispered to Barloc. He nodded his head up and down. I started a routine with him. I slid to the side, stood, and flipped on him once or twice. A cheer broke out, and I looked over to see my little audience smiling and clapping at me. I led Barloc back to them.

"The next show that opens up, I am taking you to it," Mary said with a little clap. "You are excellent, Raven."

"Thank you." I slid off Barloc. I pulled Alex into a big hug. "Bye, Alex. I love you. I'll see you soon, and you better visit me a lot."

"I love you too." We held each other a long while. Soon Jack, Ian, and Mary joined in on a big group hug. Barloc nudged my back like he wanted in on the hug, making me laugh.

"Come here," I said to the horse. He put his nose in the middle of us.

"You better still do dumb stuff with us sometimes." Ian shoved my brother.

"Who else would I do it with?" Alex laughed.

"I had this great idea yesterday," Jack said, his eyes lighting up.

"Save it. I promise. I'll be back. Don't do anything stupid without me at least watching." Alex punched Jack in the arm.

"I wouldn't dream of it." Jack grabbed him into a hug and then Ian did after him. A red sporty car pulled up into the driveway, and I saw Grim get out. He made his way over to us, his eyes covered by a pair of sunglasses. Mary stepped forward to meet him, her hand extended.

"Hello, Grim. It's nice to see you again."

"You as well." Grim nodded, smiling at the woman. It was still really weird to see Grim as a man, but I thought he was rather handsome.

"This is your great-uncle?" Jack stared at Alex. Grim did look rather impressive in his suit, with his sports car and strong-looking body.

"Yeah. This is Grim," Alex said.

"Dang, can I touch your car?" Jack said in awe.

"Sure." Grim let out a laugh. Ian and Jack both circled the red car. I had no idea what it even was, but apparently, it was impressive.

"He's driving a Ferrari," Alex whispered to me, seeing my confusion.

"Right." I nodded my head up and down. "Our little fox friend has a Ferrari. Interesting." I ran a hand down my face. "Life is weird."

"Tell me about it."

"Ready to ride, Alex?" Grim asked.

Alex gave a nod, pulled me into one final hug, and got into the car.

"I love you, Alexander Dayton," I whispered, watching them drive away.

Chapter 31

Alex

Grim and I walked through the woods, the leaves crunching beneath our feet.

"The car was a nice touch." I tilted my head to look at my "great-uncle."

"You liked that? I had a few perks on this side of the world." He suddenly turned back into a fox, his ears twitching.

"So why a fox?" I said with an amused smile.

"Beats shaving your face every day." Grim's eyes sparkled at me.

"Yeah, shaving's a beast." I reached down and scratched the fox's ears. He let out a content sound.

"Plus, it's weird if someone gives you a scratch when you're 6'2" and a ginger." Grim jumped up onto my shoulder and rubbed up against me. I'd never seen him so affectionate, but I was loving it. I never thought I would have said this in my lifetime, but, dang, I liked having a pet fox—or friend. Whatever he was.

"So what happens now?" I reached over and stroked his soft head. His fur rippled in the light wind.

"There are many more like you, Alexander. Many suffer from the illnesses you have overcome. Using both mirrors will bring balance to Amora. The city of Drite will slowly be rebuilt over time. Healing one at a time is your calling."

If anyone else had said something like that to me, I'd probably have laughed, but when Grim said anything it was like listening to *Yoda*. You don't laugh at *Yoda*—I don't care how cute or cheesy he is.

"So finding these kids is my job? Then I tell them I'm from a world where foxes can talk?" I chuckled under my breath. How was I going to convince these kids to do anything?

"Oh, you'll have your way too," Grim said with a wink and jumped off my shoulder, barely rustling the leaves.

"Wait, what do you mean?" I turned my head as he made a barking sound. *He's laughing at me.* I found the thought amusing. Grim stepped through the portal, and I quickly followed. I watched his little form bound away, becoming a mere blur. I instantly felt the difference in the air.

"Grim, if I turn into a squirrel, I swear to God somebody's going to die!" I ran after him, hearing his echoing bark once again.

I soon got to the entrance of the Drite castle, Grim standing there with his arms crossed.

"We have a lot of work to do."

"Look at you. All work and no play. Slave driver." I smirked at him. He jumped up onto my shoulder as I shoved the door open. The room swirled with golden energy, and I drew in a deep breath, filling my lungs with happiness.

"So how do we do this thing?" I scratched his ears once more.

"First, we retrieve the mirrors." Grim pointed toward the hidden compartment I'd tucked the mirrors in.

"Right." I nodded. Endrita moved in and out of the doors, busying themselves with repairs. I smiled at a few of them.

"Not to sound like a total douchebag, but are there going to be any girls on Amora?" I grabbed the mirrors out of their hidden spot. Grim jumped from my shoulder, laughing at me again.

"When you find the people who need your help, I'm sure you'll encounter a girl or two. It's up to her if she stays in Amora or not after she finishes her training." Grim motioned for me to follow, opened a door, and stepped through it. I grinned at the back of his head.

"Then let's get busy."

* * * *

The grass beneath my feet was wet with the moisture of the night as I stood outside a rundown house. The Dagmoth Mirror had led me here, and I knew the fourteen-year-old kid inside was suffering just like I had been. How to not creep him out was the next question on my mind.

Ah, dang it. I gotta do it. I scratched the back of my head, looking up to the stars above me. *Grim, you suck.* My body shimmered with golden, energetic light. I'd learned a trick since being in the world of Amora, and I wasn't exactly proud of it either. I didn't really see another option though—I had to do it. People weren't going to believe some kid that another world existed in their backyard, but a talking squirrel, yeah, you get the picture. Golden energy pulsed through me, and my body shrunk, shimmering, until I turned completely white, four-legged, and as cute as a button.

I scurried up the side of the house, balanced on the edge of a window, and shoved it open. Sleeping in the bed was a kid, roughly fourteen, blond hair, and a journal thrown open. Snooping, I saw the last entry he'd entered.

I can't do it anymore. No one cares about me anyways. They are better off without me. It's over.

I jumped onto the kid's back, my nose twitching, my little paws rubbing together. This was going to be awesome.

"Hey, buddy, wake up. I have something you need to see."

At the sound of my voice, the kid woke up, his eyes heavy with sleep.

"Life can get better, I promise you. You gotta believe me," I continued.

"What the heck is going on?" the kid mumbled, and I knew he probably thought he was dreaming. Why else would a squirrel be talking to him? He rubbed his head, trying to sit up. I jumped onto the floor, pacing back and forth.

"Dude, you're not dreaming. I want to show you something. Will you follow me?"

The kid's eyes got slightly wider. He pinched his arm. "You're a squirrel."

"Yup."

"And you're talking to me." The kid pointed to himself. "I have finally gone completely bat crazy." His face turned ashen.

"You're not crazy. Come on." I waved him forward as I jumped onto his windowsill. "You need to see this."

Out of sheer curiosity, the kid stumbled after me, nearly falling out of the window in the process.

"I'm Alexander."

"Jake." The kid rubbed at his eyes, still not believing that a squirrel was talking to him. I led Jake through the woods. Several times I made sure he was still there behind me. When we approached one of the doors to Amora, I stopped. I turned to face him with a big smile on my face.

"You're about to have your mind blown."

"Okay." Dark circles were under Jake's eyes, and I could tell he hadn't been taking care of himself.

"Things are about to get real trippy." My body shimmered with a thousand golden specks. My human form came back, and by the gasp Jake made, I probably gave him a heart attack. "Come on." I reached for his hand, and he grasped it. With one step, we entered the world of Amora.

Chapter 32

Raven

"I can't believe you're back." My friend Ella pulled me into a bone-crushing hug, sounding like she was about to cry. We sat on the porch of my new home, hearing the horses whinnying in the background.

"Thanks, Ella," I said.

"You have got to tell me everything that has been going on. I've been worried sick about you. You never answered my texts or calls."

"I know. I'm really sorry." I launched into the story about Jill and Nelson, trying to leave most of the gory details out of it. After I was finished, she stared at me with an empathetic expression.

"Oh my god, I'm so sorry. I had no idea." She held me for a long time. Suddenly she pulled back. "Hey, what about that guy? The guy at the café? What happened with him?"

It felt nice to get all this stuff off my chest, even if I left out the part about being in another world for a while. I wasn't quite ready to tell her all of that. I tried my best to explain what happened with Colten. Ella's eyes grew wider and wider, and when I reached the part about breaking up with him because of my foster parents, she nearly started to cry.

"You need to text him. Right now. I'm sure he would take you back. Do it." She stared at me. "I'm not taking no for an answer."

"Okay, I will." I gave a smile. "I promise."

"You better." She looped her arm through mine and kissed my cheek. "I have to get going, but you better call me the moment he responds back." She jumped to her feet and headed toward her bike. She gave one final wave.

* * * * *

Later that day, I sat against my bed's headboard staring at the ceiling. Everything that had happened to me over the last few months was literally mind boggling. Although my parents' death still hurt like crazy, my time in Amora had brought me so much healing. I worried my lower lip for a moment, trying to put my thoughts in order. Living with Mary was like a breath of fresh air. Much like my own mom, she was kind, caring, and warm. I thought about what Ella and I had talked about, and I knew I had to do it.

"God?" I whispered up to the ceiling. The moment I said His name, a flood of love came over me. I thought about the giant hug we'd shared, and tears instantly sprang to my eyes.

Sometimes words aren't needed.

The thought came strongly to my mind. I gave a tearful smile, shaking my head. He was right. I didn't even know how to begin to express how I felt toward Him. I'd always thought of God as some distant figure in the sky—one who really didn't interact with me much, but now…

"I don't know how I lived without you," I whispered.

You never did, Raven.

The thought tingled through my body, and I let out a giggle. If anyone had told me I'd be hearing "God," I'd have told them they were crazy, but after everything I'd seen, it felt like it was normal.

Text him.

I slipped my hand over my face. I was still slightly terrified to reconnect with Colten, even though it was what I wanted most in the world. Even though we'd only been together a short time, I knew there was something there worth pursuing.

Text him, Raven. It'll be okay.

I grabbed my phone and held it against my chest, closing my eyes. *Okay. I'll do it.* I heard a light chuckle, and I felt the presence of someone around me. I peeked an eye open to see several Endrita, their light-filled wings filling my entire room.

"Oh!" Even though I'd expected someone was there, their physical sight still startled me. "Thanks for the moral support, guys."

They smiled at me but said nothing.

Hi. I sent the quick text.

I stared at the screen, my heart going crazy in my chest. What if he hated me? *Calm down, Raven.* I forced myself to breathe. Mary had helped me get settled the last few days, making me feel completely at home in her beautiful farm house. I had been wanting to text Colten since I'd gotten here, but I had been hesitating. I feared what would happen when I did. After Ella's pep talk, I knew I needed to confront my fear. I stared at the text again.

Hi. My phone buzzed. My heart hammered.

Can we talk? I trembled, anxious to know what he was going to do.

Sure. Where do you want to meet?

I texted him my new address.

Right now?

I looked around my room. It was now or never.

Yeah.

I'll be there soon.

I stared at my phone, a thrill rolling through me. *He doesn't hate me.*

I hurried and got ready and made my way to the front porch, plopping myself down on the swinging bench. Not more than a half hour later, I saw a figure on a horse, making his way down the road.

He's here. I was both terrified and excited out of my mind. The closer he got, the more my nerves bounced around. He slid off the horse and made his way toward the porch. He stopped once he got to the bottom of the stairs, standing before me, his dark hair perfectly messy.

Colten.

"Hi." I gave a little wave, and he looked up at me. A smile crossed his face, and I felt a thrill go all the way through my toes.

"Hi." He ran to me and pulled me into his arms. The feel of him sent warm shooting feelings all the way through my entire body. "I missed you, Raven. I was so worried about you." He buried his face in my hair, and something broke on the inside of me. I started to sob, clutching him to me so tight, I wondered if he could breathe. After a few minutes, he laughed.

"I need air." He looked at me, his blue eyes shimmering with affection. "What happened to you? Are you okay?"

"I'm amazing." I drew in a deep breath. "It's a really long story, but I want to show you something first." Before he could say another word, I grabbed his hand and yanked him toward the barn. Barloc poked his head out, nodding up and down, wanting a treat.

"Wow," Colten said. He jogged toward my horse and stroked his nose. "Is this yours?"

"Yeah." My eyes shimmered with love. "He's mine."

"He's gorgeous." Colten continued to stroke Barloc's nose. "Where did you get him?"

I knew the question would come, and I was ready for it. "That's what I wanted to tell you. He's not from around here."

"You went out of state?" Colten looked slightly confused, but I plunged ahead.

"Remember how I told you about Grim and the world of Anxious?" I couldn't help but smile, I'd been wanting to tell someone the entire story so badly. Alex and I knew telling Ian, Jack, or anyone else would probably be a bad idea, but I knew I could trust Colten.

"Yeah?" Colten held Barloc's head, looking over at me.

"He's from there." I smiled. "I have a lot to tell you."

"You can start off first by telling me why you broke up with me." A hurt look crossed his face.

"I thought I wasn't good enough for you." Tears filled my eyes. "I couldn't believe that I could love someone so fast with only a few dates. Jill and Nelson said—"

I didn't get to finish my sentence because Colten's lips were suddenly pressed up against mine, his arms wrapped around me. Tingles exploded through my entire body, and I let out a soft gasp.

"You will always be good enough, Raven." He pulled me into a kiss again, and I let myself get lost in the feel of him. His soft lips melted against mine, until we were no longer two people. Something nudged my shoulder, and I let out a giggle. Barloc wanted in on our kiss, but I didn't think his kisses would quite be the same.

What's he doing to your face? The horse nodded his head up and down.

"This may sound crazy, but my horse kind of talks to me." I squinted my eyes.

"Nothing sounds crazy to me anymore." Colten kissed me again, and I let him. After a long moment, we broke apart, and I instantly missed the feeling of his kisses on my lips. "You need to tell me everything." He grabbed my hand and led me out of the barn. "I brought someone who really misses you too." He led me over to the horse he'd ridden. I ran toward Mayfly and wrapped my arms around her neck.

"Hi, baby." I buried my face in her mane. Mayfly nibbled at my hair. I pulled back from her, stroking her nose over and over. "I want you to meet someone, Mayfly." I led her toward the barn, Colten grinning as he followed. I brought her up to Barloc and stood her before him. I unlocked the stall and let Barloc out. He turned his head, curious at the new playmate.

"Barloc, meet Mayfly. Mayfly, meet Barloc," I said. The two horses nodded at one another, letting out little snorts as they did. Colten laughed, rubbing Mayfly's neck.

"Want to go for a quick ride?" I asked Colten.

"Sure."

I ran over to the saddles and grabbed one for Barloc, even though I knew I could ride him bareback too. Once he was fitted, he turned his head and nibbled at my shirt.

Let's go.

I giggled at him, climbing up into the saddle. Colten and I got the horses moving, and as we walked, I found the words tumbling from my mouth. I went through everything—my parents' death, living with my uncle, foster care, and finally the world of Anxious.

We slid off our horses, letting them nibble at the grass they found in the woods. Our feet crunched the leaves as we walked, our fingers laced together.

"There is one thing that is kind of a mystery to me." I reached into my saddlebag and pulled out the mirror I'd retrieved from my old house. "This thing. It looks just like the Drite and Dagmoth Mirror, but I have no idea what it is." I handed the mirror over to Colten. He grasped it by the handle and frowned, peering deep into the surface of it.

"It looks a little dirty." He rubbed his sleeve against it, until the surface was clear of fog. A blue light shot out of the surface of the mirror, cascading out like a waterfall of light. Colten jumped, let out a yelp, and dropped the mirror in the process. He fell to the ground.

"What is going on?" I said with a gasp. The moment the mirror touched the earth, I felt a cold shiver go through me. The blue light swirled, creating a vortex straight up from its surface. The air pressure changed, and a violent wind rattled everything around us.

What is happening? A giant lump formed in my throat, and my stomach lurched.

Colten started to get sucked toward the spinning air, his fingers grasping at the ground.

"Raven! Get out of here!" His hair blew back and forth, his clothing getting whipped violently by the force of the wind.

"No! Take my hand!" I grabbed a branch and stretched out my fingers toward him. Colten fought against the wind, reaching his hand out as far as he could go. The blue light spun out further, a massive amount of sparking energy sucking in everything around it. I could see terror in Colten's eyes.

"You can do it!" I reached out further, my fingertips brushing his. He ducked his head down, trying to push against the sucking pull of the vortex. Our fingers brushed again, when Colten's feet slipped. I watched in horror as he struck the ground, his jacket flapping in the wind. His body spun out of control until it was hovering just above the mirror. A pale face appeared in the midst of the tornado of wind. A woman, her eyes as black as coal, stared straight at me.

"Hello, Raven," she said with a sneer. "I see you've met my brother, but, darling, you forgot about me." With those final words, Colten was sucked straight into the mirror. The moment he was gone, the wind stopped and the blue light disappeared. A sob stuck in my throat. I had finally gotten my happily ever after only to have it snatched from my grasp.

"Give him back." I ran over to the mirror and shook it, screaming at the sky. "Give him back!" My shoulders shuddered with sobs as I fell to my knees. After a minute of crying, I stood to my feet. I tucked the mirror back into my purse. Who was this woman? What did she want with us?

I don't care what it takes. I'll find you, Colten. I promise.

CPSIA information can be obtained
at www.ICGtesting.com
Printed in the USA
FFHW021801290419
52151806-57503FF